WOLF BEACH

Stephen Banister

© 1990

There are three kinds of people who roam this earth.

Those who believe there are, those who do not believe

there are, and those who are . . . werewolves.

This book is dedicated to the true believers.

About the Author

Stephen Banister resides in Central Texas, where he divides his time trying to play golf and his guitar, and connecting words to give them meaning. He sometimes daylights as a mild-mannered insurance mediator. He finds great comfort when his son and family head out on a vacation, 'cause he gets to puppysit their three Labs.

Contents

About the Author iv

1 1

2 5

3 15

4 18

5 22

6 26

7 31

8 34

9 38

10 39

11 41

12 44

13 47

14 49

15 56

16 61

17 65

18 69

19 72

20 74

21 77

22 79

23 83

24 86

25 92

26 99

27 106

28 115

29 121

30 128

31 131

32 133

33 138

34 143

35 145

36 150

37 153

38 157

39 159

40 164

41 167

42 172

43 174

44 176

45 178

46 180

47 182

48 185

49 187

50 191

51 194

52 197

53 200

54 212

55 217

56 224

57 232

58 238

59 242

60 248

61 252

62 256

63 258

64 262

65 267

66 271

67 275

68 277

69 282

70 287

71 289

72 292

73 298

74 301

75 311

76 326

1

It was a night for lovers to enjoy. The cool, early summer breeze that sailed in across the Gulf of Mexico made making out on the hot, sticky sand almost worth it.

Jennifer had met Eric at Stewart Beach that morning and had been immediately taken by the way he handled his board in the surf. The hours had flown to sundown, where she now found herself locked in mortal combat on his Coors beach towel. The first few kisses weren't so bad, rather enjoyable to the teenager, but when he slid a hand under her bikini top, all her admiration went out with the tide.

"No!" she whispered in an awkward voice as she grabbed him by the wrist.

"Come on," Eric said when he refused to relinquish his cup-like grip on her breast. "It's dark. No one's gonna see us."

Barely seventeen, Jennifer was not untouched, but her previous encounters had been with boys she had at least known for more than a day. "Not yet," she said. She jerked his wrist sideways and was able to free herself from his hold, but in doing so, the thin strap that held her top in place broke and allowed the small half of her Yaga Ragz original to fall to her waist. Before she could lift it back up, Eric was on her.

In one frightening moment, she grabbed a handful of coarse sand and slammed it, fingernails and all, into his eyes. Eric rolled off the towel, dug at his eyes, and cursed. Without trying to cover herself, she jumped up and ran.

Jennifer had no idea how far she had run or for how long when she finally fell breathless into a shallow tide pool. The cool gulf air on her small breasts reminded her that she was still naked from the waist up. She leaned back into a sitting position and reached for the loose, expensive material that lay torn in her lap. Her left hand felt heavy. She raised it out between her face and the full moon and realized she had taken Eric's towel with her. It was soaked from the tide. She let it drop from her hand as if it were soaked in blood, then jumped up and stomped it spitefully until all her anger was buried with it in the wet sand.

She lifted the bikini top up until it once again covered her breasts and tried to tie the broken strap behind her neck. As she was doing so, she looked back in the direction she had come and realized that she was no longer in the guarded confines of county-owned property. She had run the wrong way. The lights of the amusement park at the entrance to Stewart Beach seemed like an eternity away. The jubilant screams of the children on the Tilt-A-Whirl were lost to the sounds of the open surf. Somewhere beyond those sounds was her sister's Volkswagen Jetta parked in the dwindling row of cars on Seawall Boulevard. She had promised her she would have it back at the Flagship Hotel before dark; a promise she had already broken at Eric's request. And now Eric was somewhere between her and an even later return.

She gave up trying to tie the broken strap, which left her no other choice but to hold the top up with her hand. She had never before complained about the size of her breasts as she knew that in a year or two, they would fill out nicely just as her sister's had done, but now she wished that time had already come. Connie could wear her bikini fearlessly without the aid of the thin strap that tied behind her neck and broke up her natural tan line.

Jennifer stood in the dark solitude of East Beach and tried to decide how she could get back to the Jetta without having to cross paths with Eric. She knew that the road back to the park ran parallel to the beach. If she could just make it through the sea grape-infested dunes to the road, she could make it back to the car without further confrontation. If Eric was waiting for her there, she would at least have the protection of the bright lights and maybe even one of the deputies who patrolled the area.

She turned toward the dunes and stared at the sight that loomed in front of her. She had seen the building from a distance that morning, but the sight of the abandoned, three-story condotel with the full moon peering through the partially burned-out structure sent a bone-chilling rush of fear through her young body. She was suddenly very cold and very alone and wished she had let Eric go a little farther. She looked back down the beach in hopes that she might see him walking in the tide in search of her, but there was nothing between her and the half-buried, wooden pylons that marked the boundary between the two beaches except darkness.

It was then that she heard the noise. It was like the sound her asthmatic grandfather made in the spring when the high pollen count made it virtually impossible for him to breathe. She stood in the shallow water, one foot still on Eric's towel; afraid to turn and yet more afraid not to.

"It's just Eric," her frightened mind told her. "He's sorry for what he did, and he's come running through the dunes after you to apologize for his actions. He's just out of breath, that's all."

She stood with her back to the wall and waited for him to reach her, but when he didn't, she decided to give him a break. She turned and spoke. "Eri . . ."

Jennifer's mouth gaped open as she tried to finish his name, but her throat was sealed shut in a sharp vise. When the pressure eased, she tried to scream, but there was nothing left between her mouth and lungs to make the connection.

The last thing she saw was a color that never registered in her brain; the fiery, bluish-yellow of the eyes above the snarling, bloody mouth that had torn her throat away. Its next lunge ripped through bone and stole Jennifer's dying heart from her body. The beast offered it up toward the full moon before it feasted itself on the tender meat.

2

Andy Langsjoen climbed up onto his dark green and white tower through the sticky morning haze. At thirty, he was the senior lifeguard on the Galveston County Beach Patrol. His rise to that position had begun in the summer after his junior year at Galveston Ball High School when his father had pulled some well-meaning strings to land him his first lifeguard job. After high school, he attended Lamar University but returned to his beach each summer to fulfill what he considered his destiny rather than his duty. It was that same feeling that had kept him from finishing his education in favor of a full-time position with the beach patrol, a branch of the Galveston County Sheriff's Department.

The beach patrol was usually reserved for the young, but through the years, Andy had managed to preserve his station by placing high on all the tests and competitions set out by the department. Also in his favor was the fact that when summer ended and most of the other guards returned to school, Andy was still out there patrolling the beach. When the rotation schedule called for him to work the cush job at Palm Beach, he always passed in favor of remaining on guard of Stewart Beach. It was **his** beach. Although the younger guards didn't understand his reasoning, they were more than happy to take his turn at Palm Beach, where those who could afford the price of admission chose to spend the hot and humid days of their vacation lounging on a man-made playground of fluffy, white sand that surrounded two over-sized, yet shallow pools, complete with waterfalls, jacuzzies and frozen Margaritas.

This summer had started out no different than the rest. Vacationers still swam out too far and had to be rescued from the deadly undertow. Young girls still showed up wearing suits that left little to the imagination of those they were trying to impress, and the charter boats still returned in the late afternoons with a full catch of would-be fishermen, green around the gills. Galveston Island had made it through the Memorial Day crowd without a drowning, but the Fourth of July crush was fast approaching.

From his tower, Andy could see the maintenance crews as they busily raked the high tide seaweed into haystack-like piles, one step ahead of the converted brush trucks as they cleaned their way up and down the beach. He took the small, dark blue square of plywood out of his bag and hung it on the hook at the back of the tower to cover the NO on the sign so that it now read LIFEGUARD ON DUTY. His routine called for him to take his high-powered marine binoculars from their weathered yet still waterproof case. It had been two years since any sharks had been sighted along Stewart Beach, but he still felt more secure after a first look of his own.

Andy scanned the cloudy, blue-green surface in a semicircle until his gaze once again returned to shore. He followed the sand to the next tower, the last one before the pylons brought an end to his realm and the beginning of the unpatrolled East Beach. It was unpatrolled because the beach was semi-private, and few swimmers ventured into that area. The semi-private distinction meant that the maintenance crews were not obliged to clean the beach of the Sargassum weed that blotched the sand like aging liver spots. Dumping the dozen or so trash barrels was all that was required of them. Jim's Beach Rentals also did not operate on East Beach, which meant no umbrellas, beach chairs, or other such rental items, which made a day at the beach even more relaxing, could be had.

Andy found that last tower vacant. He lowered the binoculars and checked his watch to make sure he had not jumped the gun. It was three minutes after seven, and very unlike Butch to be late, even by a mere three minutes. He raised the glasses again and adjusted them for an extended look. A flash of familiar color caught his eye. It was the same color that caught the eye of most people on the beach. It was the fluorescent, lime-green color of the lifeguards' trunks that set them apart from the rest of the swimmers. Butch's tower blocked Andy's view and forced him to climb up on the railing for a better look, like the spotter on the outermost bow of a whaling ship.

Butch was bent over with his hands on his knees as if he were quarterbacking the small huddle of maintenance men next to one of the boundary pylons. Just then, one of the maintenance men turned around and unloaded his breakfast on the sand. The others backed away.

Butch turned in Andy's direction and saw him perched on the high edge of the tower more than a quarter of a mile away and began to wave his arms frantically.

Andy swung himself back down onto the platform and traded the binoculars for the red Artie, the name the lifeguards had given their rescue tubes, as in R.T. They were trained never to leave their towers without them. He jumped from his tower and received a sharp pain in his groin when he hit the beach running.

"You're getting a little too old for that move, son," the pain told him as he limped his way up the beach. Just before he reached the pylon, Butch caught him full on the shoulders before he could move in close.

"It's a body, Andy," Butch said.

"Shit! I knew it was just a matter of time," Andy said. "At least we made it through June."

"She didn't drown."

"What do you mean she didn't drown?" Andy said and shoved the younger guard aside. "Let me see."

Two dead eyes stared up at him through a ragged blanket of brownish-green seaweed when he knelt down beside the body. He slowly lifted the tangle from her face and fought back a lurch at what he saw. Her throat had been completely torn out and laid bare the tide-washed bones of her neck. He fell into a prone position and dug his fingers into the cool, wet sand in order to keep things inside.

"That's not all," Butch said. He walked around the pylon and kicked the remaining seaweed away from her upper body to reveal a cavernous opening where her chest and stomach should have been.

Andy breathed in deep and forced himself to look. A small nipple attached to a hanging piece of flesh above the gaping hole was all that remained of her breasts. He stumbled to his feet and ran drunkenly to the water's edge, and fell on all fours. The cool, salty smell of the gulf was all that kept his own breakfast down.

After a few seconds of letting the tide swirl in around him and then back out again, Andy regained enough strength to get up. Butch stood a silent guard over the body.

"Shark, you figure?" Butch asked when Andy joined him.

"Looks like it."

"That's not going to make the big boys very happy with the Fourth coming up."

"Fuck the big boys," Andy said between heavy, strained breaths. "You think she cares? How do you think she felt?"

"You know what I mean."

"Yeah," Andy said. "Have you called it in yet?"

"No, I just got here."

"Well, you better do it. We need to get them out here before the crowd arrives."

"OK. You gonna be all right?"

"I'll make it," Andy said. "You go on."

Andy had seen the gruesome aftermaths of shark attacks before, but that didn't make this one any easier to stomach. Each one always seemed more hideous than the last. After Butch left to go to his tower, where he had laid the bag that contained the department-issue radio the guards called talkies, Andy forced himself to drag away the remaining seaweed cover from the lower part of the dead girl's body.

Her legs were smooth and a bluish-white from the lack of blood and were virtually untouched. The bottom of what had once been a two-piece bathing suit was still in one piece, though the top edge was folded almost neatly into the cave of her abdomen.

Word of the grisly find made its way back down the beach like the high tide of a full moon. The crew of the brush truck stopped their morning ritual and arrived at the scene about the time that Butch returned.

"You guys got a blanket or something in there?" Andy asked as the truck was sinking to a stop.

The driver jumped out of the doorless truck with a wadded-up, sandy-wet towel. "Here," he said. "Just found it."

A soft breeze blew in over the gulf as Andy covered the body with the towel. When it died down, the middle of the towel where the faded picture of the Coors beer label was sank into the body's empty bowels like a crushed can.

"Who'd you get?" Andy asked Butch when he saw he had returned with the talkie still in his hand.

"Sheriff Danforth."

"Went right to the top, huh?"

"I thought I better."

"That means he'll have the mayor with him, and who knows who else."

"Well, he has to find out about it sooner or later," Butch said. "Might as well get it over with."

Andy motioned to the driver of the seaweed truck. "Why don't you pull your truck over here? The fewer people that see this, the better."

The driver obliged and parked the truck next to the pylons but chose to remain at the wheel.

"Looks like you called it right," Butch said and nodded his head in the direction of the pavilion where Sheriff Danforth's tan Ford had come to a stop at the end of the last entrance to the beach. The sheriff and Mayor Paschall jumped from both sides of the car before the tires had a chance to begin cooling on the packed-down sand. A rear door also opened, but the passenger did not exit as quickly as the other two.

"Yeah, but at least they had enough sense to bring Jesse," Andy said.

Jesse Spangler was the local coroner. Had been since before Andy was born. There had been talk of replacing him last year when he hit sixty-five but the talk soon died down to a whisper when the town council was given the figures of what a newer, younger version would cost them.

Jesse was also the closest thing to the family that Andy had since his father died of cancer three years before. All his life, it had been Jesse and his father. His mother had died giving birth to him. He knew that Jesse and his parents had come to Galveston after World War II, but other than that, they had just been hard and fast friends; Jesse and his father. That never stopped him from calling him Uncle Jesse when the feeling struck him.

"What kind of trouble you boys dug up this time?" the mayor asked when he walked up and almost stumbled into the towel-covered body.

Andy knew not to expect any cordial greeting from the man his father had hated, a feeling he had passed on to him like an unwanted legacy. Andy jumped at the chance to answer him in a similar fashion. "This kind," he said, and bent down and jerked the towel off without warning.

"Oh, Jesus, what is it?"

"It **was** a girl, Mister Mayor," Andy said. "Or can't you tell?"

"That's enough, son," the sheriff told him.

Andy was about to put his job on the line with a further comment when Jesse stepped in and ruined what would have been a mistake.

"Morning, Andrew," Jesse said and bent over the body for a closer look.

"Jesse," Andy said calmly and with a ring of respect.

Jesse began to poke learnedly here and there over the girl's remains. Sweat had already begun to bead up below the few strands of gray hair that remained on his head.

"Shark, Jesse?" the sheriff asked in an attempt to take control of the situation.

Jesse didn't answer. He was too busy with his examination of the remains to answer what Andy considered the obvious.

"It had to be a shark," the mayor said. "Nothing else could have torn her up like that. This is all we fucking need right now."

Andy could feel the contempt as it welled up inside his six-foot frame. He could feel his closely cropped, light brown hair, almost blonde from a life under the daily coastal sun, as it stood on end when the hatred he felt for the man forced its way upward in an attempt to escape. He held it in check, more out of respect for Jesse's presence than the possibility that another outburst could cost him his job.

Like his father, he wasn't exactly high on the mayor's list of people he would like to keep around. The feeling of mutual disrespect dated back to when his father, then the owner of Phil's Army Surplus, mounted a political attack to oust him from his Council seat two terms before he became Mayor. His father's refusal to get down and roll in the dirt of the campaign almost won him the seat, but a last-minute injection of funds from the local banking community, of which Paschall was an integral part as President and CEO of the Port Galveston Savings and Loan, paid the way for his victory.

Phil Langsjoen accepted his defeat gracefully, but not so Brian Paschall. A few well-chosen threats in the right places saw to it that the note on his surplus store was called in. In six months, the doors were closed, and three and a half years later, the man behind the threats was elected Mayor.

His father's death the following year did nothing to ease the tension. Paschall merely directed his revenge on Jesse but lost the first round when the Council refused to pay the price of a new coroner. Paschall could have thrown a few of his own dollars into the pot, but even **he** had his limits when it came to money and what it could buy in the right hands.

To Andy's way of thinking, the mayor could probably get him fired from his own job at any time, but he obviously considered that the job of a low paid lifeguard wasn't worth the effort of taking away.

Jesse remained at work over the body until the ambulance arrived, then left with it. He also left the sheriff's question unanswered.

With all the evidence gone and nothing left to hide from the crowd who was sure to come, the maintenance crew returned to their work, as did the two lifeguards.

"We better keep a close watch on the water today," Andy told Butch as they reached the first tower. "I'd sure hate to ruin the mayor's holiday."

"I just bet you would," Butch replied as he climbed the green, wooden stairs to the shaded platform.

Andy broke into a trot for the quarter of a mile to his own tower. As he climbed the stairs, he couldn't help but compare what he had just seen to the other shark victims in his past. There was something about the body, or what was left of it, that just didn't seem to fit. He shook off the feeling and exchanged the Artie for the binoculars and began his day again.

3

Eric Beckett stood in front of his third-floor office window in the Port Galveston Savings and Loan Building and watched sugar being augured into the steel belly of a tanker bound for London. His eyes still, and he had a foul taste in his mouth that even three doses of Listerine hadn't been able to remove. He had sworn off cigarettes for probably the seven hundredth time but knew that promise wouldn't hold any more water than the previous six hundred and ninety-nine. When he drank, he smoked, and that's all there was to it.

He couldn't remember drinking that much last night, but the bitter aftertaste on his tongue served as proof positive that he had. The girl on the beach, Jennifer, as he recalled, had proven to be more than he had been prepared to handle, but the beach was full of Jennifers this time of the year. He knew he could find another as soon as he mounted his board.

When the door to his office opened, he turned to see his secretary, Amy, come in. Her eyes looked as wide as golf balls with little blue dots in the center.

"Something wrong?" he asked calmly.

"You aren't going surfing this afternoon, are you?" she said.

"Why, has something come up that you can't handle?"

"No, it's not that," she said. "I guess you haven't heard the news."

"Obviously not," he said. "Why don't you be the first to tell me?"

"I just heard on the radio that they found the body of a girl who had been eaten by a shark."

"Where?"

"Between East and Stewart."

"No way. I was just out there yesterday," he said.

"That's what they said."

"Just because that's where they found the body doesn't mean it happened there. The current could have brought it in from almost anywhere," he told her rather assuredly.

"Maybe you're right, but I still think you'd be better off not going out," she said.

"They haven't closed the beach, have they?"

"Are you serious? In the middle of the tourist season?"

"Then I'll be there. If it were a shark, it's probably gone by now. If not, hey, it's a big beach. I doubt it'll come looking for me anyway. It looks like it has developed a taste for female flesh. It would probably just spit me back out."

"You're cruel, Eric," she said.

"Not really," he said. "We all get what's coming to us in the end."

"You're not just cruel, you're sick." Amy didn't know why she worked for him, other than the fact that he paid her considerably more than she had made as a salesperson at The Ivory Shop on The Strand.

"Maybe so," he said, "but I like me."

Amy did too, and for the life of her she didn't know why. Working for him was one thing, but liking him was quite another. Maybe it was physical, although during the two years she had worked for him, he had yet to put any moves on her. She wasn't altogether sure she wanted him to, for that matter, but she couldn't help but wonder why he hadn't. He always made it a point to fill her in on his nightly conquests, including the juicy parts, and although she always complained, she always listened.

"Was she a local?" Eric followed.

"They wouldn't say until they notified her next of kin."

Eric turned back toward the window, which signaled an end to their conversation. Amy watched him run his fingers through his hair that was the color of a worn penny and winged to the right just above his collar. Then, as usual, she left without saying what was on her mind. He was handsome, on the short side of thirty and obviously rich, since he had come to Galveston less than ten years ago fresh out of some college in the East and opened Port City Import-Export without financial aid, at least from any of the locals. He spent his mornings working and his afternoons surfing. He would be a prize catch if he wasn't such an asshole.

4

Andy was on his third or fifth screwdriver; it didn't matter, he wasn't counting; when Jesse walked in the front door of the beachfront condo. Jesse never knocked unless he had reason to believe Andy wasn't alone. Since he had phoned just ten minutes earlier, there was no reason.

"Help yourself," Andy said and pointed to the half-full, second pitcher of vodka and Minute Maid on the bar. "It'll keep you from catching a cold."

"I'll stick to my scotch, thank you."

"Well, you know where it is."

Jesse walked around behind the bar and took out a bottle of Cutty Sark and poured half a hi-ball glass, downed it and poured another to the same mark.

"Rough day?" Andy asked.

"Not as rough as it's going to get before it's all over."

"I know," Andy said. "His Honor didn't do too good a job keeping it quiet. It made my day pretty easy, though. The beach was crowded enough but no one got wet."

"Do you blame them?" Jesse said and ran a free hand over his nearly bald head before he downed his second and poured a third.

"Not after what I saw."

"Just what **did** you see, Andrew?"

Other than Miss Chauncy, his first-grade teacher, and Uncle Jesse, no one else had ever called him by his given name. He considered than an honor reserved for special people. Miss Chauncy had been his first love and Jesse . . . well, Jesse was Uncle Jesse.

"What do you mean?" Andy wondered whether the scotch Jesse had thrown down his neck had bypassed his bloodstream in favor of a more direct route to his brain.

"Just tell me exactly what you saw."

"You want all the gory details? I mean, you were there."

"Yeah and I got an even closer look later," Jesse said. "I just want your opinion."

"OK, well, I saw this girl who had her guts and most of her neck torn out by a shark. How's that?"

Jesse waited for more, but when nothing else was offered, he continued with his questioning. "Nothing else?"

"Like what?"

"You **have** seen shark victims before, haven't you?" he asked, and again emptied his glass and poured another helping.

"You know I've seen as many as you have in the last fifteen or so years, so what are you getting at?"

"The legs, Andrew."

It was then that Andy's memory came full circle. "That's what it was! I knew something was different." He slammed a fist down on the bar which caused Jesse to have to grab his glass with both hands.

"Then you **did** see it," Jesse said. He took another drink but didn't refill his glass until he was sure Andy was through taking his inability to remember out on the top of the bar. "I was beginning to think maybe I had been out in the sun too long this morning."

"No, I saw it, and you're right. Legs are usually the first thing a shark hits since they are usually lower in the water. Even if the person is swimming, a shark will go for the thrashing movements."

Jesse looked at him hard, as if he wanted to tell him something, but then he didn't.

"So, you're thinking it wasn't a shark?" Andy asked.

"Maybe not."

"What, then?" Andy said. "I don't remember seeing any barracuda around these parts.

"I'm not sure," Jesse said, and still held back.

"Have you called anyone else in to examine the body? You know, a marine biologist or someone like that, or some kind of a shark expert?"

"Too late. Her sister's already claimed the body and a funeral home in Dallas is picking it up in the morning. Just because I'm not sure it was a shark isn't a good enough reason to put her family through the ordeal of waiting."

"So, where does that leave me?" Andy asked.

"What do you mean?" The question took Jesse by surprise and caused his hand to shake as he lifted his glass of scotch to his mouth.

"Well, do I need to be on the alert for another shark attack or what?"

"Oh." Jesse was relieved at Andy's questioning answer. If there was a werewolf prowling the island, he would have to tell him about it sooner or later. He preferred later. He really preferred never to have to tell him at all. "It probably wouldn't hurt for you to keep your binoculars handy just in case my feeble, old brain has finally turned to mush."

"If I were you," Andy said as he watched Jesse empty the remaining scotch into his glass, "I'd worry more about my liver than my brain."

Jesse chose to let Andy's comment slide. His own well-being was the least of his worries at the moment.

5

Eric had spent the afternoon surfing East Beach just to prove his point. He would brag about it to Amy tomorrow. Right now, he had other more important matters to tend to. His expertise at handling the five-footers had gone completely unnoticed, which meant if he wanted company for the evening, he would have to find it elsewhere.

Elsewhere, for the moment, was the Sea Star, the local hangout for those between the ages of eighteen and twenty-one. It was common knowledge that Sheriff Danforth was the primary investor in the nightclub, which is where the *Star* in the name came from. It was just as much common knowledge that all you had to do was produce an ID—an expired driver's license with no photo from, say, North Dakota that showed you to be twenty-one—to be able to drink without being hassled by the law, for obvious reasons.

Eric considered himself forever eighteen and his deep tan and surfer-cut hair gave nothing about his age away. He also used a fake ID for the same, yet different reason; to show him to be younger, not older. His fake ID said he was twenty-two.

It was Rock and Roll night at the Sea Star and like the singer was saying, the joint was jumping. Eric ordered a gin and tonic and lit up his first cigarette. Tomorrow's promise would be seven hundred and one.

"You shouldn't smoke those things, you know?"

Eric turned in the direction of the voice and came face to face with a brown-eyed brunette who looked like her senior prom was still in her future.

"I don't smoke them he said. "I just hold them."

About that time the band broke into a slow song. "How would you like to hold me instead?" she asked.

"That's a fair trade," Eric said. He dropped the cigarette to the floor and stepped on it as they made their way through a maze of people to the dance floor.

"I don't believe I've seen you in here before," Eric said as they moved slowly around a small section of the floor.

"You haven't," she said. "I'm from out of town."

"Here on vacation?"

"Sort of," she answered. "And you?"

"I live here," Eric said.

"Oh, yeah? What do you do?"

"Surf."

"That's all?"

"What else is there?" Eric said. He knew his lines by heart.

"Nothing, I guess."

He pulled her closer and she offered no resistance. When the song ended they walked back to the bar where Eric planned to get their drinks and find a table somewhere in the darker recesses of the club. His plan failed.

"What the hell do you think you're doing, Karen?" The question came from a boy about the same size as Eric, though considerably younger, who met them at the edge of the dance floor.

"Just dancing, Bobby," she said.

"Well, you dance with me and nobody else," he said to her but in direction.

"You were in the bathroom," she said.

"Well, now I'm not."

Eric sized up his competition during their short conversation. He knew he could take him, but he also knew that by doing so he would run the risk of being asked to leave the establishment. He took another look at the girl and decided her baggage was too heavy.

"Sorry, friend," Eric said. "I didn't know she was taken."

The boy took Eric's apology as being founded on fear and followed up on it. "Then why don't you get your ass out of here?"

The reddish-brown hair on the back of Eric's neck bristled. It wouldn't take more than one well-placed fist to teach the boy some manners, but once again Eric weighed the situation and his options and chose the path he was unaccustomed of walking, but not totally. "If you really want to fight, I'll gladly oblige you, but we'll have to step outside first because there's not enough room in here. If I were you, though, I'd just keep my fucking mouth shut and go out there and dance, because that's what you really came here for, wasn't it?"

The boy could tell from Eric's eyes that he had bit off a whole lot more than would fit in his mouth, much less chew on and made a wise decision of his own.

"Come on, Karen," he said as he led her back onto the dance floor. "I didn't coma all the way over here just to kick somebody's butt. I could've done that at home."

Eric let the boy's saving-face shot slide and returned to the bar. After two more drinks and six smokes in spite of it all, he decided it was time to try his luck elsewhere.

6

The beast's nostrils flared as they failed to pick up a scent. From the third floor of the condotel it could see or smell anything that might venture onto the two mile stretch of shoreline between the bright lights of Stewart Beach and the condominiums at the opposite end of East Beach. The gulf breeze combed through the hump of silky-thick, auburn hair that rose on its back between muscular shoulders. It paced impatiently on all fours from opening to opening in search of unsuspecting prey.

Fear of discovery kept the beast from roaming freely along the beach. The night before, it had carelessly allowed the tide to steal the body before it had a chance to bury it along with the others. At least it had devoured her heart so she could not awaken from death to roam in its world.

Over the years, it had always been careful to single out its prey. The offerings had been plentiful. There were the vagrants who had sought refuge in the railroad yards only to end up buried, half-eaten, in the industrial zone of the port with no one to miss them. The tankers from the Philippines and Africa and South America that docked at the port to take on tons of grain, sugar, and Sulphur brought with them an abundant supply of human flesh. While their disappearances were noted, it was a common event for crewmen to occasionally jump ship for the chance of a new life in America. Some were caught by the authorities and some made it to freedom. The very unlucky ones remained buried at the port; their flesh rotting deep in the sand.

When the real estate market on the island went bust and the developer of the multi-million-dollar condotel on East Beach went bankrupt, the half-finished structure became the haven for dope addicts, winos and wandering strangers. They almost succeeded in accidentally burning down their own home one cold winter night. It was then that the beast discovered them. The growing tourist trade around the port, brought in by the refurbishing of the shops along The Strand, the clipper ships, and the paddle-wheeler that welcomed visitors at almost all hours, made it virtually impossible for the beast to roam freely. The condotel had been its savior.

Until now, its presence had gone unnoticed. It had feasted on the flesh of those the island could very well do without. Those they would have thanked it for killing had they but known. And just like the girl, it had torn the hearts from their bodies so that **it** remained the only one of its kind on the island. A wolf pack would surely have come to someone's attention, not to mention the number of deaths that would have to be hidden during the three-night cycle of the weremoon. It was the second night of such a cycle.

During the last cycle, it had dined on the flesh of the last inhabitant of the condotel. Only the dried blood stains remained in the second-floor room where it had torn the scream from the addict's throat before it devoured his entrails.

It might have changed the port or railroad yards in winter, but the summer crowd was too heavy. It was doomed to remain in its modern-day castle as the moon betrayed it across the sky.

A sound from a distance brought its ears to a point as it turned its head toward the front of the building. The hair on its hump bristled as it sprang to the nearest opening where it saw the lights of a car shining a path along the broken asphalt drive that led from Seawall Boulevard to its lair. Saliva dripped from its sneering mouth, making its teeth take on an eerie glow in the moonlight. It emitted a low growl of expectation from the pit of its stomach.

The car stopped at the edge of the building, its lights formed a beacon through the pylons below the first floor. The beast watched, protected by the shadows.

"Not here," the girl in the passenger seat said. "This place gives me the creeps."

"That's not what you said this morning," said the driver. He turned the motor off but left the lights on.

"It looked different this morning."

"Well, it's the same damn place, Karen!"

The beast's feet made no sound on the cool concrete stairs as it made its way swiftly to the first floor. It leaped out a back opening to the sand below, careful not to enter the beam of the car's lights.

"What if someone's in there, Bobby?" the girl said.

"You heard what the guy at the club said. There might be some bums sleeping off a drunk in there but they aren't going to bother us. And if they do we always have this." He reached into the glove compartment and pulled out a .38 caliber pistol.

"Put that thing away, Bobby. You know I don't like you playing with it."

"I'll put it back if we can stay here a while."

"OK, but at least leave the lights on."

The beast could feel the mosquitoes as they attacked the bare skin on the inside of its pointed ears as it crouched just behind the front passenger door. It knew it wouldn't be long before the mosquitoes found their way into the open car window and drove its prey to safety. It would have to move now.

Bobby was kissing Karen on the neck when the first swarm of insects attacked the left side of his face through the open passenger window. "Shit!" Bobby said. He slapped at the mosquitoes as they drew first blood, and then sat in silence with his hand glued against his cheek. He could feel the warm urine trickle down one pant leg.

The beast's front paws were on the door just below its snarling, wrinkled mouth. The first growl should have been a warning but it came too late for Bobby. Its powerful jaws seized him by the neck and pulled him slowly across Karen's body and out the window. It tore the young, muscular flesh away as the body fell and gave the mosquitoes easy access to a fresh blood supply.

Karen was confused by the movement, but not for long and screamed when the beast returned to the window, where it still chewed on newly torn meat. She began to kick her feet madly as the beast's fiery eyes bore into her own. The glove box door sprang open under the force of a wild kick, and the pistol fell out onto the seat. She continued to kick at the ugly, animal-like being in the window as she grabbed for the pistol and held it tight in both hands.

The smell of death filled the car when the beast leaped through the window on top of her. It jerked backward at the sound of a muffled gunshot and snarled at the sight of blood that oozed from a small hole in the left side of the girl's T-shirt. It lifted its head and howled at its loss. It had been robbed of the sweet, pleasurable taste of the kill. The girl's brown eyes were still open and there was a life-like smile on her face, but the beast had been around death all its life and knew her heart was not rightfully its.

The beast leaped back through the window and dragged the boy's body between the cement pylons beneath the first floor of the structure. For the next hour, it gorged itself on the remains of its honest and rightful kill.

7

The sound of thunder jerked him from his sleep. From the third floor of the condotel, he could see that dawn was about to break far out over the gulf. He could also see that he had changed back into his human form. He stepped cautiously into the opening and looked down at the car below; its lights still on but barely shining. He dressed quickly and ran down the stairs, and jumped from the first-floor landing into the soft sand. He felt only a mild pain; something the beast had not been bothered with. He slapped at the swarm of mosquitoes that attacked him, as hungry for blood as he had been. He found the comparison amusing.

His first thought was to turn the car lights off before the battery was too far gone. He saw the remains of the boy that awaited burial as he ran through the substructure. He found the girl's body just as he had left it, both hands still in a death-grip around the gun. Her white T-shirt was now stained a deep crimson. He reached in, turned off the lights, and shook his head at the sight.

He returned to the boy's body and dragged it by the feet to a pylon not yet marked. He went to the back section of the structure and dug into the sand until he reached the shovel he kept buried under a heavy sheet of plastic, and then returned to the body. He dug a vertical trench down the side of the pylon and then lowered the body head-first into it. After he filled the grave with sand, he scrawled a small X into the concrete pylon just above the ground with the shovel.

While he had dug, he had planned his next move. The girl's death provided him with an excellent scheme. He returned the shovel to its usual place as rain started to fall. Nature would wash away all the traces of his activities. He opened the driver's door of the late model, red Chevrolet and climbed in. He had to lift the girl's head up to get into the seat, but laid it back down on his right leg when he settled in. He knew it would be best to move the body as little as possible. She needed to be found just as she had died.

He turned the key, but the engine answered back with a click. "Come on, you son of a bitch!" he said with a growl as the rain started to come down even harder. The motor favored him when he tried it again. He backed up, and then made a U-turn to go out the same way they had come in. If he went in the other direction, he would run the chance of being seen by an early morning jogger from the condominiums down the beach. Rain never seemed to bother them.

He took a left on Seawall Boulevard and headed back along the edge of town. The heavy rain would be his ally. It would give him the perfect cover should he pass someone he knew along the way. Even if they thought they recognized him, they would not give him a second look. The red Chevrolet was a far cry from his usual mode of transportation.

He drove down the boulevard to the first light, stayed to the right at the Y, and headed toward the ship channel. When he reached the row of vacant warehouses near the railroad yards, he parked the car in an alley. He took out his handkerchief and wiped the car clean of his presence. He left the windows down to let the rain take care of any traces of evidence he might have missed.

His office was a six-block run in the rain. The fact that he had changed into a jogging suit the night before for his late evening run to the beach would also give him the perfect excuse for being drenched. He had simply driven to work early or maybe even spent the night at his office, both he had done on any number of occasions, and decided on an early morning run and just flat-out got caught in the sudden downpour.

When he reached the parking garage, he found it empty, with the sole exception of his own vehicle. He unlocked the door and slid in. The leather upholstery squeaked in defiance when the wet fabric of the jogging suit was forced across its expensive skin. He had more than enough time to go home and shower last night's memory from his body.

8

Andy sat at one of the picnic tables on the second floor, covered patio of the pavilion that overlooked Stewart Beach, and tried to think of something he hated more than rain. Rain meant no swimmers, and no swimmers meant no lifeguards. He loved being a lifeguard. It was his job, and yet it wasn't. He enjoyed it too much to consider it work. It was more of a pleasant experience he got paid for going through. When he couldn't do it, he was unhappy, and when he was unhappy, he was bored. Right now, Andy was bored.

"Hi, Andy," Michele Molson, a willowy, muscular girl with long, platinum hair and tawny skin, said when she sat down at the table across from him.

"Hi," was all he said back to her, typical of the mood the rain had dropped him in.

"You think it's gonna stop any time soon?"

Andy could feel the gray cloud above his own head begin to dissipate with her presence. She reminded him of a song his father used to listen to about a girl who was described as five-nine-beautiful-tall.

"It better," he said. "I've had about all the relaxation I can handle this morning."

"I know what you mean," she said. "I've been at Palm Beach the last three days. Nothing exciting ever happens over there."

"You're lucky," Andy said. "You should have been here yesterday."

"I know. I heard about the girl," she said. "I don't think I would have been able to handle it."

"You'd be surprised what you can handle when you have to, especially on an empty stomach," he said. His own personal storm cloud had now given way to a brighter day. "You going back to UT in the fall?" he continued in an attempt to change the subject to something more enjoyable.

"Sure am," she said with a smile that revealed two rows of perfect teeth. "I've got two years left on my scholarship."

Michele was a local girl who had won the State Championship in the butterfly as a senior in high school. She was awarded a full-ride scholarship at the University of Texas, where she continued to excel in that event plus the being on the two-hundred-meter relay team.

"Then what?" Andy asked.

"I have no earthly idea," she said. "Maybe I'll land a job as a swimming coach somewhere."

"You can always come back here and do what you're doing now. It's a good life and the pay sucks. What more could a beautiful girl want?"

Andy's comment caused Michele to blush, but her golden-brown tan hid most of the evidence. She was pleased that he had noticed, although it would be hard for Andy or anyone else who had been born with two eyes in fairly decent working order not to. She had been born beautiful, raised beautiful, and would probably die beautiful many years down the road.

"Maybe I'll just do that," she said. "Will you still be here?"

Now it was Andy's turn to feel the warmth of flattery. He was fourteen years her senior, not quite old enough to be her father but wise enough to recognize a little flirtation when it was thrown in his general direction.

"You'll have to ask the mayor about that," he said.

"What do you mean?" she asked. A frown hid her photogenic teeth.

"Nothing," he said and wished he could retract what he had just let slip. "Sometimes my mouth starts in motion while my brain's still in neutral."

They were both enjoying their conversation so much that neither one noticed that the rain had moved on and was now out over the gulf. It wasn't until a herd of bathers stampeded across the sand below them that they realized the weather had changed for the better.

"Looks like it's time for us to go to work," Andy said.

"Can we continue our conversation later?" Michele asked.

"Sure, I guess so." It wasn't one of his better responses, but his mind was still playing the age difference game with his feelings.

They walked down the stairs together with their department issue bags fill with the tools of their trade slung over their shoulders. When they reached the bottom Michele told him she would see him later and then jogged to the right toward the tower nearest the amusement park.

Before he headed to his own, Andy detoured to the wooden pylons where they had found the girl yesterday and breathed a sigh of relief when he found that history had not repeated itself.

He walked along the shallow tide and then up to his tower and unloaded his bag. He made his usual sweep of the gulf with the binoculars, and when the semicircle ended at Michele's tower, he saw her wave. It was not the kind of wave Butch had given him the day before. It was more in the form of a thanks-for-looking wave.

"Pull yourself together, son," his mind warned him. "There ain't no future there."

An hour later it was business as usual. Two young boys, barely old enough to swim, had been sharing a rented raft and found themselves too far out in the surf to be able to maneuver their way back to shore. Michele ran from er tower, Artie in hand, and towed them back to the safety of their mother who immediately returned the raft to the rental stand and promised them each a butt blistering when they returned to their room.

Andy had watched it all through the binoculars, not sure if he was doing it in case she might need help or whether he just couldn't pull his eyes away from her slender form as she swam gracefully through the surf. Either way, business or pleasure, he was glad he had done it.

Michele flashed him a smile when she strolled out of the water and caught him red-handed.

9

The alley between the vacant warehouses looked like a police convention when Jesse pulled up behind the red Chevrolet. He was greeted by Sergeant Offatt who stood by the passenger window of the car.

"What have we got here, Sergeant?"

"Looks like a suicide, Jesse," he said and backed away from the car window to give Jesse room to work.

Jesse bent over and looked through the window, and shook his head at the sight. It was the second young girl he had seen dead in the same number of days. This one still had all her body parts, but she was still just as dead.

"Any ID?" Jesse asked when he stood back up.

"We haven't gotten that far yet. We called in the plates and the car's registered to a Kenneth Hollack in Houston."

"Can I have her yet?" Jesse asked.

"Yes, sir. We're gonna take the car back to the garage and go over it good just in case."

"Good." Jesse turned and motioned for the ambulance crew to bring the stretcher.

"It's a shame, huh?" the sergeant said.

"Yeah. Sort of makes me glad I never had any kids."

The attendants removed the girl's body and were careful not to touch anything they didn't need to. They loaded the body and left immediately. Jesse stayed until the wrecker arrived and towed the red Chevrolet away.

10

It was only ten o'clock, but Eric was famished. "I'm going over to The Kettle to get something to eat," he said to Amy as he walked out of his office.

"There's some *kolaches* by the coffee," she said as a reminder of an earlier invitation.

"I'm thinking more along the lines of a greasy burger," he told her.

"Oh, that'll do your heart good."

"My heart's not what's hungry," he said.

"You probably don't even have one," she whispered to herself.

"Say what?"

"I said are you coming back when you're done?"

"Of course," he said. "Where else would I go?"

"Just checking," she said. She turned to her typewriter and began to work on a stack of bills of lading.

Although Eric usually took the stairs for his three-floor trip to keep in shape, he decided on the elevator this time. When the door opened, he stepped in and found he wasn't alone.

"Morning, Mister Mayor," he said to the man who not only occupied the penthouse suite on the fifth floor, but also owned the building.

"Good morning, Eric," he said. "How's business?"

"Got 'em coming and going," Eric said.

"Good," Paschall said. "I can't think of a prettier sight than all those tankers lined up out there waiting to get in here."

"I can't argue with you there, sir."

The door opened to the first floor, and Eric waited for the mayor to exit first. "Have a good one," he said.

The mayor made no reply as he hurried off toward the savings and loan lobby.

"And you have one too," Eric said to himself, sarcastically.

The parking garage was full but he had no problem finding his car. Even if he didn't have an assigned parking space, a silver BMW with a surfboard racked on top wouldn't be too hard to spot. He checked the Wolfe surfboard to make sure it was still latched on tight before he got in. The board was like family and if he had a family he would make sure their seatbelts were on tight also.

His journey to The Kettle took him by the row of vacant warehouses at the same time as the wrecker was towed a red Chevrolet out of the alley. He stopped and let the wrecker pull out in front of him. His stomach growled in disagreement with his courteous move. He followed the tow truck for three blocks until it turned left toward the police impound yard. Eric turned right but caught a parting glance of the red car in his rear-view mirror.

11

Jesse had never grown accustomed to the heat of the Texas coast. He preferred the semi-frigid conditions of his own lab. He knew before beginning that when he cut the girl's T-shirt off he would find a bullet hole in her chest. The bullet would probably be lodged somewhere in or behind her heart from the amount of blood that covered her clothes. There had been no exit wound. He had seen that when they removed her body from the seat. Nevertheless, he took the surgical scissors and started at the bottom of the shirt and began to cut upward. As he cut into the sticky and somewhat dry material, he stopped when his eyes caught a glimpse of something stuck to the blade. Something that should not have been there. He searched the tray until he located a pair of tweezers and picked out what looked to be several strands of hair. He held them up into the bright, operating light, and then looked at the girl's head.

From first glance, they seemed to match her bark, brown hair, but as he looked closer, he realized there was a slight color difference. The length was also not right. The girl's hair was almost shoulder length with no bangs, while the strands in the tweezers looked to be no more than three, maybe four, inches long. He turned back to the tray and placed the hair in a plastic bag, then extracted some strands of the girl's hair and placed them in another bag.

"I'll look at you two later," he told them.

Jesse made the necessary surgical cuts in the body's chest cavity and located the bullet, extracted it, and laid it in a stainless-steel cup on the tray. He made several more expert cuts to make sure nothing else might have been involved in the girl's death. He found none. He dictated his findings, which included a series of scratches on her legs, into an overhead microphone, then covered the body with a hospital-type sheet. He purposely left out the part about finding the strands of hair.

He took the two plastic bags over to the microscope on the table behind the desk. He took out one of the shorter hairs first and placed it on a glass mounting plate and adjusted the scope until it was clearly in view. He followed the same routine with a sample of the girl's hair and found they were nowhere near alike. Just to be sure, he took another sample of each and mounted them side by side and came up with the same conclusion.

Had he been a smoker, he would have left the room and lit up before he made his next move. Since he wasn't and since he had finished off the bottle of scotch in his lower, left-hand desk drawer after yesterday's autopsy, he had no other alternative but to continue.

He went to his desk and unlocked the lower, right-hand drawer and took out a third plastic bag. He laid the bag on the table by the microscope and took a deep breath before he opened it. When he did, he took out a strand of hair taken from inside the body cavity of the alleged shark victim and placed it on the slide next to the hair found on the girl's T-shirt. He didn't want to look but knew he had to. He adjusted the scope until the matched set came into unmistakable view.

"No! No! No!" he screamed deeply into the side of the microscope and slammed both palms down on the table. One of the slides fell onto the floor and broke into too many pieces.

The old man felt a wave of nausea break over him. He gripped the table as tight as he could and fought back the urge that tried to control him. He lifted his head until he stared into the glass cabinet door in front of him.

"No!" he uttered with a growl when his bluish-yellow eyes stared back at him.

12

Andy stepped out of the shower just as the phone rang. It interrupted his train of thought, that was stationed on Michele and their upcoming date. She had caught up to him when they closed their towers and had continued where she had left off. Before he had had time to collect his thoughts and debate the pros and cons of why he should or should not accept her invitation of lobster at Gaido's, his mouth had said yes.

Since he lived alone, he saw no reason to have more than one phone, and it was on the wall by the bar. This was usually a convenient location, but in this instance, it required a short trip to answer. He wrapped a towel around his waist, which he thought rather silly of himself since the only one who would see the white flesh of his butt would be him and not without the aid of a mirror, and went into the living room and grabbed the phone off the wall.

"Hello?"

"Andrew?"

"Well, hello, Uncle Jesse."

"We need to talk," Jesse said rather abruptly. "I'll be there in fifteen minutes."

"I've got a date," Andy advised him.

"Break it."

"Why?" he said. His previous thoughts of dinner with Michele had now formed a knot in the pit of his stomach.

"I'll tell you when I get there."

"Come on, Jesse. Can't it wait?" he begged.

"No!"

The phone went dead before Andy could argue further.

"Damn!" he whispered into the phone before he placed it back on the vertical cradle. He reached under the bar and took out the phone book and tried to recall Michele's father's first name. He couldn't, but since there were only two Molson's in the book he had as much chance of being right as he did of being wrong.

He took the phone again and dialed the first number. He got lucky, if you could call having to break a date with a beautiful girl who was buying lucky, as Michele answered on the first ring.

"Hello?"

Andy didn't really know what to tell her since Jesse hadn't told him why he had to meet him, so he lied.

"Michele, this is Andy."

"I know," she said. "I recognize your voice." She wasn't making it easy for him.

"Listen," he said. "My uncle just called and he's sick. I need to go see him to make sure it isn't anything serious." Andy thought that his lie may very well turn out to be the truth. If what Jesse had to tell him could have waited, Jesse would damn sure need a doctor when he was through with him.

"So, you'll be a little late? That's OK. We'll just get a window by the seawall and look out into the darkness while we eat," she said sweetly.

"Damn you, Jesse," he thought, but to Michele he said, "Uh, no. I think we better just forget it for tonight."

There was silence from Michele's end of the line.

"Michele?"

"Well, at least you didn't say you have to stay home and wash your hair," Michele told him.

"You're mad, huh?" Andy said.

"No, just disappointed," she said.

"Listen. I'll make it up to you. I promise," Andy said.

"You damn sure will," she told him. "And you'll pick up the check when you do. I only offer once."

"That's fine," he said. "Whenever you want."

"I'll hold you to that promise, my friend," she said, "and don't think for one minute that I won't."

Andy could tell from her tone that it would be in his best interest to close their conversation before he either made a promise he couldn't live up to or told Jesse to go fuck himself and went out with Michele anyway.

"OK," Andy said. "I'll see you tomorrow."

"If you're lucky," she answered and hung up.

It was the second time in too short a period that someone had hung up on him before he could get in the last word.

13

Andy's call left Michele in a semi-useless funk. Back at college that meant it was time for her to grab any or all of her three suitemates and head for Sixth Street and party until the mood passed, which was usually when the bars closed. Since her parents didn't exactly meet those qualifications, she chose the next best thing and called Julie Archer. Julie was a high school friend who had also come home from college for the summer.

"Jules," Michele said when her friend answered. "What's happening?"

Julie knew it was Michele because of the pet name. Julie had one for Michele also. "Nothing out of the ordinary, Mick," she said. "I've got three guys standing outside my door waiting for a chance to bang my brains out. Why?"

"Oh, I don't know," Michele said. "I thought we might head on over to Kokomo's and see who we can latch onto."

"That sounds good to me," Julie said.

"What about the three guys?"

"Let 'em eat cake," Julie said.

"That would probably be better for them anyway," Michele said.

"Oh, really?" Julie said. "You been talking to my gynecologist?"

"No," Michele said, "but I did get a call from the Health Department."

"Damn! They told me that was all confidential."

"That's OK," Michele said. "I narrowed their list down to thirty for you."

"Thanks," Julie said. "Listen. Can you pick me up? My parents have both cars tied up tonight."

"No problem. How's eight?"

"Super," Julie said. "That'll give me enough time to take care of two of the guys anyway."

"How are you going to decide who goes without?" Michele asked.

"Shortest straw."

"Shortest straw?"

"Yeah, you know . . ."

"Nevermind. I'm sorry I asked. I'll see you at eight," Michele said and cradled the receiver to disconnect the call.

14

Andy threw on a pair of shorts and a muscle shirt. It was a far cry from what he had planned to wear that evening. He was about to mix up a pitcher of screwdrivers when Jesse came through the front door and saw him.

"No drinking," he announced.

"Bull **shit**!"

"You're going to need a clear head about you for what I'm about to tell you and I'm not so sure that's gonna help."

"If it's not gonna help then I'm gonna drink," Andy told him.

Jesse stepped up to the bar and yanked the bottle of vodka from his hand. "You can drink all you want when I'm finished and I'll probably join you but for right now you're gonna do what I tell you."

"Have it your way but it had better be good."

"It's not going to be. I'll tell you that right now, so sit down."

Andy did as ordered and plopped down in a padded, wicker chair hard enough to break it had he not reinforced the base after a similar incident. Jesse remained on his feet.

"Have you heard the news about the girl who committed suicide down in the warehouse district last night? Jesse asked.

"Yeah, I caught some of it, but what's that got to do with me?"

"Just listen," Jesse said. "You remember I told you I wasn't sure the girl yesterday was killed by a shark? Well, she wasn't."

Andy started to butt in again and ask what one had to do with the other but Jesse was too fast for him.

"They were both killed by the same think, or at least one of them was. The other was probably driven to it." He reached into his pants pocket and pulled out two plastic bags and pitched one to him.

"Those are hair samples. I found one in the bite wounds of the girl you saw yesterday and the other was taken off the clothes of the girl who was supposed to have committed suicide."

Andy looked at the hair through the plastic. As far as he could tell, that's exactly what it was. "So, you're saying somebody killed them? Uh, uh. That girl yesterday wasn't killed she was eaten."

"That's right," Jesse said. "And what you're holding is the hair of the thing that ate her."

"What the hell do you mean thing?"

"A wolf."

An air of unexplained silence filled the living room as Jesse gave his revelation time to soak in.

"A wolf?" Andy said. Like in *Little Red Riding Hood*? The big, bad wolf? How many Cutty's did you finish off before you came to that conclusion, Jesse?"

"You can joke if you want to, son, but you might want to wait cause I'm only just beginning this story."

"I hope for your sake that I'm the only one you've told this to so far, otherwise you're history, old man. The mayor's gonna see you locked up in that building with the padded walls and no windows."

"That might not be all bad," Jesse said. "But you're going to hear me out before they do."

"Go ahead then," Andy said. "You've already fucked up my evening. You might as well add to it."

Jesse took a deep breath and yearned for the scotch he wouldn't touch until he was through. "I wasn't exactly being truthful when I said it was a wolf." He paused and then forced the next words out. "It was a werewolf."

Holy shit, Jesse! You're fucked! You are pure D, absolutely, certifiably fucked!" Andy threw the plastic bags at him and stormed up out of the chair. The force sent it back against a bar stool.

Jesse looked at him as tears formed in his eyes. He wished Andy's father was still alive. They had talked about ways to tell him together and hoped the time would never come. For Phillip Langsjoen, it never did. Death had freed him from that responsibility.

"You're not making this easy for me, Andrew."

"What the hell do you want me to say? 'Oh, jeez, Uncle Jesse. The town's been overrun by werewolves. Let's go get us some silver bullets and kill the motherfuckers?' Huh?"

"That wouldn't work," Jesse said calmly.

"What wouldn't work?"

"Silver bullets," Jesse said. "Silver Bullets only kill werewolves in the movies."

"Oh, I see. And you're speaking from experience. Is that it?"

"I'm afraid so."

"OK, I've come this far. I'll bite. You tell me how you can kill a werewolf, then I'll sit down and have a couple of drinks and you can tell me what the punch line to all this is and I'll laugh and then you can get the hell out of here. Maybe it's still not too late for me to call Michele and go out."

"Only a werewolf can kill another werewolf," Jesse informed him and looked him square in the eye.

"OK, now that we got that behind us, give me the punch line."

Jesse's eyes never moved. "I'm a werewolf," he said. "And so are you."

"Yeah? Well, OK then. Let's me and you go out and hit a couple of bars and do a little howling at the moon, or does the moon have to be full?"

"It is full."

"Then what are we waiting for? We're cutting into some prime howling time."

"You're leaving me no choice, Andrew," Jesse said.

"What kind of a choice are you giving me? You walk in here with come cock and bull story about werewolves. You tell me that not only do they exist, but lo and behold I'm one of them. Where'd you put that vodka? If we're not gonna go out then I'm gonna stay here and drink and do a little howling of my own."

Andy found the bottle on the floor by the couch and took it behind the bar. While he poured an ample amount in a pitcher, Jesse walked around the living room and closed the blinds.

"Now what are you doing?" Andy asked and set the bottle on the bar.

Jesse didn't answer. He closed the last blind and positioned himself in the middle of the room where he began to undress. His words had failed so the time for action had come.

"A naked **man** is not exactly the gender I'd hoped to end up here tonight," Andy said.

"You'll have to forgive me if I don't get this right. It's been three years so it may take me a little longer than usual," Jesse explained.

"To do what?"

"I'm going to change into a werewolf. That seems to be the only way I can make you believe me," Jesse said calmly. "Oh, and don't be afraid. I won't hurt you. And by the same token, please don't try to hurt me because in your human form you won't stand a chance. I'll try to change back as quickly as I can."

"Wait a minute, Jesse. I need to get the orange juice out of the fridge. I want a drink if I'm gonna be watching a show."

"It's too late," Jesse said.

The low, raspy sound, not the words they formed, that came from Jesse's throat stopped Andy dead in his tracks and he headed for the kitchen. He turned just as the metamorphosis began.

Jesse's eyes were the first to change as they went from a deep brown to a bluish-yellow. A thick, gray mat of hair began to form over his partially bald head and spread rapidly down over his body that was now stooped over as if he had just been stricken with a terminal case of arthritis.

Andy couldn't move. It was as if his brain had suddenly ceased to send out signals to the rest of his body. He could have been brain dead for all practical purposes, but his eyes still worked, only what they saw did not register. Not yet.

Jesse's one-hundred-and-sixty-pound frame had now been fully transformed into what could have been a large, gray wolf. The only difference was the large hump that grew between its shoulder blades. It was not ugly. As a matter of fact, it was quite a handsome creature. Although it growled lowly, as if it were trying to speak, there was no menacing snarl. No curling of its mouth to reveal razor sharp teeth that could tear the throat from a human in a fleeting instant.

As if to prove a point, the creature sprang from the center of the room to the top of the bar that separated the living room from the kitchen, a distance of no less than fifteen feet. It stood there on all fours like the proud beast it had become.

Andy still couldn't move. It wasn't fear that draped on him like a heavy chain. It was the realization of what he had just witnessed. The realization that had finally worked its way into his brain and lay there like a bomb ready to explode.

When it understood that Andy had seen enough, the beast leaped off the bar and back into the center of the living room where the transformation began to reverse itself.

"Are you satisfied now, Andrew?" Jesse asked when he began to dress.

"How?" The word came out alone and hard.

"How is the rest of the story," Jesse said. He walked over to the front of the bar.

Andy found a way to move his feet and met him on the other side and again spoke. "How, Jesse?"

"Why don't you pour us those drinks now," Jesse said. "Then I'll finish the story."

15

Kokomo's was more in tune to the older crowd, those legitimately over twenty-one but under the mistrusting age of thirty. IDs were examined more thoroughly but exceptions were made for gray areas at the management's discretion. Michele and Julie were gray areas. Although they were not quite yet twenty-one, they were well into their twenty-first year and locals. They both ordered a beer then walked around the dark and crowded dance floor to the back, outside deck that spread out above the beach beyond the seawall. They found a small table next to the railing and took a seat.

"So, Mick, how's your love life been so far this summer?"

"Well, I haven't exactly had them lined up outside my bedroom door like some people I know," Michele answered.

"Don't give up yet. The summer's still young and you're not exactly a toad."

Michele enjoyed Julie's company. She hadn't been blessed with near the natural beauty as Michele but she made up for it in the wit department. She wasn't bad looking by any means, just a little too top-heavy for her own good. She found it hard to carry on a conversation with a male and have him keep eye contact with her. His gaze always ventured about a foot south. Her response to this was to fix her own gaze on his crotch and see how long it took him to realize that two could play that game.

"I know," Michele said. "And I've sorta got my eye on someone."

"Oh, really? Who?"

"One of the guys I work with."

"Oooh. One of those stud guards?" Julie said.

"Well, sort of."

"What do you mean, sort of?"

"Well, he's a little older," Michele said.

"Like what, twenty-five? Twenty-six?"

"Thirty-four."

"Shit, Mick. That's not older. That's old."

"Not really," Michele said defensively. "He doesn't look it."

"God, I hope not," Julie said. "Does he know you're after his ass?"

"I'm not after his ass. I just like him."

"So, who says you can't like someone and be after their ass at the same time? Looks to me like that would be the perfect relationship."

"I don't know," Michele said. "It's just not like that."

"Don't tell me you've given up on sex. I mean, I know you're a jock and all that but we all gotta eat to live."

"I haven't given up on sex. We just haven't gotten to that part yet."

"What part **have** you gotten to?" Julie asked.

Michele looked out over the railing where two surfers were practicing their art in the dark.

"Come on, Mick. This is Jules you're talking to. No secrets, remember?"

"Well, I did ask him to dinner."

"All right, a liberated woman after my own heart. Where'd you take him?"

"Nowhere," Michele winced. "He broke the date."

"You're shitting me, when?"

"Tonight."

"Tonight? You mean I'm sloppy seconds?"

"Fraid so," Michele said. "Sorry."

"Hey, no big deal," Julie told her. "That's better than being third." Julie paused for a few seconds. "I **was** your second choice, right?"

"Number two on my list but number one in my heart," Michele said.

"Whoa. Don't go getting kinky on me now," Julie said. "I don't think I'm ready for that yet."

"And here I thought you were game for almost anything."

"Yeah, but even us free spirits gotta draw the line somewhere," Julie said.

They had both been buried so deep in their shallow conversation that they had failed to notice a chair being placed at their table until its owner took a seat.

"I hope you don't mind if I join you," Eric said. "You looked like you were having a pretty good time."

"Not at all," Julie said. "You got a friend for my friend?"

"Uh, no," Eric said. "Is that going to pose a problem?"

"Not for me," Julie said. "My friend's got her eye on someone, anyway."

Michele just grinned and shook her head.

"My name's Eric."

"I'm Jules and the shy one over there's Mick, or Julie and Michele if you're not into cute names."

"Whatever," Eric said.

"I like a man who knows how to make a decision," Julie said.

Eric wasn't sure how to take Julie's comments but it wasn't that important. His eye had been on the other one, anyway.

"You want to dance?" he asked in Michele's direction.

"I thought you'd never ask," Julie answered instead.

Before he had a chance to set the record straight, Julie was up out of her chair and waiting. He knew that if he refused the one he might never get a chance with the other, so he got up and followed her back inside.

Michele took a sip of beer and thought about Andy. Maybe she **had** come on too strong with him. Maybe older men didn't like women who made the first move. Maybe she had scared him right out of their date. Maybe she had ruined it already.

Before she could maybe herself right out of Andy's life, Eric and Julie returned. Julie sat down but Eric remained standing. "Your turn," he said.

"Well, you did come here to have a good time," she told herself. To Eric she said, "So, I'm your second choice?"

"All right, girl," Julie said with a loud laugh. "Go to it."

Eric took her by the hand and led her inside.

16

The screwdriver Andy had poured himself two hours ago sat untouched in a wet pond on the end table by the couch. His gaze was hard-fixed on the old man who had just filled his mind with a story too unbelievable to be true and yet it had to be. He had seen the transformation with his own eyes or at least his brain told him he had.

Jesse's story ran across the screen of his mind like an old B movie. One where a husband, his wife and a war buddy, an army surgeon in his own right, had moved to Galveston Island and had lived supposedly normal lives until the birth of a son. While giving birth, the main artery near her womb had ruptured and caused the woman to bleed almost to the point of death before she fell into an irreversible coma.

Death would have been a blessing, but the woman, like the two men, was a werewolf, incapable of such a humane and natural death. For a werewolf can only die at the hands of another werewolf. She would have been forced to live forever in a death-like state.

The two men, understanding her fate and the pleading in her vacant eyes, had done what any loving husband and friend would have done. With her newborn son asleep at her side, the good doctor surgically removed her heart and allowed her to find peace.

This same good doctor, the county coroner, had been able to keep the truth of her death a secret, until now.

The storyline had faded at that point and resurfaced some thirty years later to find the husband's body racked with cancer. The disease would have eaten away at his body until he would have been forced to spend his painful days hidden from the eyes of the public. The good doctor again found he had no choice but to end his only friend's life in the same manner.

When Andy finally spoke, the words tore at his heart. "How many people did you and my father kill? And my mother?"

"Your mother was never forced to use her power, at least not to my knowledge. She was not born into it as your father and I were. She was human, but she had been so in love with your father that she allowed him to bring her into the fold. A simple bit had been all that was required," Jesse explained.

"How could she?"

"How could she not? It was her own choice and she never regretted it, just as I am sure she never regretted giving up her life to give you yours." There was a long silence before Jesse continued. "As far as your father and I, we killed but not for the sport. Not for the taste of the flesh."

"How have you kept from it? What about the moon?" Andy asked.

"We were born into it, as you were. We belong to the bloodline, the true werewolf."

"What's the difference?"

"First off, you must forget everything you've ever read about or seen in the movies. The only thing they have managed to get right is the fact that the moon does control our cycle, but in different ways. If you were born into the bloodline you have the power of control over your beast during the cycle."

"Then what kept my mother from changing?" Andy asked as he tried to comprehend the full measure of what was being force fed into him.

"We did, your father and I. We transformed ourselves with her with each cycle and kept her from the outside world."

"And me? What's kept me from changing?"

"Your of the bloodline. With each new offspring a werewolf becomes more human again. The power to control your beast becomes even stronger," Jesse said.

"So, if all this hadn't happened, I might have never known?"

"That's what your father had hoped for and so had I, but when we found out he had to die, we knew you would have to be told some day."

"Why? Why should that make any difference?"

The room grew deathly quiet as Jesse prepared to answer. "There may come a time when you will have to kill me," he said.

"No way, Jesse."

"I appreciate that, but if the time comes I hope you will do it," he said. "I hope you will do it out of love if nothing else."

"You don't even know if I **am** a werewolf." The words tore their way out with an ugly sound. "You said yourself that the bloodline weakens every time another one is born. I may be too human to change. After all, my mother was human once."

"No, your father's heart was too strong and your mother was of new blood."

"Then I'll kill myself first."

"You can't."

"Then I'll mess myself up so bad you'll have to kill me."

Andy's words bit deep into Jesse's lost soul. "You won't make me have to do that again. Not after you have felt the power."

"I don't want to feel the power," Andy said as he rose from the couch.

"I pray you won't have to," Jesse said. "But right now we have a more urgent matter to discuss."

"And what might that be?" Andy asked. He took his weakened drink from the table and headed out of the living room to dispose of it and start anew.

"We have another werewolf to kill."

The wet glass shattered when it slipped from Andy's hand and fell to the tile floor in the kitchen.

17

Michele pulled into the driveway of Julie's parents' Each Beach condo and killed the engine.

"I still say you should have gone on with Eric?" Julie said.

"And how would you have gotten home, walked?"

"Hey, I could have gotten a ride and who knows, I might have gotten lucky."

"Well, I didn't feel lucky," Michele said.

"You didn't have to," Julie said. "You already had him hooked. All you had to do was reel him in nice and easy."

"I wasn't fishing."

"You baited the hook."

"I most assuredly did not," Michele said.

"Well, what do you call dancing almost every dance with him?"

"We didn't dance every dance. You danced with him too."

"Oh, yeah, the first dance. Whoopie shit," Julie said.

"I don't want to discuss it anymore," Michele told her. "I just wanted to go out and have some fun. I wasn't looking for someone to jump in bed with."

"Prude."

"Fuck you, Jules."

❧

"Oh, so now you want to talk sex. You don't want to have sex, you just want to talk about it."

"Just shut up and go in," Michele said. "I'm tired and I gotta be on duty at seven."

"So, you can see your older man, huh?"

"Maybe."

"One of these days I'm gonna give up on you, Mick," Jules said when she opened the door and got out.

"Not anytime soon, I hope," Michele said.

"Not if you're lucky."

Julie shut the door and Michele started the engine and backed out of the drive. She waited until she saw her friend safely inside before she started up the street. Her mind was jumping between Andy and Eric when she came to the turn that would have taken her back to Seawall Boulevard and then home, had she not failed to negotiate it. She realized her mistake when the moon peered at her through the empty openings of the castle-like condotel on her left.

The beast had watched her from the minute she had left the condo. It had hoped for another easy victim as it had the night before. It sniffed at the air as it circled about the opening of its third-floor lair.

Michele brought the car to a slow stop. Her windshield was gritty from a buildup of sand from leaving it parked at the beach all day. She turned the wipers on but that did nothing more than spread the sand into thin lines across the glass. She pressed the washer button but all she got was a whining sound that reminded her she still hadn't refilled the reservoir she had noticed was empty that morning when she had tried to wash off the coat of overnight spray.

She wasn't sure if the road she was on would keep going and eventually lead her back to the main drag. She put her lights on bright but still couldn't see well enough through the sand scratched windshield. She got out for a better look.

The beast made its move. It barely felt the concrete floor beneath its feet when it took the stairs in long, graceful strides. It was on the sand almost immediately. The sweet scent from Michele's body filled the beast's nostrils as it waited momentarily in the cool substructure. Its lips quivered into a snarl as it imagined the taste of her flesh. It moved low to the ground toward the rear of the car as it stalked its prey.

Michele's body grew cold in the hot summer night. The chill brought her nipples to a point behind her shirt.

Saliva dripped from the beast's mouth as it took in her scent and prepared for the kill. It crouched at the rear of the car and prepared to lunge, but Michele lunged first.

The sound of the door as it slammed shut just before the rear wheel sent a spray of tar and gravel into its face sent the beast into a fit of uncontrollable rage.

When Michele drove down the broken asphalt path she thought she heard the sound of a dog howling but paid it little mind. For all she knew, it was just part of the background music from the new Van Halen tape that blared at her from the rear speakers.

The beast clawed at the ground as the tail lights that carried the young girl disappeared into the night. It charged at the rain-soaked stack of decaying sheetrock and tore the outside layer into a gaping hole of chalk and dust. The taste enraged it even more. It wasn't the taste it had yearned for in those fleeting moments. The taste it had been so close to. It shook the torn paper from its mouth and lumbered heavily toward the beach. It understood that the chances of another such opportunity would not prevail itself again that night.

18

Jesse found himself faced with no other choice but to play his last card. They had argued to the point where he was afraid he would lose him. Andy had threatened to leave the island and never return.

"Your father would have done it," Jesse said.

"Leave my father out of it," Andy said. "He's dead."

"That's precisely my point, Andrew."

Andy didn't respond. Jesse took his silence as a positive sign and began to plot his course of action in the lull.

"Tonight is the third and last night of the cycle which means he will probably kill again, if he hasn't already. The fact that we found the first body means he may not be of the bloodline. They don't leave their kill to be found."

"Don't you mean **we** don't leave **our** kill?"

Andy's comment was unexpected but welcomed nonetheless. It meant he was now ready to at least accept the fact that there would be a change in his life whether he wanted it or not.

"OK. As I've explained to you, if the victim's heart has been taken they are dead, plain and simple. The bloodline will then bury the evidence or destroy it in some way. If they don't take the heart then a new line is started, and for the want of a better explanation, a pack is formed. In this case he took the girl's heart but left her body."

"I'm sorry, but you've lost me," Andy said.

"You see, Andrew, the bloodline can still think like a human even while they are in the form of a wolf. So, if they aren't starting a pack . . ."

"Then they take the heart and destroy the body," Andy finished.

"Right, but in this case . . ."

"He fucked up."

"That's one way to put it, but only if he was of the bloodline. If he was once a victim himself then he would not have the power to reason while in the form. He would just kill, ravage and leave the remains as he did here."

"So, then he's not a bloodline werewolf."

"Right, except his kind don't usually take the heart. They don't understand anything other than killing and eating the flesh, and that's when all hell breaks loose. They kill, and then their victims kill and so on."

"Why don't we see or hear more about those if they do exist?"

"We do," Jesse said. "It's just that nobody believes it. You can go into any grocery store and pick up one of those colorful tabloids at the checkout counter and read about werewolves in pretty much every other edition. What you won't see though is anything about them being over here. They're all in Europe or South America or someplace like that, so everybody just laughs about it."

"Maybe he was just hungry," Andy said and forced a laugh for the first time that night.

"I'd rather believe otherwise," Jesse said.

"How's that?"

"I'd rather he be a bloodline werewolf who, as you put it, just fucked up. Otherwise, we could have a real mess on our hands."

"So, what do we do? I don't guess there's any way to recognize one, is there?"

"No, and don't ask me about garlic either because that's also something Hollywood made up just like showing a werewolf walking upright."

"I was gonna ask you about the garlic bit, as much as you like eating Russo's lasagna," Andy joked. "So, what's next?"

"We wait."

"Wait for what?"

"To see if another body turns up tomorrow," Jesse said.

"You mean today, don't you?" Andy said when he looked at his watch and saw their meeting had taken them to the other side of midnight in more ways than one. "And if one doesn't turn up?"

"Then we've probably got us a bloodline werewolf who has never lost the taste for flesh," he said. "Either way, there's not much we can do about it right now."

"Why?"

"This moon's cycle is about over."

19

The beast had roamed the beach and stayed carefully close to the low-rising dunes. It had stopped every hundred feet or so to lift its snout and test the air. Now, its patience was about to be rewarded.

A night fisherman and his black lab had decided to brave the dark beach in search of a new, untested spot to try their luck under the hypnotic glare of the full moon. The black lab could smell the danger even before the beast made its move from the dunes.

"What is it, Spook? You smell some fish? This must be the place then," the man said when his dog growled and began to make tight circles around him.

The beast waited until the man had entered the water to just below his knees and cast a heavy line into the surf. It crept over the sand, dragged its hairy chest over the cool surface and kept both eyes trained on the big dog. As it neared the animal the dog attacked. The beast caught it in mid-air and tore the black head from its body. The roar of the ocean drowned out the dog's final warning yelp to its master.

The taste of the animal's flesh and the warmth of its blood only heightened the beast's craving. It had tasted animal flesh before but only when the cycle was ending and the choice, human flesh could not be found. It inched its way to the water's edge and waited for the right moment.

"I got one, Spook," the fisherman said as he pulled back on the rod and set the hook. He started to walk slowly backward out of the surf and pulled the rod back and reeled in with each careful step.

The beast poised itself for the kill. It would wait until the man was out of the water.

With the next jerk the line snapped and the man was sent sprawling back onto the sand. "Son of a bitch!" he shouted and leaned up on his elbows. He turned to where he thought he saw his trusted companion watching him and started to speak to the animal. He started to tell him about the big one that had just gotten away.

Before the moon hit his eyes he was dead. The beast feasted on his strong heart but remembered its earlier loss. The cycle was now over but a new one would begin.

20

Michele was sitting on the bottom step of Andy's tower when he arrived ten minutes early. "How's your uncle?" she asked.

He hadn't expected to see her so soon, much less expected to be grilled when he did. Not that he shouldn't have, it just that after last night Andy didn't know what to expect anymore. He sure hadn't expected to be told he was a werewolf, whether he was or not.

"Huh?" he answered.

"Your uncle? You remember, the one who was so sick you had to go take care of him rather than go out to eat with me?"

"Oh, yeah," Andy said. "He'll be fine."

"He's not going to die, then?"

"No. Only a werewolf can kill another werewolf," Andy thought but didn't say. "Not in the near future," he said instead.

"Well, that's good," she said. "Did you take him some chicken soup?" she said sarcastically.

Andy's brain finally caught up with the conversation. "No, but I fed him enough scotch to kill what ailed him."

"So, you two just sat around and got drunk, huh?"

"That's what usually happens," he said.

"Well, I hope you had fun." She grabbed her bag and stormed off toward her tower.

Andy let her go. His mind was too tired and confused to argue. He had argued enough last night and that hadn't gotten him anywhere. He climbed up onto his tower and hung his shingle over the NO on the sign. He went through his morning ritual of scanning the gulf, which now made exactly no sense at all. There were no sharks, just werewolves, and for all he knew they probably couldn't even swim. They could kill. He knew that.

When his sweep ended on East Beach he saw one of the maintenance crewmen fiddling with an object near the surf. He adjusted the glasses until the man came into clearer view. He held what appeared to be a deep-sea rod and reel and looked up and down the beach, obviously in search of its owner. Andy scanned the beach himself but other than the truck driver there was no one else to be seen.

"Finders keepers, buddy," he whispered.

Andy swept back over the gulf and ended up at Michele's tower where he found her bent over and applying a sun block on her legs. Andy watched until she rose back up then laid the binoculars down and picked up the talkie.

"Tower three to tower five," he said into it.

He saw her turn in his direction then pick up her talkie. "Tower five. Go ahead," she answered in a business-like manner.

"I didn't," Andy said.

"You didn't what?"

"I didn't have any fun."

"Good," she said.

Andy had said what he needed to and laid the talkie back down before their conversation could be picked up by any of the other guards.

21

Eric slept in as he sometimes did, though not often. It was one of the perks of owning his own business along with leaving for the afternoon to surf. That he did more often and on a regular basis. Today would be a regular basis day. Michele had not only told him she was a lifeguard but had mentioned in passing that she would be at Stewart Beach today. He would be too.

While he shaved he decided to extend his perk and not go into his office at all. When he was done he went to the phone by his bed and called in. The receptionist put him through to Amy.

"You got the handle on things, Moneypenny?" Every once in a while he would throw Amy a curve just to see if she was listening to him.

"Yes, James. I just sent Q out for breakfast." This time she was.

"In case you haven't noticed, I'm not there," he said.

"Rough night?"

"No, rather enjoyable."

"I'll bet," she said. "When can we expect you?"

"Tomorrow."

"Tomorrow? Does that mean we can shut it down here and all go home?"

"Not if you like getting paid on a regular basis," he said.

"Where will you be if I need you?"

"Why, you've never needed me before?"

Amy wasn't sure how to take that comment, so she tested the water. "I didn't think you were interested." She found it easier to trade Freudian slips with him when they had a mile or so of optic cable between them.

"What if I am?" he said.

She suddenly realized she had ventured out past the last sand bar and could feel the undertow as it grabbed at her ankles. "Are you?"

"It depends on what you have in mind," he told her.

"How about dinner and a movie?" she said.

"I was thinking more along the lines of greasing each other down with Wesson Oil and rolling around on the kitchen floor," he said.

"I believe that could be considered sexual harassment." She back-peddled when she realized he had just been toying with her.

"Then I guess you **aren't** interested," he said.

"No and it's a shame too.

"Why's that?"

"A dirty mind is a terrible thing to waste," she said. "See you *manana*."

Eric cradled the phone and reminded himself that he had made it a rule to never mix business with pleasure. "But if she's really interested," he told himself, "I can always fire her afterward."

He threw his most expensive pair of jams and headed for Stewart Beach.

22

Andy was lunching on his usual cold submarine sandwich from the pavilion snack bar. There was something about microwaves he just didn't trust. He thought that if you ate enough microwaved food you would probably nuke yourself in the end.

"No need to worry about that anymore, son," he told himself. "Only a werewolf can kill a werewolf." He threw the half-eaten sandwich in the trash.

From his table on the pavilion patio, he could see Michele's tower. She was leaning against the side railing with her head tilted back to catch the full effect of the sun's rays. Andy grinned when he thought of what his father had told him about turkeys. How when it rains the stupid birds tilt their heads back to catch the falling water and eventually drown. He pictured a field of turkeys with their heads back catching raindrops while a turkey lifeguard ran around trying to save each one from the inevitable. But, it wasn't raining and Michele wasn't a turkey and for all he knew she wasn't stupid either.

"That's debatable, son," the voice in his mind told him. "After all, she does seem to be interested in **you**."

"Go fuck yourself," he told himself, then realized what he had just said and to whom.

While Andy had been carrying on his one-sided conversation, Eric had parked his BMW in the lot near Michele's tower. He unlatched his cream-colored Wolfe board with the brown and green stripes down the middle and hoisted it off the roof and over his head. He walked to the side of Michele's tower and leaned the board against it.

"Hi, Mick," he said.

The sound of someone other than Julie calling her by that name startled her. Even though she had been worshipping the sun with her eyes closed, the ultra violet rays had still managed to penetrate her eyelids enough to cause sun spots when she opened them. She put a hand above her eyes as if saluting whoever had spoken to her and looked down.

"It's me, Eric."

"Oh, hi," she said. "What are you doing here?" She felt a nervous twitch work its way up her body.

"Same thing I do most every afternoon," he said and reached over and pulled his surfboard toward him.

The twitch turned to a chill that seemed to jell at the ends of her nipples. She didn't notice but Eric did and took it as a feeling of excitement at his presence.

"Are you planning on surfing here?" she asked.

"I can't think of anyone I'd rather have around to save me from drowning," he said.

Michele knew the rules about fraternizing with the beach-goers and she knew Andy knew them as well. "If you must talk to the people, do so when your watch is over." Or as Andy put it, "If you're gonna flirt with 'em, do it on your own time."

She knew Andy was at lunch, but she also knew he took lunch at the pavilion so he would still be close by if he was needed. Right now, he wasn't needed, but she could feel him watching. She fought the urge to turn in his direction to confirm her feeling.

"Listen," she said. "I'm not allowed to talk to anyone while I'm on duty."

"OK," he said. "How about when you're off?"

"What do you mean?"

"Let's go somewhere when you get off."

"Oh, I don't know," she said, nervously.

"Then I'll just stay here and talk."

"No, you can't do that."

"Then let's go out."

Michele could feel herself being backed into a corner of her tower. Maybe she had been wrong. Maybe she did need Andy right now, or maybe not. She had had a good time with Eric last night but he had been her second choice of sorts. It would give her something to do, plus, if Andy had it in his mind to ask her out to make up for breaking their date last night, she could tell him she was sorry but she already had a date. This all might work to her advantage.

"OK," she said, "but I'll have to meet you somewhere."

"That's fine," Eric said. "How about The Black Pearl at eight?"

"OK," she said, "but please go on before I get in trouble."

"You got it," Eric said. "Just don't let me drown." He grabbed his board and headed victoriously into the surf.

Andy had his hand on his talkie and was about to call Michele's tower and remind her of the no flirting rule when he saw the surfer run for the water. He was relieved he didn't have to make the call.

23

Eric straddled his board out in the flat behind the breakers and saw Michele pack her bag in preparation to close her tower for the day. The waves had pretty much played out by the middle of the afternoon. He had stayed around and rode the three-footers just to keep an eye on her. He assumed she had been doing the same. He bellied down on the board and caught a shallow wave in and jumped off on the last sand bar. He lifted the board over his head and flexed his muscles to give her one last look as he walked to her tower. She was descending the wooden steps when he got there. He shoved one end of the board into the soft sand until it stood upright on its own.

"You sure I can't pick you up?" he said.

Michele gave serious thought to breaking the date since her watch was over and the pressure was off, but realized he would probably just show up tomorrow and again the next day until she gave in.

"No," she said, "that's OK. I'll just meet you there."

"If you insist," he said. "Can I walk you to your car?"

"No, I have to check out. I'll see you later." She jumped off the bottom step and onto the sand and hurried toward the pavilion. She didn't need to check out as she had told him, but she didn't need to be walked to her car either.

The afternoon had been quiet, so quiet that Andy had had too much time on his hands. He had also had too much time in his head and had spent much of it debating on whether to ask Michele out that night or not. When he closed his tower "or not" was ahead, but when he saw Michele waiting for him in front of the pavilion stairs "whether to" jumped into the lead again.

"Another day, another dollar," Michele said just to get a conversation started.

"Give or take a quarter or two," he answered.

"For you, maybe. You make more than me."

"Stick around and you'll be in the big money one of these days too," Andy said.

When Michele failed to come up with a continuation to their conversation Andy took a deep breath and nervously forced out his question. "I know this is kinda short notice, but are you free tonight?"

"It is and I'm not," she said. What she had hoped for had materialized.

"Oh," Andy said. He now wished that the other side had won the debate. Asking had been hard enough on him, now he would have to live with her rejection.

Michele did leave the door open, however. "Maybe another time."

"Sure," Andy said. "No problem."

They both stood awkwardly on the concrete walkway, unsure of who was supposed to make the next move. Andy just wanted to get into his Bronco and home, but he didn't know how to leave properly and still save face. He could just tell her he would see her in the morning, but somehow that wasn't enough.

"I've got another date," Michele said.

Instead of saving face by waiting, Andy got a door slammed in it. He still managed to come up with a parting shot. "I guess that makes us even then."

"Nope," Michele said. "You still owe me."

The door cracked open just enough for a ray of hope to shine through, but Andy knew he would have to wait a while before he would be allowed to walk through. "OK, then. I guess I'll see you in the morning."

From where she stood, Michele had watched Eric pack up his board and drive off. Had he not, she was prepared to continue her conversation with Andy even if it meant opening the door even wider. "I'll be here," she said. "I need the dollar."

She headed toward the lot to the left of the pavilion. Andy went in the opposite direction. Being the senior lifeguard meant he got to park on the shady side next to the building. It was a small perk, but a perk just the same.

He opened the Bronco door and threw his bag inside and cursed Jesse for making his life miserable in more ways than one. It was the first time that afternoon that his thought had centered on Jesse, now he had the whole night to think about him. The werewolf too.

24

Eric was leaning against his BMW when Michele drove up and parked next to him in The Black Pearl lot. He had taken the surfboard off and left it on a wall rack in his garage next to his two others.

"Nice car," Michele said when she got out of her late model Malibu.

"It gets me there," he said.

"Mine does too," she said, "but it doesn't always get me back."

When they started to walk toward the front door, Eric took her hand. She felt a chill again but her nylon jacket hid the evidence on her arms.

A tall, bleach-blonde hostess in a revealing evening gown greeted them when they entered. There were at least a dozen others standing about waiting for tables.

"Two for dinner?" she asked.

"Yes," Eric said.

There'll be about a thirty-minute wait," she informed them.

"I don't think so," Eric told her rather abruptly. "The name's Beckett and we have an eight o'clock reservation." He slid his left thumb up against his forefinger to reveal the business edge of a twenty-dollar bill to the girl.

The hostess made a one-eighty turn, walked to her station and checked a list on top of the stand. She took her pencil and made a mark on the sheet and then motioned to them. "If you'll follow me please, Mr. Beckett. Your table is ready."

Eric made a sweep of the waiting area with his eyes and smiled before following her. She seated them by a front window with a view of the gulf and lit the candle in the middle of the table. "Milo will be your waiter and he'll be right with you. Enjoy your meal."

Eric didn't reply. He slipped the twenty into her hand instead.

"It's a good thing you made reservations," Michele said.

"I always do."

"You eat out a lot, do you?"

"I don't cook, if that's what you mean," he said.

It wasn't, but she didn't say so."

A young man who looked to be of college student age came to their table and introduced himself as Milo and asked if he could take their drink order.

"I'll have a gin and tonic and the lady will have a . . ."

"Beer," Michele said. "A beer's fine."

"We have . . ." The waiter started to go through their list of imported and domestic beer, but Michele didn't care to listen.

"Miller Lite," she said.

"Bottle, can or draft?"

"Only at the beach would beer be offered in a can," Michele thought and told the waiter a draft and waited for the next decision she would have to make.

"I'll bring them right out," Milo said.

"We'd also like two dozen oysters on the half-shell," Eric told him before he could make a clean getaway.

"Not me," Michele said and made a curling gesture with her upper lip.

"You sure?" Eric said. "You know what they say about raw oysters."

The waiter did what waiters are known for. He waited.

"You mean that they make you horny?" Michele said.

"That's one way to put it," Eric said. "They're an aphrodisiac."

"Whatever," Michele said. "But they don't make me horny. They make me puke."

The waiter held back a laugh at her direct choice of words.

"Better make that just one dozen then," Eric said.

"I think you're right," Milo answered.

"You really don't believe that?" Michele asked when the waiter was finally set free.

"They've never failed me before," Eric said.

"You're awfully sure of yourself," she said.

"Not really," he said. But it never hurts to be prepared."

"Funny," Michele said.

"What is?"

"You don't look the Boy Scout type."

"What type do I look like?" Eric asked. The thrill of the chase was beginning to excite him.

"I don't know, but didn't you sell me my car?"

"Ouch."

Michele made a note to play back their conversation to Julie the next time they talked. Julie would be proud that she had learned at the feet of the master, although mistress was a better fit for her friend. She smiled at the double-edged thought.

"Just joking," Michele said to take some of the sting off.

"Never do that," Eric said.

The serious tone in his voice frightened her for a minute. "Never do what?"

"Once you've stuck the knife in don't pull it right back out. It spoils the victory," he explained.

"Sorry," she said. "I didn't know we were fighting."

"We weren't," he said. "But you won anyway."

"I always heard that it doesn't matter if you win or lose but how you play the game."

"Yeah, I read that once."

"Did you now?"

"Yeah. It was on the tombstone of a loser."

The waiter returned with their drinks and a big plate of raw oysters. He set the drinks in front of them and the oysters in the middle of the table. Eric moved his drink to the side and slid the plate in front of him.

"Yuk," Michele said. "Are you really going to eat those?"

"It would be a waste not to," he said.

"Then you won't mind if I look out the window until you're done."

"Have it your way." He reached down and plucked a shell from the edge closest to him, tilted it above his mouth and let the meat drop straight down his throat.

Michele grimaced and took a long drink of beer. She looked out the window and watched a flock of seagulls hover above a small girl who was pitching pieces of bread into the air. "I hope you don't get shit on too," she told the girl in silence.

When Michele finished her beer she looked back at the table in enough time to see Eric throw the last oyster into his mouth. "Good timing," he said after swallowing it whole.

"Not good enough," she said. "Can we get rid of that thing now?" She pointed to the plate of empty, yet slimy shells.

Eric motioned to Milo who had just set a round of drinks on a nearby table. He nodded and returned to them.

"How were they?" Milo asked Eric, but looked at Michele for an answer.

Michele wanted to say something derogatory but didn't.

"I think they'll do the trick," Eric said.

"You ready to order?" Milo asked as he picked up the plate.

Michele realized she had missed her chance. She could have been hiding behind the rather large menu and deciding what to order rather than just gazing out the window. She picked it up and ordered the seafood pasta. "And I need another one of these," she said and held up her empty glass.

"Very good," Milo said. "And you, sir?"

"I'll have the oysters Rockefeller."

"You would," Michele said.

25

"Thanks for a lovely dinner," Michele told Eric when they walked out of The Black Pearl and toward the parking lot. She hadn't meant it.

"That's just the beginning," he said and walked to the driver's door of the BMW.

"The beginning of what?" she asked as she stood between her car and his with her hand on her own driver's door.

"Get in," he said and unlocked the doors.

"What about my car?"

"Leave it here," he ordered. "I don't think anyone is going to steal it."

"No, but they might have it towed away," she said.

"Then I'll pay to get it out."

"Thanks, but I don't need the hassle." Michele was looking for a way out of what he said was going to be just the beginning.

"Then park it out on the street," Eric said. "Nobody will bother it there if you're that worried about it."

Michele found herself out of excuses. She got into her car, backed out of her space and drove to the rear of the lot and parked on Sealy Street. She could have driven out the front onto Seawall Boulevard and been gone, but her old Malibu would have been no match for his BMW if a chase had surely ensued.

Eric waited for her in the lot until she returned and got in.

"Where are we going?" she asked as she buckled up.

"The Beacon," he said.

"That's way over in Port Bolivar," she said. "Can't we just go some place around here?"

"You got something against ferry rides?" The only way to get from Galveston Island to Port Bolivar was by ferry. It was a twenty-minute ride after at least a twenty-minute wait in traffic to board.

Michele didn't have anything against a ride on the ferry, as a matter of fact she thoroughly enjoyed riding the ferry at night, but she also enjoyed turning right around and riding it back. She did have something against leaving the safe confines of her island though. She could get back to her car from anywhere on the island. From elsewhere, she wasn't so sure.

"No," she told him. "I'd just rather spend my money locally."

"It's my money spending tonight," he said. "So, just sit back and enjoy the ride."

Before she could come up with another excuse; one he would probably have another answer for; Eric backed out and turned left onto Seawall Boulevard.

The ferry was docking when they stopped in the fairly short line of traffic. After the boat unloaded the returnees, they followed the line of cars on and parked about mid-deck next to the cabin that housed the engine room. Eric lowered

the power windows then shut off the BMW's motor
like the sign on the cabin wall told him to do.

Five minutes later they headed out into the
channel. Eric turned the key to auxiliary and put
a Creed disc in the CD player. "You like Creed?"
he asked.

Michele did, but she wasn't going to admit it
any more than she was going to admit that she
liked moon-lit ferry rides. "They're OK," she said
instead.

"Would you rather hear something else?"

What she wanted to hear was the captain telling
them that Port Bolivar was closed so they would
have to return to the island, but she knew that
wasn't likely to happen on this trip.

"No, that's fine."

From where they had parked, all Michele could
see was the side of another car. When she turned
to ask Eric if they could get out and go stand by
the railing she found herself face to face with
him. He put a strong arm on her shoulder and kissed
her on the lips. It wasn't a bad kiss, but it
didn't do anything for her either, other than
catch her by surprise. When their lips parted,
Eric looked her in the eyes for some kind of sign,
and then kissed her again.

This one was different. Eric slipped his
tongue in and touched hers. Michele jerked back
as far as the seat would let her. "You behave,"
she said.

"Come on, Michele," he said. "Just sit back
and enjoy the ride. We've only got about fifteen
minutes left."

He leaned over farther and tried to kiss her again, only this time he put his hand on her right breast and squeezed lightly. She tried to push him away but he was too strong. She tried to turn her head away but that only served to give him another target. He went for her bare neck and bit into the tan flesh. It wasn't hard enough to draw blood but it hurt just the same.

"Stop it!" she yelled over the music and grabbed for the hair on the back of his neck.

The man in the next car looked in their direction, but turned back just as quickly when Eric backed away and caught his stare. That was all the time Michele needed. She unlatched the seat belt that had held her prisoner and shoved the door open hard enough to slam it against the side of the other car.

"Hey!" the other driver said. "Watch it!" But his warning fell on fleeing ears.

Michele slid out quickly and ran down the row of cars to the back of the ferry. Eric jumped out but didn't chase after her. He went around the front of his car to the other side and looked at the door. There was a deep bend along the edge and an even deeper gouge in the dark green metal of the car next to it.

The other driver tried to open his door to get out and inspect the damage but Eric pushed it shut, then gently closed Michele's door. The other driver, an elderly man with an unshaven face, who probably worked on the island and had stayed for a few beers before taking the ferry home, tried to get out again. Eric put both hands against the door and held it shut. "I think you better stay put, old man. You don't want to bite off more than those false teeth of yours can chew."

The old man didn't answer. Instead, he reached down between his legs and brought up a beer can he had nestled in his crotch and took a long drink.

"Good idea," Eric told him and patted him on the cheek then walked down the row of cars toward the back of the boat. He knew he didn't need to hurry as Michele had nowhere to go. While she was a lifeguard and probably an expert swimmer, she wasn't expert enough to dive into the swirling waters of the channel and try to swim back.

He found her in a small crowd. She had a death-grip on the heavy chain that guarded the entrance ramp. He gave a light but threatening shove to the man who stood beside her and took his place.

"I'm sorry," he said, but to Michele the words sounded plastic.

"Touch me again and I'll scream," she told him without looking in his direction.

"I won't," he said. "Just cool down and come on back to the car."

"I have cooled down," she said, "but I'm not going back anywhere with you."

"You have to eventually," he told her. "We'll be at the port in ten minutes."

"I don't have to do shit," she said and gripped the chain even tighter.

"Look, we're even, OK?"

"Like hell we are!"

"You put a two-hundred-dollar dent in my car, so I'd say that makes us about even," he told her.

"Fuck your car!" she told him back.

Eric could feel the stares of the people around him from her comment. What he didn't need was an audience. "OK," he said calmly. "I said I was sorry, now come on back. We're almost there."

Michele finally looked him in the eyes, unaware of anyone else's presence but his. "The only time I'm going to get back into your car is when this thing has docked back on the island and then you're going to take me back to mine."

"You're not serious?"

"I'm serious as death."

"What if I just decide to drive off at the port and leave you?"

"Why don't you just do that," Michele said. "As a matter of fact, that's a done deal."

"No, I'm not going to leave you stranded like that," he said. He finally decided it was time to admit defeat and regroup.

"Don't worry about me," she said. "I can get a ride."

"I can't let you do that."

"Why not, it was your idea?"

"You know I didn't mean it."

"Well, **I do** and that's all that matters."

"OK," Eric said. "I'm going back to my car. When the boat docks, I'll turn around and get back on. You can stay out here until we get back, then I'll take you back to your car.

"I don't give a rat's ass what you do," Michele said.

"All right. I know you're mad. Maybe the night air on the way back will bring you to your senses," Eric said. "If not, you can do what you want to."

"If I had any sense I wouldn't have agreed to go out with you in the first place," she said. "I should have told you to go to hell this morning."

"But you didn't"

"That's obvious."

"So, you must like me a little bit."

"I may have then, but I sure as hell don't now."

"You'll get over it," he said.

She let go of the chain and turned to face him, still oblivious of the crowd that had grown around them. She lifted her right hand up in front of his face and showed him a slim, middle finger.

The applause of the crowd was drowned out by the ferry's horn as it signaled their arrival at Port Bolivar.

26

Andy was watching the local news when the phone rang. He got up from the wicker chair and grabbed the phone off the wall above the bar. He knew a call at that time of night would not be good news. It seldom was.

"Hello?" Andy said and leaned on the bar.

"Andy? It's Michele."

Andy was glad his assumption had been wrong. Maybe this would start a new trend in late night calls. "What's the matter?" he asked. "I thought you were on a date."

"I was," she said. "That's why I'm calling."

Andy stood up and backed away from the bar and tried to figure out what she had just said, but before he could unscramble the message she continued.

"Listen. Can you come pick me up?"

"Uh, yeah. Sure. Where are you?" Andy asked.

"At the ferry dock."

"You alone?"

"Uh, huh," she answered. "And Andy?"

"Yeah?"

"Could you hurry?"

Michele hung up the pay phone after Andy had told her he was on his way. She walked from the booth and stood in front of the tourist building that was closed for the night. She could still see Eric's car parked in the small lot across the way reserved for folks who took the ferry just for the sake of taking the ferry. They weren't going anywhere once they got to Port Bolivar other than back to the island without so much as stepping a foot on that far shore. Eric, on the other hand, had other reasons to be parked there. She hoped he was still in the car and that he would stay in it until Andy arrived.

Eric hadn't spoken to her again on the return trip even though their audience had departed at the port. When they had docked at the island, she had run off the boat as soon as the chain had dropped and had taken shelter at the corner of the tourist building. She had watched as Eric drove off the ferry and had hoped he would just keep on driving. Had he done so, she was going to call Julie to come pick her up. Since he hadn't, she had called Andy instead. She could have called her father but then she would have had to explain her predicament and face the music. With Andy there would be no music to face, at least none with penalties attached to the end of the song.

She had hopefully watched more than a dozen cars come up the road toward the dock in the ten minutes before Andy's green and white Bronco appeared. Eric's car was still there. She walked out from the shadows at the side of the building to where Andy could see her, and Eric too, for that matter.

Andy pulled to a stop by the curb where she jumped in immediately. "Let's get out of here," she said.

Andy made a U-turn in the lot and headed back up the road. Michele didn't look in the direction of the parked BMW when they passed.

"You got a story behind all this?" Andy asked.

"Yeah and I'll tell you about it if you'll let me buy you a beer," she told him.

"Hell, buy me a pitcher and I'll let you kiss me on the lips." Andy didn't know where that comment had come from. He didn't even like beer, but at least he had made her laugh and she looked like she needed it. She looked like she needed them both, the laugh and the beer.

"If he was lucky, she would need him too," he told himself before he realized she already had.

Just before they reached Seawall Boulevard, Michele told Andy to pull into the Circle K convenience store near the intersection. When he obeyed, she jumped out and ran in and returned with a six-pack of lite beer.

"A six-pack's more than a pitcher, isn't it?" she asked when she got back in.

"If it's not, we'll just have to pretend," he said.

Even though she felt safe with Andy, Michele still felt a chill engulf her when Eric's BMW drove by in front of them as they were about to exit the Circle K lot.

"You OK?" Andy asked when his previous comment failed to muster up the response he thought it would bring. He saw she was sitting upright in the seat and clutching the sack containing the beer like a security blanket about to be taken from her and headed for the wash.

"I will be," she said when she saw the BMW take a right on Seawall Boulevard. "Let's go to your tower."

"It's a little early to be going to work, don't you think?" Andy joked.

"Not when you enjoy it, she answered.

Andy drove into the entrance to Stewart Beach, through the sandy lot and around to the far side of the pavilion where he usually parked. The remnants of a full moon hung over the ocean like a pale reminder, but Andy paid it no attention. They got out of the truck and walked around the pavilion and onto the beach. Michele kicked her shoes off and wrinkled her toes in the cool sand.

When they got to Andy's tower, Michele sat down on the bottom step and took the beer out of the sack and handed the first one out of the rung to Andy. Rather than telling her he had never developed a taste for beer, he accepted it and pulled back on the tab. Since she was watching him he took a drink and sat down beside her. She took one for herself and leaned back against the second step. Andy allowed her time to relax and rolled the cold can of beer around in his hands.

"I guess you want an explanation?" Michele said.

"Only if you want to give me one." Andy really didn't care about what had happened to bring them together like this. The fact that something had was all that mattered to him.

"I might as well since we're here." Michele went on to tell him about her ill-fated date with the surfer he had probably seen talking to her that day.

Andy didn't admit he had but he didn't admit he hadn't either. He just listened and nursed his beer and when Michele was all through she ended by saying, "So, you see, it's all your fault."

"What do you mean, my fault?" Andy said.

"If you hadn't broke our date last night none of this would have happened," she said.

"I see," Andy said. "And we wouldn't be sitting here on the beach in the moonlight either. Sorry about that."

"That's not what I meant," she said in a hurry. "I'm glad we're here."

"Then just relax and enjoy it."

"You could've gone all night and not said that," Michele told him when she remembered those very words spoken to her earlier.

"Why? What's wrong with that?"

"Nothing, I guess," Michele said. "Coming from you anyway." She leaned her head back and closed her eyes. Andy took the chance and lowered the beer can that had become warm in this right hand and poured its contents onto the sand by the steps, then crushed the can to show he had allegedly finished his first one, a mistake he instantly regretted.

Michele opened her eyes and leaned forward. "Ready for another one?"

"Guess so," he said sadly.

She took a final drink and said, "Me, too." She took two more beers out of the rung and handed him one. "Better slow down," she continued. "We gotta make these last a while."

"I'll see what I can do," Andy said.

It was after one o'clock when the last can was crushed. Michele and the beach had tied with three each. Andy had come in a distant third and thirsty to prove it.

"I guess we better go," Michele said. "We gotta be back here in a couple of hours."

"Yeah," Andy said. It's a shame we can't just stay here. It would save time."

"I'd consider it if I thought you were serious," she said.

"We're hardly dressed for work," he said.

"I know, but it's the thought that counts."

"Come on and I'll take you home," Andy said when they stood up.

"My car's at The Black Pearl, remember? Or weren't you even listening to my sob story?"

"Oh, that's right," Andy said. "I'd almost forgotten about your date.

"I wish I could." Michele put the cans into the sack and threw them into a trash barrel on their way back to the Bronco.

They drove to Sealy Street and found her car just as she had left it. When Andy parked behind the Malibu, Michele leaned over and gave him a kiss on the cheek.

"Thanks for picking me up," she said

"Does that make us even now?" Andy asked when she opened the door.

"No," she said. "Now you owe me double."

"How's that?"

"I called you, remember?" She closed the door before he could muster up an argument, not that he would have.

He waited for her to get in and drive off before he pulled from the curb and made a U-turn and headed in the opposite direction. About a block down the street, he passed a parked, silver BMW with an empty surfboard rack on top. Andy didn't see the driver but the driver saw him.

27

Andy didn't mind having to work on the Fourth of July. It meant he wasn't expected to make a showing at the Ashton Villa's Ice Cream Crank-off and listen to another boring speech by Mayor Paschall. As far as he was concerned, the less he saw or heard of him the better off he was. He was sure the feeling was mutual.

The real fun didn't start until the sun was about to go down anyway. At that time all the lifeguards would parade down Seawall Boulevard in their two-tone, emerald green and white Jeeps, Blazers and Broncos and park at the far end of the Flagship Hotel pier to watch the fireworks display.

Michele had drawn the duty with him at Stewart Beach again and had gotten there early to make sure she got the tower nearest his. It would have been an automatic on any other day, however there was an extra guard assigned to the beach for the Fourth crowd and she didn't want to take the chance of being bumped to the far end; a hot, sandy mile away.

There had been no more alleged shark attacks although the jury was still out on the missing fisherman who had last been seen after the park closed, casting out from the waist-deep surf of Stewart Beach. That had been two weeks ago and the local authorities had given up the search after three days when his trusted black lab had also failed to return to their house on Avenue M. A meal of them both would have been too much for even a hungry shark to handle without leaving some scraps around for the crabs to nibble on. His disappearance was still a mystery since his rusty, old Datsun pickup was still parked in his driveway.

It wasn't a mystery to everyone; however, Jesse was not at liberty to divulge his theory on the man's sudden disappearance. He was sure of how he had died and why. He was also pretty sure where, especially since Andy had tendered the evidence to him when he told him about the maintenance man finding the rod and reel on East Beach the following morning.

The authorities were also torn between declaring the dead girl found in the car a suicide or not. Her boyfriend, one Bobby Hollack, had also turned up missing, leading them to believe she might have been murdered; but the authorities didn't know about the hair.

Jesse added the missing fisherman and boy to the supposedly shark victim and counted the werewolf's coup at three, the same number of nights in the full moon's cycle.

That grisly thought had been sitting wearily on Andy's mind when Michele jogged passed him on her way to her tower earlier that morning and asked him if he would be her date for the fireworks. He had said yes without even realizing what it was he was agreeing to.

It had been a little over a week since Michele had split the six-pack with the beach in Andy's company, and although they had worked together the following day, Michele had been assigned to Palm Beach the following week. He hadn't seen her in all that time. Michele had left the next move to him, but he had yet to make it. Seeing him that morning had changed her mind.

Andy was taking his usual lunch of a cold submarine sandwich at his usual place on the pavilion deck when an all-too-familiar voice called his name from the top of the side stairs that led to the parking lot. Andy bit into his cheek when he turned and confirmed what he already knew.

"Mister Mayor. I thought you'd be back at your office practicing your speech." There was no feeling in his voice to hide the fact that he knew the speech would be the same one the mayor had lulled the crowd to sleep with year after year.

"There's plenty of time for that," the mayor said. He took a seat across from Andy. "I just thought I'd come down here and check out the crowd."

"Well, as you can see, all the chairs and umbrellas are spoken for again this year," Andy commented.

"Good. Good. We need the money."

"Oh, really? I didn't know we were hurting."

"That's because you don't know that much about operating a city like ours."

"My daddy did."

The may looked at him hard for a few heated seconds. "I didn't come down here to open up old wounds," the mayor said.

"I know," Andy responded. "You came to check out the crowd."

"Well, not really."

"Oh?"

"I really wanted to speak to you about Jesse."

"What about Jesse? You gonna try and get him fired again?" Andy could feel his temperature rise. The shade of the pavilion offered him no help against the mayor's words.

"No, I'm really kind of worried about him."

"That's so much bullshit," Andy said.

"No, I'm serious, Andy. I know your family and I haven't exactly seen eye to eye about things and that's probably not going to change, but I've got a job to do around here and neither the city nor the county can afford to hire a new coroner right now."

"So, what's the problem? As far as I know, Jesse's got no intention of retiring in the near future."

"I don't think his mind's been in the right place lately," the mayor said.

"How so?" Andy asked. He watched as beads of perspiration formed at the point of the man's red widow's peak.

"Well, for one thing, he's been sort of wishy-washy concerning that girl."

"What girl?" Andy asked. He knew full well who he was talking about but he wanted to hear the mayor say it. He wanted to drag every little bit of information out of him while he sat there sweating.

"The girl they found in the car."

"Oh, the suicide."

"That's just it," the mayor said. "The sheriff's not convinced it was a suicide and Jesse's not exactly helping matters by saying that it is."

"What do you want him to do, lie?"

"No, I don't want the man to lie. I just want to make sure he's doing all he can to find the truth." He took a handkerchief out of his back pocket and wiped off the sweat that trickled down into his eyebrows.

"Look," Andy said sternly, "if Jesse said it was a suicide then that's exactly what it was. He may not be some big city coroner but he's seen enough in his day to know what he's talking about."

"Has he talked to you about it?" He ran the handkerchief down both sides of his face and flattened out his reddish-gray sideburns in the process.

"Jesse and I don't discuss business," Andy answered, "but let me ask **you** a question?"

"OK."

"Why do **you** think it wasn't a suicide?"

The question caught the mayor off-guard as he worked the handkerchief over his face. "I . . . . I just want to make sure Jesse's doing his job."

"That's exactly what I would expect from a politician."

"What do you mean?" the mayor said.

"You didn't answer my question."

The mayor took a deep breath and shoved the handkerchief back into his hip pocket. "Let's just forget we ever had this conversation."

"Now who's being wishy-washy?" Andy pointed out when the mayor got up to leave.

"You can tell Jesse I'm watching him," he said as he began to walk away.

"And who's watching you?"

With that comment hanging in the air between them like a bad aftershave, Mayor Paschall threw him a searing glare. The sun that shined through the overhang of the side stairs seemed to turn the mayor's green eyes a fiery yellow just before he turned and left.

"What was that all about?" Michele's voice asked him from the top of the opposite stairs as she headed in his direction.

"Nothing important," Andy said. "The mayor was just trying out his speech on me."

"You mean the old fart's finally gonna break down and give a different one?" she joked.

Andy didn't answer. He just laughed along with her. It felt good to laugh, even for a short while. He hadn't had a reason to in the last couple of weeks.

"So, what time are you picking me up?" she asked after their laughter trickled off into silence.

"What?"

"Tonight. The fireworks, remember?"

"Oh, yeah." He suddenly recalled their earlier fleeting conversation. "Uh, is eight too early?"

"No, that's fine," she said. "You gonna bring the beer or shall I?"

"I don't drink beer," he said without thinking.

She tilted her head in a question-like manner. The sudden move allowed her ponytail to dip around her left shoulder. "You did the other night."

"That was just on the spur of the moment," he explained.

"I thought all you macho guards drank beer," she said with a wide grin that showed off her perfect set of teeth.

Andy had never thought of himself as the macho type, but it pleased him that she thought of him in such a manner. "I drink," he said. "I just don't drink beer. I'm more into healthy drinks."

"Oh, a health nut. I didn't know. Sorry," she said. "What kind?"

"Screwdrivers," he said.

"Shit, Andy, I thought you were serious."

"Speaking of serious," Andy said. "Who's minding the store?"

"Larry and Yann," she said.

"When did Yann get here?"

"About ten minutes ago. He said they got the Palm Beach schedule all screwed up and had too many of them over there, so they sent him over here. I let him take my place so I could go to lunch. It's OK, isn't it?"

"Yeah," he said. "I'll take you over the mayor any day."

"Thanks, I guess."

They both shared another laugh at the mayor's expense. Michele reached into her bag and pulled out an apple.

"That's your lunch?" Andy asked.

"What, you think you're the only one who's into the health food scene around here?" she said. She took a quick, healthy bite into the apple to keep from laughing.

Andy watched her as she slid the piece of fruit into her right cheek and began to chew. She watched him watch her and slid her tongue across the top row of her perfect teeth for affect. It was obvious to both of them that a game of cat and mouse was in progress, but the program didn't list which player was which.

Andy looked at his watch. He hoped it would tell him he still had enough time left to sit back and enjoy their game, but it didn't. The mayor's unscheduled meeting had taken more time than he had realized. "Hey," he told himself, "if it was the mayor then that counted as business time, not lunch time." Then he told himself, "But Michele doesn't know that and you don't need to be setting any bad examples, son."

"Whoa! I gotta get back out there," he said to Michele this time. He wadded up the half-eaten sandwich into a sloppy ball and chunked it at a nearby trash can. It missed its mark by a good foot, hit the wall and sent a spray of lunchmeat and garden fixings across the concrete floor.

"Never played basketball, huh? Michele said.

"Guess that sort of ruins my macho image," he replied as he cleaned up his mess.

"That's OK," she said. "That just means you're better at other things."

Andy decided he had better hurry on back to his tower before he stuck his almost middle-age foot in his mouth and spoiled the mood. "See you at eight."

"I'll be ready," she said.

He took the stairs three at a time and wondered just what it was she would be ready for.

Michele took another bite of her apple and scanned the beach. So far, she had been lucky. Eric hadn't shown up the day after their so-called date. She hadn't expected him to show up at Palm Beach since he was into surfing and the surf was never up in the man-made pools there. She had lain awake most of last night wondering if he was waiting for her to return to Stewart Beach. So far, he hadn't.

"Maybe he got the message," she said, as if saying it out loud would make it so.

28

Eric had spent the last week in Houston on business. He could have commuted but he had tried that once before and found the daily drive not to his liking and quite ugly in places. Besides, he figured he owed himself a week of tittie-bar nights. It would have taken him a year of nights to hit them all but he made a stab at it anyway.

Once he got his fill of breasts and business he came home. He also missed the surf. There weren't too many waves in the bayous that meandered their way through Houston, although he would have gotten an argument from many of the locals who had seen their cars washed away during an average rainstorm. But it hadn't rained and he also hadn't taken his board. It was just as well as it would have been stolen anyway.

He hadn't bothered to go by his office on the holiday. Amy wouldn't be there to harass him and he had called her twice a day while he was gone, so he knew there was nothing on his desk that required his immediate attention.

It was noon-thirty and July hot, with just enough breeze blowing in off the gulf to keep old folks from dying in the streets. Eric took the Wolfe board down off the garage rack and mounted it on the BMW. He backed the car out into the street and reached up to the visor and pressed the remote box to close the garage door. He could smell the salty air as he drove down the side street that ran parallel to Seawall Boulevard. Traffic was lighter along this route.

The Stewart Beach lot looked to be full, but he paid his five dollars at the gate and drove in anyway. It would be worth the investment if Michele was there. His plan wasn't to confront her, but rather just make his presence known. He hadn't forgotten their last encounter and he wanted to make sure she hadn't either. He knew his week away had probably made her think she had seen the last of him and he relished the idea of being somewhat of a holiday surprise.

It was a quarter to one when he drove down the crowded aisle next to the beach. He wasn't looking for a parking spot at the moment which was a good thing since there were none in the entire lot. He was looking for her. He saw the first tower was manned, literally speaking. The next tower was empty but there was gear on the platform. He drove to the far end and found the last tower also literally manned.

"She'll be in the middle one," he whispered to himself. He made a U-turn and drove back to just behind the middle tower and stopped. He rolled the BMW's windows up, turned on the air and waited patiently.

The sight of the fluorescent, lime green suit at the base of the pavilion caught his eye first. His heart quivered then jumped against his chest when he recognized the lifeguard. It wasn't Michele, but the one who had picked her up and had finished **his** date. He gunned the BMW's engine and threw it into gear. The car's tires slid over the loose sand and left a rooster-tail of fine particles in their wake. He left the lot just as fast and almost hit a family of four who were walking to the amusement park.

Eric's fit of rage hadn't gone unnoticed. The siren and flashing red and blue lights in his rear-view mirror told him so. He pulled to the shoulder of Seawall Boulevard and slammed both palms against the steering wheel.

The policeman pulled up behind him and got out of his car first. He adjusted his aviator sunglasses and walked to the side of the BMW just as Eric was got out. "You in a hurry, son?" the officer asked.

"No, sir," Eric told him. "I just wasn't paying attention."

"You know you could have killed those people?"

"Yes, sir." He tried to remain calm and polite. "And I'm sorry. It won't happen again."

"You from around here, boy?"

"Yes, sir." Eric handed him his license as if to offer him proof.

"Thought so," the officer said. "Thought I'd seen this car before. Sort of hard to miss."

Eric thought he heard a sound of leniency in his voice so he decided to drop a name for the officer's benefit. "I have an office in Mayor Paschall's building."

"Oh, so you know the mayor?"

"Yes, sir. I probably talk to Brian almost every day."

"That right?"

"Yes, sir." Eric figured he had the policeman right where he wanted him.

"Hmmm," the officer said. "You got proof of insurance on this baby?"

"Uh, yes, sir. It's in the glove box."

"Mind gettin' it?"

"No, sir. Just a minute." Eric got back into the car and opened the glove box but failed to find his liability insurance card at first glance. He rifled through the papers then threw them out onto the passenger seat. The card was still nowhere to be found. He slid back out of the car.

"I know it's in there," Eric said. "I just can't seem to find it right now."

"You got the registration?" the officer asked politely.

Eric couldn't remember seeing the registration card either. He knew he had kept them together for just this purpose. "Look, officer, I can't find the registration either, but this **is** my car."

"OK, just a minute." The officer walked back to his patrol car and got in.

Eric watched him get on the radio and knew it would be just a matter of a few minutes before the police dispatcher would confirm his ownership, and then he'd be gone.

The policeman replaced the mike, wrote something down on his pad, then got back out and walked toward Eric. "The car's yours, all right."

"Yes, sir," Eric said. "And I assure you I carry insurance on it."

"How much did this baby set you back, if you don't mind me asking?"

"More than you can afford, asshole," Eric thought, but to the officer he said, "Fifty grand, why? You in the market?"

"No, but I guess if you can afford that price tag you can afford to buy insurance for it, so I'm not going to give you a ticket for not having your card," the officer explained to Eric satisfaction.

"Thank you," Eric said and waited for the man to return his license.

"But I will need for you to sign here." The officer handed him his ticket pad with his license inserted in the perforation at the top.

"What is it?"

"That's your ticket for Reckless Driving, son. You should be able to afford that too," the officer said and smiled.

"Well, fuck," Eric said as he looked at the ticket.

"Now, you wouldn't want me to add Public Profanity to that ticket, would you, boy?"

Eric quickly signed the ticket and handed it back to the officer without answering. The policeman tore off his copy and handed it to him along with his driver's license. "You have a good day now, you hear?" the officer said and tipped the front brim of his hat.

Eric remained silent again and got back into his car and closed the door. He was about to start the engine and leave more slowly and carefully this time, when the officer tapped on his window. Eric rolled it down and the officer leaned down to where the two were face to face.

"I understand the mayor's over at Ashton Villa," he said slowly and drew each word out to its full measure. "If you hurry, not too fast though, you can probably catch the tail end of his speech, being that y'all are good friends and all. I know you'd hate to miss it."

Eric hit the button and closed the window, then started the motor and drove back onto Seawall Boulevard. He also signaled his intent to do so just in case the officer was watching. He wadded up the ticket and threw it on the pile of papers in the passenger seat.

When he got to the entrance to the burned out condotel he pulled in and stopped the car. He watched out the passenger window for the policeman to leave and when he did, Eric backed out and headed back into town. The hot, afternoon sun blazed through the windshield, so he pulled down the visor. Next to the vanity mirror and under the garage door opener clip was his insurance card and registration.

"Well, fuck me," he said and slammed the visor back up.

29

Andy poured the second batch of screwdrivers into the plastic, gallon milk jug he used when he spent one of his few days off fishing at Seawolf Park. He thought about the conversation he had just had with Jesse concerning the other conversation he had had with Mayor Paschall.

"You think he's trying to hide something?" Andy had asked.

"I wouldn't put it past him," Jesse had answered. "But I don't know what it could be."

"Well, just be on the lookout."

"I will, but right now that son of a bitch is the least of my worries."

Andy hadn't needed to be reminded of what had been prominent on his mind since that night two weeks ago. He screwed the plastic cap on the jug and checked his watch in a nervous sort of way. He had been out with plenty of women over the last few years but this one wasn't exactly a woman. She was more of a girl and the last thing he needed was to have to go in and meet her parent. That was something he had **not** been accustomed of doing in quite some time. He could imagine the cold stares he would probably receive from her father when he took notice of the age of the man who was picking up his young daughter. At least he had kept himself in good enough condition to probably hide the fact that he was on the opposite side of thirty than his daughter.

Andy unscrewed the cap and took a nerve-settling drink from the jug. He breathed deep then took another and decided he better go on and get it over with. If he stayed there sucking on the jug much longer he might wind up half in the bag on her door step, which certainly would prove to be to his advantage.

Andy took the more indirect route to Michele's house. He steered clear of Seawall Boulevard which he knew would be choked with cars trying to find the best spot to park and watch the festivities.

Michele's Malibu was parked in front of her house and the driveway was empty. With any luck at all, her parents would have already left to claim their own spot. He pulled into the driveway and noticed that the garage door at the back of the house was shut. He sat in the Bronco with the motor running. The closed garage door could mean that their car was still parked inside to protect it from the salty, sea air until the last minute. If that was the case, he needed another swipe from the jug. He was reaching for it when he saw movement at the front door.

Michele closed the front door behind her and hopped down the steps while Andy breathed a sigh of relief. That same feeling of deliverance turned into one of excitement when the summer breeze lifted Michele's wind-breaker off her shoulders and revealed the white, light cotton undershirt she wore underneath. Like most girls her age who hung around the beach, she wore one a size or two too big. Before she could pull the jacked back down, he also noticed that she had nothing on underneath the loose shirt.

Michele opened the passenger door, jumped into the bucket seat and threw her guard bag onto the back floorboard. Her lime green, nylon running shorts strained tightly against her upper thighs when she slid over and placed an easy kiss on Andy's cheek.

"You're late," she said as she eased back over and buckled herself in.

"I took the long way," he said, apologetically.

"Why?" she asked as she kicked off her sandals and planted her feet on the dash to reveal even more of the tawny flesh beneath her shorts.

"Traffic," he said and moved the lever into reverse.

"Oh, yeah."

"Why'd you bring your bag?"

"You never know when it might be needed," she reminded him. "Gotta be prepared for emergencies."

"Have your parents already gone?" Andy asked bravely, now that the obstacle of their meeting was safely behind him.

"They're not here," she said. "They go to my grandmother's in Marble Falls for the Fourth. They won't be back until this weekend.

Over a third of Andy's life had passed since he was Michele's age but he realized that some things never changed, especially casual hints. He continued his detour that took them through The Strand and arrived at the entrance to Stewart Beach where the other guards anxiously awaited his arrival. He considered himself the old man of the group but they looked on him more as their leader. And like every good leader, it was up to him to lead. He wondered just how long they would have waited.

The guards met him with a round of applause which turned into cat-calls and whistles when they got their first look at his passenger. Andy felt a twinge of embarrassment that quickly turned into pride when Michele unbuckled her seat belt and climbed into the open window and began to circle a right hand high above her head. It was the guards' sign to head 'em up and move 'em out.

Two guards, whose Jeep was already parked in the right direction on the opposite side of the street, took their positions and began to stop traffic in both directions. Few horns sounded as the locals understood the meaning of the procession. Those who didn't, mostly unsuspecting tourists, would certainly know the next time around.

The procession of emerald green and white four by fours paraded their way down Seawall Boulevard for twenty-five blocks. The guards waved to the crowd who waved and cheered back. When Andy reached the Twenty-Fifth Street entrance to the Flagship Hotel a Galveston policeman stopped all the other traffic at the intersection to let them turn in.

Andy parked the Bronco in the tow facing the west side jetties while the others filled up the pier lot behind him.

"Well," Andy said when he turned the motor off and reached for the jug. "Here we are."

Michele caught him as he reached behind her seat and planted a soft kiss on his lips.

"What was that for?" he asked, then looked out the side window to see if anyone had caught the sudden event.

"For a while," she said.

He didn't understand her answer and yet he did.

The guards were already crowding around Andy's truck when they got out and not a moment too soon. The local hotels were beginning their own fireworks displays, although nothing would compare to what the city had in store, but a show of spirit nonetheless. It was also against the law, since there was a city ordinance against shooting off fireworks within the city limits. It was a law that was not enforced during this particular evening.

Andy put the jug on the hood of the Bronco and leaned back against the grille and used the front bumper as an uncomfortable seat. Michele crowded in next to him like a queen with her king. Andy had a good feeling about him and for the first time in two long weeks there were no thoughts of werewolves lurking in the anxiety closet of his brain.

The fireworks went of without a hitch and twenty short minutes later it was all over. Most of the guards hung around the pier and exchanged beer and the usual stories about what had happened on their particular beach that day or the day before. Mostly it centered around the lack of swimwear the girls paraded around in, except when the few female guards entered the conversation with stories of their own.

The jug had remained untouched on the hood of the Bronco, forgotten by the one who had so carefully concocted it. Andy found he preferred the warmth of Michele's body to the mixture in the jug.

"Where to now?" Michele asked softly when the crowd began to filter away.

"I don't know," Andy said. He realized, to his dismay, that he hadn't planned that far ahead. "You feel like dancing?"

"Not really," she said. "I'm sort of tired."

Andy suddenly felt like a sailboat with no wind. "You want me to take you home?" he asked out of instinct and cursed himself for it.

"I guess," she said. "If you want to."

He didn't want to but he had already committed himself to the task. He eased off the bumper and stretched his aching back and rubbed at the numbness in his butt. He walked to his door, then walked back and took the jug off the hood. If nothing else he could always polish it off when he got home.

Only two Jeeps remained on the pier when they drove away, but Butch and another guard were too deep in conversation with a group of giggling girls to notice. When Andy put his left turn signal on at the intersection Michele hit him with a question.

"Where are you going?"

"You said you wanted to go home," he said and stopped, even though the light was green.

"I said I wanted you to take me home," Michele said.

Andy looked at her in the dark cab with a confused expression on his face.

"Your home, silly," she said.

Andy's sails billowed with the sudden breeze and he made a quick right turn in direct disagreement with his turn signal. The driver of the car across the intersection who had also signaled for a left turn and was halfway into it laid on his horn and barely avoided hitting them.

Andy never heard the horn.

30

Eric had been more than a little pissed off after his brief encounter with the law. So much so that he had completely blown off the planned afternoon of surfing and had gone to his office instead. He had found Amy there hard at work. She had told him that she had nothing better to do and that she could use the over-time.

Amy had been able to tell from the get-go that Eric was not in one of his better moods and had mentioned the fireworks display to him and the fact that if he would cool down she might see fit to let him go with her. She had been joking; sort of; and had no idea that he would accept her invitation. But he did.

To Eric's way of thinking he would at least be able to take his anger out on someone other than himself. They had stayed at the office until almost time for the show. Amy had already been in casual dress but Eric had still been in his surfer jams. This, however, had posed no great problem since Eric kept several pairs of clothes in the antique wardrobe in his office for just such emergencies.

Amy hadn't considered their make-shift date as an emergency. To her it had been more along the line of fate, no matter how fine the line.

"That's all there is?" Eric said when the skies around the Flagship Hotel grew dark again. "No wonder I never bothered to come here before."

"I thought it was beautiful," Amy responded. They had arrived in just enough time to find a parking space on the town-side of Seawall

Boulevard and were able to watch the display while leaning against the side of the BMW.

"Yeah, I guess it was better than being poked in the eye with a number two pencil."

"Did anyone ever tell you you're a son of a bitch?" Amy said suddenly and without warning.

"My mother," he said, "but only once."

Amy had tried to make a point but had failed miserably, and in doing so she had opened the door on a subject she didn't care to walk through. So, she changed the subject. "Why don't we go somewhere for a drink?"

"Are you asking me to go get a drink or why we should?" Eric said.

"Never mind," Amy said. "Just take me back to the office so I can go home."

"No, we can go for a drink," he said, "if you think you can handle me."

"I don't want to **handle** you. I just thought you might want to have a drink. You've obviously had a bad day."

"If you don't want to handle me then what's the point of getting a drink?"

"For one thing it will help you to relax."

"And then?"

"Who knows?"

"OK," Eric said. "Let's go have that drink."

"That's better," she said. "Where?"

"Your place."

"No," Amy said. "You don't want to go there. The place is a mess." It was the best excuse she could come up with on such short notice.

"It's your place or no place," Eric said as he walked around to the driver's side of the BMW. "Get in."

31

Andy's condo was pitch dark when they entered. He reached for the wall switch and brightened the room.

"Cozy," Michele said. Her eyes were immediately drawn to the wicker furniture that surrounded the large, padded couch.

"I like it," he said. "You want something to drink?" Andy suddenly remembered the traveling jug was still in the Bronco.

"What do you have besides your health?" she asked as she surveyed his surroundings. She took note that everything that either hung on the wall or sat on a shelf had something to do with the fact that his life was made up of the beach or the ocean and nothing else. There was scuba gear in one corner and half a broken surfboard in another. There were only two pictures on the wall. One was a picture and the other was a poster. The picture was of an old, three-masted, sailing ship in a storm. The poster was of a surfer carrying his board above his head. He was looking out over the water as the sun was going down. The words ENDLESS SUMMER were embossed on the horizon.

"I've got some scotch, unless Uncle Jesse's been here while I was gone."

"No, that's OK. I'm fine."

"You sure?" he asked. "I can run to the store for some beer if you . . ."

"No, I really don't feel like drinking," she said as she slipped out of her wind-breaker.

Andy noticed that his first sight had been correct as her erect nipples pressed unrestricted against her undershirt as she walked over to where he stood beside the bar and looked up at him.

"You haven't kissed **me** yet," she said.

"What was that we did earlier?"

"I kissed **you** then. Now it's your turn."

Andy weaved his muscular arms around her and kissed her. When their lips parted Michele forced his arms open and backed away from him just long enough to lift her shirt off and reveal her young, evenly tanned breasts. She slid her arms down her sides and caught her thumbs in her thin shorts and removed them along with a pair of bikini panties as perfectly white as her teeth. She stood in front of him, almost as Jesse had done in that same spot two weeks before, but that comparison never entered his mind. What did enter his mind was the fact that, like her breasts, there was no trace of a tan line anywhere on her slender body.

There were no thoughts of tomorrow in either of their minds as they made their way into the bedroom where Michele undressed Andy with as much ease as she had undressed herself. They explored each other's body until they could wait no longer. They made love as the soft beam of a half-moon covered their nakedness in a thin shroud.

32

Amy lived on the top floor of a two-story house on Broadway that had weathered several hurricanes in its time and looked the worst for it.

"Will my car be safe here?" Eric asked when he pulled up to the curb in front of the house.

"Mine always is," she said.

He started to tell her that the two hardly compared but he realized he didn't know what kind of car she drove. Still, hers certainly couldn't be as expensive as his. Not on her salary.

When they got out Eric looked up and down the street. Traffic was fairly heavy with people leaving the fireworks display and heading for other places about town to continue their celebrations. If nothing else, the passing cars would keep any would-be thieves indoors. He turned back around to lock the car.

"Shit!" he said.

"What's the matter?" Amy asked.

"This," he said and pointed to the surfboard that was still mounted on the top of the BMW.

"It's just a surfboard."

"It's not **just** a surfboard," Eric told her. "This board costs more than I pay you a month."

"I don't doubt that," she said. "If you're worried about it then bring it up."

She hadn't meant for her suggestion to be taken seriously, but it had. Eric began to unlatch the board from the rack.

"You aren't really going to bring it inside, are you?"

"No. I've got a better solution." When the board was loose he opened the car door and got into the back seat and sprung a latch that allowed him to recline the seat forward. He got out, opened the trunk and slid the board in. The nose rested up against the stick shift but the fins were safely tucked away in the trunk.

"There," he said when he locked the doors. "That ought to do it."

Amy just shook her head as she walked to the front porch. Eric followed her onto the porch, through the screen door and up a flight of creaky, wooden stairs to the second floor. She opened the door without the aid of a key.

"You don't lock your door?"

"I don't own a surfboard."

Amy had been right. Her apartment was a mess, but Eric figured that in this part of town it would still be a mess even when it was clean.

"All I've got is some wine," Amy said.

"I don't want anything to drink right now."

"Well, I do." Amy reached into the fridge and took out a three-quarter full bottle anyway.

"No, you don't," Eric said. "That's not what you got me up here for."

"I didn't **get** you up here," she said. "Coming here was your idea."

"Well, you certainly didn't put up any resistance."

"You didn't give me much choice."

"That's because you gave up too easily," Eric said.

"Fine," she said. "Then let's leave."

"No, we're here, so let's make the best of it."

"The best of it? Just what the hell does that mean?"

"I think you know what it means," Eric said. "You wanted me here and now I'm here. Don't try and play coy on me now."

"Get out of here!" she yelled.

"You don't mean that," Eric said as he began to walk toward her.

"The hell I don't," Amy said. She turned the bottle of wine upside-down and gripped it by the neck like a club.

"OK, OK," Eric said. "If you want to have a drink first, fine. We'll have a drink."

"No, I want you out of here now."

When Eric took another step toward her, Amy swung the bottle around. The condensation caused by the humid night air in the non-air-conditioned house on the cold glass bottle caused it to slip from her hand. It crashed through the front window in full flight.

Eric knew the party, such as it had been, was now over. Somebody had to have heard the noise; the first-floor tenants at least, if no one else.

Amy took breaths in rapid succession and looked about the kitchen for something else to grab.

"OK, that's done with," Eric said. "You've made your point."

His statement didn't make Amy breathe any easier. "Now get out," she said again.

"I'm going, but no hard feelings, OK? I'll even pay for the window."

"There aren't any feelings at all," she told him.

"Fine. That's even better," he said. "We'll just forget this whole thing. It never happened. When you come to work tomorrow we'll start all over again. OK? We got a deal?"

Amy wanted to tell him to take his job and shove it up his dick until it broke, but she was already late on her rent payment and he did seem sincere. "Just get out," she said.

"All right, I'm going," he said. "But I expect to see you in the morning." He opened the door hurriedly and left. He had been sincere. A secretary like Amy was hard to come by and cheap too.

When Eric got to his car he was relieved to find that their fight had gone unnoticed. The lights were off in the first floor living quarters which meant the tenants were either still out celebrating or blessed with the ability to sleep through a hurricane; though not exactly a blessing for a Galveston Island resident. His relief turned to anger when he saw the broken glass scattered about in purple pools on the scratched and dented hood of his BMW. He was more pissed that the alarm hadn't gone off than he was with the damage. The damage could be repaired but not his trust in the car's expensive alarm system.

When he sped off from the curb a purple rain covered the windshield. He turned on the wipers and heard the sound of glass being ground into glass.

The sound of the BMW tearing away down the street reminded Amy that her own car was still parked at the office. "Well, fuck him," she said out loud. "I'll just be late."

Andy woke with a start. He had been used to sleeping alone, at least the vast majority of the time. He was also accustomed to sleeping in a ten-year-old pair of worn-out gym shorts, but through the early morning light that dawned its way into the room he saw that they still hung recklessly on the arm of the rocker where they had landed yesterday morning.

He looked across the bed at the clock, but took a detour first as his eyes were drawn to the body sleeping next to him, covered only in a sheet. The digital numbers told him that sometime in the next sixty seconds the alarm would go off. He reached across Michele's body to shut it off before it sounded, but he overestimated the allotted time. The alarm began to buzz loudly in mid-reach and caused him to lose his balance and fall on top of her.

Michele's eyes danced open and she smiled. "You didn't get enough last night?"

"I'm sorry," Andy said. He felt somewhat embarrassed and was not sure what to say to the girl, a little more than half his age, on this particular morning after.

"I'm not," Michele said. She dragged her arms out from under the sheet and hung them around his neck.

"That's not what I meant," he said.

"I know. I'm just teasing you."

He could feel the warmth of her body through the thin material. His own body began to tell him one thing and common sense another. "We can't," he said.

"Why not?"

"In case you've forgotten, we've got about an hour before we have to be on watch."

"So?"

"So, I've got to get you home so you can get ready."

"My stuff's in my bag, so I don't have to go home," Michele said and refused to loosen her grip.

"So, that's what you meant by needing it," Andy said.

"And I was right, wasn't I?" Michele advised him.

"What about your car?"

"It'll be OK where it is."

"No, I don't think it would look too good for both of us to show up together," the boss in him explained.

"Why not, Jeff and Candice do?"

"That's different," he said.

"How?"

"They're engaged."

"They weren't always," she said.

"I'd still rather not," Andy said and tried to ease his way out of her hold even though his body was still not in agreement with his mind.

"I'm not letting you go until you give me a better reason," she said and squeezed even tighter.

"What would your parents say if this ever got back to them?

"I'm a big girl now," she said. "I can make my own decisions."

"I won't argue that point with you, but your father might not take too kindly to it and he's probably got enough stroke downtown to get me fired."

"He wouldn't do that," she said.

"How do you know?"

"Because I'm a daddy's girl and daddy's girls always get what they want or didn't you know that?" she said with a giggle.

"Well, he might not mean to but Paschall's got it in for me already and something like this brought to his attention might just be the icing on the cake."

"I thought there was a little more going on between you two yesterday than just a casual conversation," she said. "What's the problem?"

"We just share a mutual disrespect for each other. It goes back to before your time."

"And you don't want to talk about it, right?"

"Right. Now, let go so I can go take a shower," Andy ordered, though not in a tone that would have made her jump to attention.

"Nope," she said. "I just thought of a better idea. We can just say my car wouldn't start and I had no choice but to call you."

"None of that is going to work," Andy said. "They all saw us together last night, so if we show up together no one's going to believe anything we tell them."

Michele figured she had teased him enough already so she reminded him that she wasn't even on his beach today but at Palm Beach instead. "Gotcha," she said and took her arms away to supposedly set him free. However, she followed with a *coup de gras* and threw off the sheet to give him a look at what he was passing up in the early daylight.

Andy just shook his head.

"You know you want to," she said and pointed between his legs as he stumbled backward toward the bathroom.

"Wanting to has nothing to do with it," Andy said when he entered the bathroom and closed the door. He stepped into the shower stall and adjusted the spray to lukewarm. A cold shower was definitely called for but his body was not yet ready for such a rude awakening. He stood with his head under the nozzle and let the warm water ease his aching body into submission.

"Mind if I join you?" a tender voice said from behind him, already stepping into the shower.

"Michele," he whined.

"Hey, if we shower together we can be done in half the time." She reached around him and took the soap from the tray and began to rub it up and down his back. "Besides, if you didn't want me in here you would have locked the door."

Andy turned slowly, his mind realized that his body had finally won and took the soap from her hand. Michele leaned back against the tile wall and let him caress her breasts with his soapy fingers.

"If you keep this up you're defeating the purpose," Michele said with her voice breaking under his touch.

"That's OK," Andy said. "We've still got your shower time left to work with." He let the soap squirt from his hand and reached under her arms and lifted her up. She wrapped her dangling legs around his waist then allowed him to slowly ease her down into position.

"What about the mayor?" she joked when he entered her.

"Let him get his own girl."

Michele bit into his neck then spit out the soapy taste.

"That'll teach you," Andy said and cupped his hands on her butt for a steadier hold. It wasn't her weight that was causing her to slip. She weighed next to nothing in his arms, but the soap had filled in any trace of friction on their skin.

Michele lifted her head up to his and kissed him hard and gave him a soapy taste of his own medicine with her tongue. "So much for good, clean fun," she giggled and kissed him again.

Andy arrived at the pavilion with two minutes to spare. Butch was leaning against one of the outside shower posts and looking the worse for wear.

"What color is the sky in your world today, Butchie?" Andy asked when he remembered that Butch had still been on the pier when he left last night.

Butch lifted the wraparound sunglasses up to reveal two blue dots submerged in an ocean of red. "That depends," he said. He lifted a finger toward the sky. "Are those clouds or pink cotton candy."

"Pink cotton candy," Andy told him. "You're all right."

"That's easy for you to say," Butch said and dropped the glasses back down over his eyes in self-defense. "You ain't wearing my head."

"What's the matter? You don't like having to pay the fiddler?"

"Not when I didn't even get to dance."

"You seemed to be holding your own when I left," Andy said. He took Butch by the shoulder and pointed him in the general direction of his tower.

"And that's all I got to hold," Butch said.

"Don't tell me you struck out?" Andy said and gave him a light shove to get him on his way.

"Shit, man, I never even got to bat," he said. "What about you and Miss Michele? You two seemed to be getting along pretty well."

Andy sensed that their friendly conversation was about to take a turn in a direction he didn't care to take. He thought quickly and put an end to any speculation on Butch's part. "Oh, she just wanted to ride in the lead. It wasn't any big thing."

"Uh, huh. So, you struck out too," Butch said. "Now I don't feel so bad seeing as how yours looked like a sure thing."

"Yeah, well, looks are deceiving," Andy said. "Now get your butt to work and try not to fall off the tower." He turned and walked to his own tower and wondered if Michele was also on the receiving end of the third degree at Palm Beach.

35

It was almost nine when Amy walked into the parking garage of the Port Galveston Savings and Loan building. She wanted to make sure her car was still there. The old Dodge wasn't much in the way of transportation but it was all she had and it was still there. She turned and headed for the door to the building but stopped behind Eric's assigned slot. In the place of his silver BMW was a red Mustang with a green and white Enterprise Rental sticker in plain sight. She had heard him drive away last night so she knew his car hadn't been stolen.

"Maybe he had been in an accident," she thought. "If he did, I hope he totaled out his damn car." She stopped short of hoping that he might have been seriously injured. "Maybe just a broken leg," she thought again. "That would keep him off his beloved surfboard until winter."

She walked cheerfully into the building and took the elevator to the third floor. She usually took the stairs in an effort to stay in shape, but the mile and a half walk from her house to work had been more than enough exercise for one day.

"Where have you been?" the receptionist asked her when she walked in. "You've had us worried half to death."

"Just late," Amy answered. "That's all."

"But your car's in the garage," the girl answered. "We thought you might have been kidnapped or something."

Amy wanted to tell her how right she almost was, but not this morning. Instead, she tried to make light of the situation by saying, "You didn't pay the ransom, did you?"

"Oh, Amy," the girl said. "You don't know how worried we were."

"Well, thanks for worrying but my battery was dead when I tried to leave last night and I didn't have the cash for a tow."

"What were you doing here last night? It was a holiday."

"Tell me about it. There wasn't a sole in the garage to give me a jump either. You know I just can't get enough of this place," Amy said. "Is the boss in?" Her question was a loaded one. If Eric had been in an accident or injured she would find out about it before having to face him.

"Yeah, he's here."

Amy waited for all the gory details that never followed, so she asked another question. "Has he been looking for me?"

"Nope," the girl said. "He got here about fifteen minutes ago and walked right past me without saying hello and went straight into his office and slammed the door.

"One of his better moods, huh?" Amy joked.

"You'd know better than me."

"You got that right," Amy said. And walked over to her desk and laid her purse down under it. She sat down and shuffled a few papers to see if Eric had left any message of apology, but found none.

She really hadn't expected to, so she wasn't all that put out by the fact that he hadn't bothered.

On the long walk to work she had mulled over what she was going to say when their eminent confrontation finally took place. She was about to start the mulling process over again when she saw a deliveryman from Island Florist come through the front door with an armload of red roses.

"Must be somebody's birthday," she thought and watched to see whose desk the receptionist directed him to. When she turned and pointed in her direction, Amy looked behind her even though she knew no one sat there.

"There must be some mistake," Amy said when the deliveryman brought the roses over to her and set them on her desk.

"Are you Amy Kingston?" the deliveryman asked.

"Yes, but these can't be for me. I don't . . ."

"They are unless there's two of you here," he said.

"But who are they from?"

"I don't know," he said. "But you might try reading the card."

By that time everyone in the office had crowded around Amy's desk. Almost everyone. Eric's door was still closed.

"You been holding out on us, girl?" LaShonda Reynolds, a filing clerk and often-times lunch buddy, asked. "Who are they from?"

Amy reached for the small envelope that was attached to one of the long stems with a small

plastic clip. She opened the envelope and took out
the card. All it said we peace. There was no name
but she recognized Eric's handwriting.

"Well?" LaShonda asked again.

Amy slipped the card back into the envelope
and slid the evidence into her purse. "Secret
admirer," she said.

"No, no," LaShonda followed. "You aren't
getting off that easy. Who is he?"

"He wouldn't be a secret if I told you."

When the crowd left, slightly disappointed,
Amy realized that all her mulling had been for
naught. She pulled out her computer keyboard and
made like she was working until everyone else
seemed to be doing the same. She grabbed her steno
pad, got up and knocked on Eric's door, then
entered.

Eric was on the phone so she waited by the
door. When he told the caller he would call him
back she walked over and sat down in one of the
chairs in front of his desk.

"I got the roses and the message," she said.

"Then I'm forgiven?"

"Not quite, but you're on the right track."

"I'll accept that for now," Eric told her.

"Did you have a wreck on your way home or
something?"

"No, not exactly," he said and hesitated.
"Someone vandalized it."

"You're kidding," she said. "Where?"

"On the hood."

"No, I mean where was it when it was damaged?"

"In front of your place," he said.

"No way," Amy said. "It wasn't there that long."

"Long enough for someone to bust a wine bottle over it," Eric said with a message-like gleam in his eyes.

Amy began to laugh out of control. Eric tried not to but soon joined her. When they were both teary-eyed and out of breath, Eric tried again at a final peace offering. "But you're in clear," he said. "I'm not going to press charges and the insurance will pay for the damage."

"Then I guess you're forgiven," Amy said.

36

Andy stirred nervously in the pitcher of Minute Maid orange juice and vodka. Jesse was due any minute and he didn't look forward to his arrival. Michele hadn't been all that thrilled either when Andy had told her they couldn't be together for the first night in almost two weeks. Although they had worked Stewart Beach together today, Andy had waited until their watch had ended before he had given her the news.

Their conversation had gone something like this:

"I hope you didn't have anything planned for tonight," Andy said when Michele jogged happily toward him.

"Just the usual," she said. "I'll be over as soon as I go home and tell the folks I'm gone."

"That's what I meant," he said. "We can't hang around my condo tonight."

"You mean we're gonna go out for a change?"

"No, we can't do that either."

"Well, if we can't go out and we can't stay in that doesn't leave much room for anything else, unless you're figuring on coming to my house," Michele said. "I guess we could do that but it'll be a little crowded with my folks there and all."

Andy dug a semi-circle in the sand with his right foot. He wished he had broken the news to her sooner. At least it would have been all over by now.

"Why can't we go to your place?" Michele followed.

"Jesse'll be there," he said.

"Oh. Which one of you is sick this time?"

"Neither. I just need to spend a little time with him, that's all. I'm the only family he's got."

"That's OK," she said. "I understand."

"Good," Andy said.

"But you call me when he leaves and I'll come on over."

"I don't think that'll work. Jesse's visits usually last until the wee hours of the morning and by then we're both pretty much in the bag."

"That's OK by me. "I sort of like you in the bag anyway."

"Yeah, but I think these old bones of mine are due for a rest and it wouldn't hurt you to catch up on some beauty sleep."

"Thanks for nothing," she said. "Why don't you just come right out and say you don't want to be with me?"

"You know that's not right," he said. "And I thought you said you understood?"

"I changed my mind," she said. "I'm allowed to do that, you know."

"You can always call up your friend, what's her name?" Andy told her. "You don't need me around to have a good time."

"Jules gets a little tired of being second choice," she said.

"So, don't tell her."

"She'll know when I call her this late."

"I'm sorry," Andy said. "I guess I should have told you earlier."

"That would have helped," she said. "When **did** you know?"

Andy used his left foot and completed the circle in the sand. "This morning."

"You shit. Why'd you wait?"

"I don't know. I just . . ."

"You just didn't want me to have time to get another date, huh?" She decided to put him on the biggest spot she could find.

He decided to let her have her fun at his expense. "Yeah."

"Liar."

Andy laughed. "So, are we still OK?"

"I don't know," Michele said. "We'll have to see what tonight brings." Michele reached over and patted him on the shoulder. Andy would have preferred a kiss but that would be a little too much to ask for under these circumstances.

"See you tomorrow," she said and headed across the lot to her car.

37

Andy stopped stirring when the front door to his condo opened. He reached under the bar for the Cutty Sark bottle and set it next to the pitcher.

"I hope this isn't going to be another one of those no-drink nights," Andy said when Jesse walked over to him and took the first stool.

"He's out there somewhere, Andrew," Jesse said. He looked at Andy first, then at the bottle of scotch.

"So you've told me."

"I wish your father was still alive right now."

"I do too but not for the same reason."

"You know what I mean," Jesse said roughly.

"Sorry."

"Have you made your decision yet?" Jesse asked. He still hadn't reached for the whiskey crutch on the bar.

"Yeah."

"Then you're ready to do it?"

"Nope."

"Damn it, Andrew! We've been over this and . . ."

"I've made up my mind Uncle Jesse. I've gone this long without having to and I don't want to have to start now."

"Are you afraid? Is that it?"

"That's got something to do with it," Andy said.

"Is it the girl?"

"What girl?"

"Don't bullshit with me, Andrew. I know you've been screwing around with Ed Molson's daughter. For her sake, I hope you've been using some sort of protection."

"What are you gonna do now, give me a lesson in safe sex? You're a bit late, don't you think?"

"I guess I didn't make myself very clear when I told you about your parents," Jesse said. He finally reached for the bottle of scotch and poured a healthy serving into a glass.

"I thought you did a pretty good job of it," Andy said.

"Well, evidently some of it didn't sink in."

"What are you driving at, Uncle Jesse?"

"Why do you think your mother had to become one of us?"

"You said it was because she loved my father enough to," Andy said.

"That's the main reason but when it came right down to it, it was because she **had** to."

Andy poured a drink of his own from the pitcher. "I think you skipped over that part."

"Maybe I did or maybe I just thought you understood. Either way, you better pay attention because someone else may be depending on what I have to say."

Andy took his drink around the bar and sat on the vacant stool while Jesse continued. "I'm going to be blunt with you on this because there's no easy way to say it."

"I wouldn't have it any other way."

"If you impregnate a human it could kill her."

Andy shivered as the blood in his veins turned cold. "Why the fuck didn't you tell me this before?"

"I figured your father would have told you about being careful, just like any other father."

"He did, but shit, this is different," Andy said.

"I just assumed . . ."

"You assumed shit! Damn!"

"Look," Jesse said. "You must have been taking some type of precaution over the years."

"Well, sure, sometimes, but if I'd known . . ."

"What? What would you have done? Don't tell me you would have gone without sex entirely. Even I couldn't have done that. Your father couldn't and you're no different from us. You just have to be more careful, that's all."

"You make it sound like it's no big deal now. Why the change?" Andy asked.

"Oh, it's a big deal, all right, but it's not one you can't handle," Jesse said. "I thought with AIDS and such out there, you kids were a little more careful than we were."

"I'm hardly a kid," Andy said. "But it's still different."

"No, it's not. They can both kill you just as dead."

"It's not me we're talking about here."

"Yes, Andrew, it is. You've got to think of yourself as a carrier. The only difference is you **know** you've got it, which is more than other people can say. You just have to make sure you don't give it to someone else."

"You make it sound like some kind of a disease," Andy said.

"If that's what it takes, then think of it that way."

Andy slid his glass down the bar and laid his head on the cold surface. He had never paid too much attention to his sex life before. Sure, he had taken the necessary precautions when he had felt there was a need to, but Michele hadn't been a need-to, at least not before.

"What are you thinking about, Andrew?"

Andy answered without lifting his head. "I'm thinking you ought to finish the job."

"What job?"

"Killing me."

38

Eric had surfed at Pirates Beach until just before dark. He had chosen this particular strip of beach because it was near his condo. It was also less crowded which meant he wouldn't have to contend with those less qualified to ride. The waves were larger but the undertow was a killer. Only those of his caliber dared to match their skills there. The novices preferred Stewart Beach. Those and the ones who rode just to pick up girls.

Eric hadn't been in a pick-up mood when he left work that afternoon but that had been six hours ago. Now he was hungry. He drove into his garage and unlatched the board and placed it on the wall rack with the other two. He went inside and opened the refrigerator. Other than a bottle of vodka he kept in there with a loaf of bread to keep them both fresh, it could have passed for the cupboard at the Hubbard house. He pulled open the crisper at the bottom and found a package of opened hot dogs that he figured had been in there since sometime before the first of summer. Since he didn't cook very often, he could have figured wrong.

He took the raw wieners out and smelled the package. He withdrew one and put it in his mouth like a pale cigar. He threw the rest of the package on the counter and pushed the refrigerator door rather hard. He heard the crisper drawer crack just before the door sealed shut. He chewed on the tube steak as he walked to the bedroom and was done with it before he hit the shower. The day had been hot so his choice of shower was cold. The water heightened his senses and awoke his flesh.

He got out of the shower and returned to the kitchen and left a trail of water on the floor in his wake. He grabbed another hot dog and made quick work of it before he returned to the bedroom. He stood in front of the full-length mirror on the back wall of the walk-in closet and admired his glistening body until the water dried. He dressed slowly in front of the mirror as if each piece of clothing had a reason to be worn.

He went back to the kitchen and ate the last of the wieners and left the wrapper on the counter. He wasn't big on cleanliness as far as his digs were concerned. He paid a maid to come in once a week to take care of that part of his life.

The moon overhead was full when Eric backed the BMW out of the garage and into the street. He put the car through two sharp turns and stopped at the light for Seawall Boulevard. When it turned green he took a left and headed down the beach where he knew the action would be.

39

Like all other college boys, Jimmy considered himself invincible. He was young, strong and with half the summer gone he had every intention of squeezing the very last drop out of the remaining days he had left before the time came for him to strap his surfboard to the top of his van and head back to school. It was that unconquerable feeling, aided by a recent quart of Budweiser that carried him between the wooden pylons and onto East Beach.

"You coming or not?" Jimmy shouted back to his friend, Drake, who had stopped at the boundary.

"Why out there?" Drake answered.

"Because it's there, dumb ass."

"It's also dark," Drake shouted and leaned on his board.

"You ain't gonna pussy out on me now, are you?" Jimmy yelled.

"I ain't pussying out. I just can't see shit over there." Drake referred to the fact that there were no lights on East Beach, other than a full moon.

"You don't have to **see** the waves, man. You can feel 'em. Now, come on."

Drake saw that he had no other choice but to follow. Either that or have Jimmy tell the other guys what a wuss he was. He finished off the last of his own beer and let the bottle fall from his hand onto the sand. He would pick it up on their way back out if he remembered and if he didn't drown first.

"Wait up," Drake said. "I'm coming." He plucked his board from the sand and ran to catch up to his friend.

The full moon danced along the white caps as a volley of waves broke about fifty yards off shore. Other than that, Drake couldn't tell where the ocean stopped and the night sky started.

Before Drake could reach him Jimmy broke for the surf in a dead run. When the water got too deep to run through he slapped the board down on the surface and jumped on top. He began to paddle as soon as his belly hit the board.

Drake stopped when he reached the point where Jimmy had headed out and watched him rise and fall over the smaller waves until he was out of sight. "Stupid shit," Drake thought. He wished he had another beer or any other lame excuse to keep him from having to follow. Since the quart he had just finished had been his first and his last he just shook his head in disgust over his predicament and headed out into the surf. He caught sight of Jimmy about halfway out. He had stroked onto a four-footer and was balancing his way up the board. He shouted to him as he sailed by about twenty yards away, but either the beer that was in his belly or the excitement that was on his mind kept Jimmy from hearing.

Drake decided that if his friend could do it so could he and began to paddle harder in order to reach the set before Jimmy had a chance to finish his ride and return.

Jimmy knelt down on the board as the wave played out and looked toward the beach for the friend he had hoped had seen his ride. He found the beach empty. He turned and looked back out, but just like **he** had been a few minutes before, Drake was out of sight.

"That shit's chickened out on me," he said below the noise of the waves that broke on the shore in front of him. He spread his legs and straddled the board and when he could feel sand on his feet he let the board slide out and dismounted. As he walked toward the shore he strained his eyes to the left to see if he could make out Drake's shape outlined in the light of the amusement park, but the only shapes he saw were the pylon fingers that reached up through the sand.

"Dumb shit," he said as he un-strapped the safety line from his ankle and laid the board upside down on the wet sand.

Drake was too far out and too concerned about his own safety and the hope of catching a wave soon to see what his friend saw. Jimmy saw a dog, or what he thought was a dog, running toward him from the shallow dunes. His brain tried to tell him to run. It tried to tell him that the animal was running too fast to be a dog. It was running too fast to be anything he had ever seen. His brain knew he should run and the water was close enough to provide a quick and safe opportunity, but the beer had thrown up a stop sign somewhere on the road to his feet. By the time the warning had negotiated the sign it was too late.

The beast's powerful jaws and the impact from its speed were enough to tear Jimmy's neck clean away. His head fell into the shallow surf and bounced along with the tide like a deflated beach ball.

Drake caught the next wave. It was not as good a wave as his friend had lucked upon, but he was scared. Scared of being out there alone in the dark. Scared of what might be lurking in the night water below his board. He remembered the girl that had been found chewed to pieces by a shark on that same beach no more than a month ago. The wave played out less than fifteen yards into his ride and caused Drake to go to his knees to keep from falling off. The last thing he wanted to do was fall off. Three things could happen if he did and none to his liking. He could drown, he could be eaten or he could drown and then be eaten. He looked around and expected to see Jimmy paddling out. He wanted desperately to tell him that he'd had enough for one night and was hauling ass. If Jimmy wanted to tell everyone what a pussy he was, then so be it. A live pussy was a damn sight better than being supper for some hungry shark. He couldn't see Jimmy.

A flurry of waves broke around him so Drake put his belly against the board and let them carry him back to shore. The sight of Jimmy's board that rocked back and forth with the tide gave him a moment of relief. It meant that he too must have had enough and was ready to head back to the pavilion and break open some more brew.

"Jimmy?" he shouted above the sound of the surf as the high tide began to inch its way up the beach. That same sound was the only response he got.

The beast watched him from the first floor of the burned-out section of building nearest the beach. Blood dripped from the corners of its mouth and onto the headless body that lay on the sand.

The head he held hostage under a heavy front paw. It would let the other one go if he came no closer. The strong one would be feast enough for one night.

Drake yelled Jimmy's name again. He had to be there somewhere. "Come on, Jimmy," he begged. "This ain't no fun anymore." He pulled his friend's board out of the water as the high tide continued to eat away at the sand. "Jimmy! Get your ass back here now or I'm leaving! I've had enough of this shit!"

The beast snarled as if smiling and kicked the head off the concrete and onto the sand. It came to rest just above the shoulders it had once been attached to and in the shadows the body looked almost whole again.

"All right, Jimmy. I'm gone. You can play your stupid, fucking game by yourself." Drake picked up his board and stomped madly back toward the lights. He turned back for a parting comment. "And you better get your ass back and get your board or you ain't never gonna find it."

The beast watched the lone figure until he reached the first tower, then jumped from the first floor onto the sand by the body. It kicked at the head until the eyes stared blankly at the estranged body. It let those same dead eyes watch as it tore into the chest cavity and came out with the heart in its mouth.

40

There was only a splash of scotch left in the bottle when Jesse offered his final plea. "You're a werewolf, Andrew, so you better get used to the idea whether you like it or not. That doesn't mean you have to be a monster. "You've got the power over it, not it over you, but you've got to learn how to use that power, otherwise it'll eat on you forever."

"I will not become a werewolf! Not tonight, not tomorrow, not ever!"

"Oh, but you will," Jesse told him. "We all do."

"You just said I had the power over it."

"You do, but you have to learn how to control the power. You have to learn how to use it."

"No."

"If you won't do it for yourself then do it for me."

"You don't need me."

"How do you know?"

"I've seen you, remember?"

"Yes, I do," Jesse said. "And do you remember what you saw?"

"That's not exactly something I'd tend to forget."

"What color was my coat?"

"Your coat?"

"My hair. What color was my hair?"

"Gray, I think," Andy said. "Yeah, dark gray."

"That's because I'm old, Andrew. Even werewolves get old."

"You're not that old."

"One hundred and ninety-two is old," Jesse said. "Take my word for it."

"What?"

"I told you we just couldn't die. We can only be killed. In the old days the pack killed the elderly and the weak, just like wolves do. It was their way of keeping the pack strong."

"If you're as old as you say, then just when were the old days?"

"A thousand years ago, give or take a century," Jesse advised him.

"How old was my father when he . . . when he died?"

"Let's see. We met in Germany during the war and . . ."

"Which war, Uncle Jesse?"

"Oh, the first one. Ah, yes. He had just turned a hundred a year or two before, so I guess he would have been about a hundred and seventy-five. More or less, when he died."

"Jesus!"

"He was still young compared to some others I've known. The one we're dealing with is a lot younger than that," Jesse said.

"How young, a hundred?" Andy asked.

"Probably less. His coat's still a fresh color and **that**, Andrew, is why I need you. That is why you **must** become a werewolf."

"Just so I can kill you when your time comes?" Andy asked. "If that's the case then I can wait until then."

"Not to kill me," he said calmly. "To kill him."

"We may never find **him**," Andy said.

"Oh, we'll find him. Maybe not in this cycle or the next, but we'll find him; o, you better prepare yourself for him now."

"I'm just not ready. Too much has happened too fast. I still need some time."

"If we're lucky we won't have time."

"What do you mean?"

"I'm sure he's already killed tonight. I can feel it. If we don't find him he'll just keep on killing. I don't want that and neither do you."

"He's sort of giving us werewolves a bad name, huh?" Andy poked Jesse in the ribs. It was their first hint of humor in a long night of grave discussion.

"Did you just hear yourself, Andrew?"

Andy was silent.

"You said **us**."

41

Andy found his usual parking spot had been taken when he pulled around the side of the pavilion. There were four cars with the sheriff department emblems on the doors and another unmarked vehicle. The mayor's bright yellow Cadillac stuck out like a diamond in a goat's ass among the tan Fords. Andy didn't consider the mayor as a diamond; more of a pain but in the same location.

Since his Bronco was a four by four it sat almost twice as high as the cars parked in front of it and offered Andy a better vantage point than had he gotten out. He took the binoculars from the bag on the seat next to him and focused them in the direction of the group of men on the beach. He counted two men in uniform, the sheriff and the mayor, himself, which made for too many cars and not enough drivers. One of the men in uniform was looking away from the group so Andy scanned the sands of East Beach until he located two more. They were walking with a third man, a boy actually, who seemed to be doing a lot of talking with his hands. The boy pointed to the surf, then to the beach and then to the surf again. He finally held his hands out in a yielding manner.

Andy reversed his direction back toward the group of men, only more slowly this time. He was looking for a body, but he didn't see one.

The sound of a flat hand being slapped against the side of sheet metal almost made Andy drop the glasses. He held onto them but hit his head against the door frame.

"Caught you," Butch said as he walked around the side of the Bronco he had just hit. "What're you looking at?"

"You just scared the piss out of me," Andy said and rubbed the top of his head.

"Serves you right for spying."

"I'd have served you something else if you'd made me drop these binoculars," Andy warned him.

"No problem," Butch said. "You didn't."

Andy saw that the mayor's group was looking in their direction. They had obviously heard Butch pound on the side of the truck.

"I guess we better get out there," Andy said.

"You never did tell me what you were looking at," Butch said.

"Take a look at the cars."

"Oh, shit."

"My sentiments exactly."

Mayor Paschall was his usual chipper self when Andy and Butch joined the crowd on the Stewart Beach side of the pylons. "You just now getting to work, Langsjoen?"

Andy checked his watch and noticed it was ten past seven. "Guilty as charged, Your Honor, but at least I'm dressed properly." His remark was directed at the mayor's jogging suit which was a far cry from his usual three-piece, Italian silk, business suit.

"Settle down, Andy," Sheriff Danforth told him.

"Yes, sir." Andy flashed a smile in the mayor's direction.

"The kid down there says he and a friend were surfing last night." The sheriff nodded toward East Beach. "Says his friend disappeared and he thought he was just joking around, but he never showed back up."

"Drowned?" Andy asked.

"Don't know. No body yet."

Andy remembered what Jesse had said last night and knew they'd never find the body, at least not in the near future. "Who was he?"

"Jimmy Covington. A local boy," the sheriff said. "His daddy works at the airport. Don't know about his mama."

"She works at the Donut Palace on Broadway," Butch said. "Who is that, Drake?"

"Uh, huh," the sheriff said. "You know him?"

"Yes, sir," Butch answered. "He was a year behind me in school. So was Jimmy."

"You think he'd make any of this up?"

"No, sir. He's a pretty straight kid."

"Then I guess we better get the word out and start combing the beach," the sheriff said.

Andy wanted to tell his boss that it would be a waste of time and the tax-payers' money. They could drain all the water out of the gulf and they still wouldn't find his body. What he really wanted to do was tell the mayor all he knew and watch him shit in his fancy jogging suit, but he didn't do either one. He did speak to the mayor as he turned to leave.

"You have a nice day now, you hear?"

"Are you just looking for trouble?" Butch asked him as they walked up the beach to their towers.

"I don't have to look very far where the mayor's concerned."

"No, but you aren't exactly shying away from it either."

"I'm not a shy person."

"How about stupid?" Butch said.

"How about you remembering who you take orders from," Andy told him.

"Just asking."

"Well, don't worry about me. The mayor and I have a relationship built on a common bond."

"Oh, yeah, what?"

"Hate."

Michele was standing by Andy's tower when he and Butch got there. "They find another one?"

Her question had been directed to Andy but Butch answered. "You remember Jimmy Covington?"

"Sure," she said. "He's in Austin with me."

"Well," Butch said, "he probably won't be graduating with you."

"Oh, no. What happened?"

Rather than lie, Andy let Butch continue answering. "Tried to surf in the dark and drowned it looks like."

"What do you mean, it looks like?"

"His body hasn't washed up yet."

Michele looked at Andy who just nodded in agreement. "It isn't a lie if you don't actually say the words," he thought, but said, "Y'all hit your towers. We're already late."

When Butch started to jog toward his Michele started in on Andy. "So, how was your night?"

"Boring as usual," he said. "Yours?"

"You mean you can't tell?"

Andy looked at her and tried to find an answer. "No," he said.

"Then I guess it wasn't worth it," she said. She turned and started to walk toward her post.

"Wait a minute," Andy yelled after her. "Aren't you going to tell me?"

"I got a little beauty sleep," she yelled back and then started to run.

42

When Amy heard the news about the Covington boy on the radio she went immediately into Eric's office to break the news to him. "Do you know a Jimmy Covington?" she asked as she closed the door behind her.

"Should I?" he said from behind the solid glass desk he had made especially for him in New Orleans.

"He's a surfer, or was," she said. "I just thought you might have met . . ."

"I don't make a habit of introducing myself to everyone who owns a board and thinks they can surf."

"Unless they're female," Amy said.

"Precisely," Eric said. "Why?"

"They think he drowned on East Beach last night," she said.

"How can they **think** somebody drowns?" he advised her. "Either they drowned or they didn't. It's just like being pregnant. You either are or you aren't."

"They haven't found him yet."

"Have they checked the motels?"

"Why would they do that?"

"Maybe he got lucky," Eric said.

"You're hopeless," Amy told him and turned to leave.

"They find his board?"

"The radio didn't say."

"Probably wasn't worth much anyway," Eric said.

Amy opened the door but Eric stopped her with a question. "We got anything to eat out there?"

"I think there might be a sausage biscuit or two left. Ruth stopped by McDonald's on the way in."

"Would you bring me one?"

"Why? Talking about death make you hungry?"

"No," he said. "I'm always hungry after a good night."

"I'm sorry to hear that," she said.

"Why?" Eric reminded her. "You had your chance."

It was the first time Eric had brought up the subject of their ill-fated Fourth of July celebration since the roses. Amy had the glass in her window replaced and had placed the bill on his desk two days later, along with a bill from Gerland's for a bottle of wine. When she had returned from lunch she found a check on her desk along with a note. The note had explained that since the bottle hadn't been full he had deducted half.

"No," Amy said. "I took a chance."

"Same difference," Eric said.

"Not the way I look at it."

"And how might that be?"

"You'll never know," she said and walked out of his office.

43

Jesse paid Andy a visit at noon. He found him, just as the mayor had done, chewing on a cold submarine sandwich on the pavilion balcony.

"If you've come to say I told you so, Uncle Jesse, you can just turn around and head back to your stiffs," Andy said. "That is, unless you've brought me something better to eat. Then you can stay."

"Would it help?" Jesse asked. He paid close attention to who might be eating close enough to overhear their conversation.

"What, the food or the I told you so?"

"The latter."

"Nope," Andy said. "We don't know for sure yet what happened to him. They might find his body anytime now." Andy thought about how five hours before he had wanted to tell the mayor how they would never find the body, and now, enter Jesse, and he had done a complete flip-flop.

"Suit yourself," Jesse said. "I don't know where you got your hard-headedness from. Your parents sure weren't that way."

"Maybe there was a human in the woodpile they didn't know about," Andy joked.

"Maybe so," Jesse answered. "Or maybe you're just trying to convince yourself.

"Convince myself of what?"

Jesse bent over and pressed his palms on the table and spoke just loud enough for only Andy to hear. "That so long as you don't become a werewolf, you aren't one."

"Maybe you're right," Andy said. "And so far it's working."

"Be that as it may," Jesse said. "I'll be over tonight around eight."

"Well, make yourself at home," Andy told him. "But just be gone by midnight. You know what they say about three being a crowd."

"You can't go out tonight!"

"The hell I can't," Andy said. "I had enough of you last night to last me a while."

"We have things to discuss," Jesse said.

"Nothing we haven't discussed already. I'll pick you up a fresh bottle of scotch on my way home so you won't get lonely. Just be gone before I get there."

"I hope you won't regret your decision," Jesse said. He stood back up and left before Andy had a chance to tell him he wouldn't.

Andy looked at the soggy sandwich on the table in front of him. It looked even less appetizing than it had tasted. He wadded it up and threw it in the direction of the trash can and this time it went in.

"Where is Michele now?" he thought.

44

Eric had been forced to give up his afternoon of surfing when a heavy rain settled in just after lunch. He might have chanced it had not the storm been accompanied by lightning. Three years ago, he had seen a surfer broiled in a wetsuit by a lightning strike and it hadn't been a pretty sight. He also knew the rain would have driven away any possible audience he would have been able to attract otherwise, so he had just stayed in the office and tried to act busy. Work had never been one of Eric's strong suits. He preferred to over-staff his office and let them do all the work.

The mid-morning biscuit had been enough to carry him through lunch, but now, with the workday behind him, he found he was famished. From his office window he could see the early evening crowd entering Fisherman's Wharf near Pier 22 and decided a dozen or so of his favorite shellfish and a few well-meaning vodka tonics would put him in the right frame of mind for the evening.

His office was vacant when he walked through it. Even LaShonda, who was first in line for overtime, was gone. He noticed that although Amy's roses were gone she had kept the polished bronze vase and was using it as a pencil holder. He was glad he had decided against the much more expensive crystal vase. It would have been such a terrible waste.

Eric locked up and took the elevator down. When the doors opened he stepped out into the face of the mayor. "Excuse me," he said and waited for a similar response.

Mayor Paschall just grunted some sort of reply and stepped into the elevator and hit the penthouse button. The doors slid shut and brought an abrupt end to their conversation.

Eric walked by the main entrance and across Water Street to Pier 22. The Colonel's crew was preparing the paddle-wheeler for the dinner cruise. He walked on past and onto the front deck of Fisherman's Wharf.

The waterfront tables were already filled with tourists who were washing down boiled shrimp with beer. He preferred the air-conditioned climate inside to rubbing elbows with strangers, especially those with children who had not yet learned that screaming and crying are better left at home.

Inside was happy-hour busy, but the hostess graciously accepted Eric's five-dollar reservation and found him a table by a window that over-looked the channel. When a heavy-chested waitress came to his table, Eric ordered a dozen raw oysters and a vodka tonic and told her to hold another of the same in abeyance.

The waitress, though confused, wrote something down on her pad anyway.

Eric swept his eyes over the busy crowd and noticed there seemed to be several unattached females in attendance. With any luck he might find just what he was looking for without having to venture elsewhere.

45

The Colonel had been docked at Pier 22 for almost ten years and Andy had yet to embark on one of its daily, two-hour cruises, but that was about to change. Michele had parted with almost fifty hard earned dollars and made reservations for the eight o'clock dinner cruise aboard the one-hundred-and-fifty-foot paddle-wheeler.

Ever since her parents had returned from their Fourth of July trip, Michele had either met Andy somewhere or had just gone straight to his condo. Andy began to realize that maybe she wasn't as free to do as she pleased as she had led him to believe. He made a mental note to bring that subject up later as he parked the Bronco on Twenty-Fourth Street to avoid the parking fee at the pier lot. That made two things he needed to ask her about, the other being her hopeful use of some sort of birth control measure.

Andy crossed Water Street and onto the spacious and usually empty pier parking lot. It remained that way since the city fathers were so proud of it that they set the fee based on their pride and thus no one could afford to park there. Even the most ignorant tourist only made that mistake once.

As he walked the two blocks across the barely-worn asphalt, still wet from the afternoon rain, he noticed a familiar figure in an even more recently familiar jogging suit headed in the opposite direction on the other side of the street. Andy started to yell out some sort of cordial greeting that would have come from somewhere other than his heart, but the mayor

178

looked as though he was deep in thought and in somewhat of a hurry, so he let it slide. After all, he **had** gotten in the last greeting that morning.

Michele was waiting impatiently at the wide entrance to the dock where The Colonel was moored. "Nice of you to show up," she said.

Andy looked at his watch. "You said it leaves at eight. It's ten till now."

"I also said you could board at seven for drinks," she reminded him.

"No, you didn't. You said you could board an hour ahead of time. You never said anything about drinks."

"You should have understood what I meant, regardless," Michele stammered.

"If you want to make sure I get someplace when you want me there, then why don't you let me pick you up?" He had one of the questions already up for discussion and they hadn't even boarded the boat yet.

Michele chose to sidestep the issue, but in doing so it meant she had to let him win this minor disagreement as to who was to be where and when. "Oh, never mind," she said and reached for his hand. "Let's get on board before they leave us altogether."

Andy hadn't gotten his answer but he had gotten her calmed down, so he was no worse than when he had started out. Still, he wished he had listened better about the drinks.

46

He knew there would be a good chance the authorities would be working late in the East Beach area, if nothing else but to watch the tide for the possible regurgitation of the body that wasn't there. He knew that killing one of them, even if their body was never found, would be too hard for them to swallow. It would mean investigations that would lead to searches and all in his own back yard, so to speak. For that reason, he chose to remain at the port where he knew there were at least two tankers docked in the channel at that moment. He had watched the crews scramble off like rats once they had been granted shore leave. The sight of so many brought back a rush of exciting memories.

He had hidden his clothes then waited between the stacks of wooden pallets and watched as the full moon replaced the sun. Then its hunger grew as the rays of the moon grew brighter.

Four young seamen, probably no older than the boy last night, left the tanker. They jabbered to each other in a language it couldn't understand, not that it was necessary that it did. One of the boys stopped and slapped his hands against his thighs and said something to the others. They went on ahead without him as he hurried back to the ship.

The boy had no sooner gone up the metal gangplank and into the side door than he was out again. His forgotten camera now hung heavily around his neck. He ran down the gangplank and onto the pier, hoping to catch up with his buddies before they lost themselves on The Strand.

The beast growled hoarsely when it saw its chances of an early prey vanishing before its eyes. But his low outburst had been premature. The boy stopped at the sight of the full moon as it shown through the masts of the Elissa, a 19th century clipper ship docked at Pier 21. He raised the camera and set the flash but he was too close to get the full ship in the picture. He began to walk backward as he carefully watched through the viewer for the entire ship to fall within its boundaries. When it did he smiled and mumbled something in his native tongue.

When the shutter opened it caught nothing but the flash as it ricocheted off the wet surface on the pier after the strap was torn in two. The camera beat the body to the ground, both objects being instantly and violently void of a part of their make-up that kept them together. The camera broke open when it hit the pier. The body didn't, but it was just as dead.

The beast dragged the body deep into the mountains of pallets until all light was gone and gorged itself on the taste of human flesh. It saved the young heart for last.

47

"Now, that wasn't bad, was it?" Michele asked when they negotiated the gangplank and onto the dock.

"I never said it was going to be," Andy answered.

"That's the trouble. You hardly said two words the whole trip. It seemed like all you wanted to do was stare at the moon."

"At least I didn't howl."

"I beg your pardon?"

"Nothing."

"Andy, is something wrong? Did I do something to make you mad at me?"

"I've just got a few things on my mind, that's all," Andy said.

"Like what?" she asked as she motioned him in the direction of her car. She had paid the price and parked in the pier lot to be close to the boat.

"Well, for starters, you haven't told me why you don't want me to pick you up at your house. We always have to meet somewhere."

"I thought that's what you wanted." Michele had had two hours to prepare an answer she knew would resurface before the night was over. It was a good answer too. Probably the best one she could have come up with, short notice or not. It **had** been the way Andy had wanted it. He had serious doubts about her parents accepting him due to their age difference.

Michele went a step further to strengthen her position. "Hey, if you want to come over and meet my parents, then you can pick me up there tomorrow night. I'll make sure they're there with bells on."

Andy accepted her answer and told her that wouldn't be necessary.

"Is that it, then?"

"Not quite," Andy answered. He didn't really know how to ask the next question without sounding stupid. Had she been closer to his age he wouldn't have had the problem. Most women he had gone out with had just come right out and told him what method of birth control they were using. But Michele wasn't a woman, though she was trying hard to be. She was still a girl, so he was at a loss.

"Well," she said. "I'm waiting."

Andy gave up trying to think how to word the question and just blurted it out. "Are you on the pill or something?"

The question made her laugh which embarrassed Andy even more. "Of course, silly. If I got pregnant I would lose my scholarship."

Andy breathed a sigh of relief big enough for the both of them, which is exactly what it covered. He wouldn't have to worry about any little werewolves clawing their way out of Michele's tummy. "That's it then. Let's go."

"Not so fast, Andrew. What brought that on? Why are you just now asking me about that?"

It was the first time she had called him by his given name, not that he minded. He just wished it would have been in a different tone of voice.

"I. . . I just wanted to make sure, that's all. I figured you probably were, but I. . ."

"But you what? You didn't want to knock up the little college girl?" Michele looked Andy square in the eye to let him know that she would be giving him no quarter.

Andy had been through such a conversation when he was a little more than Michele's age and had learned something from it. "That's exactly right," he advised her. "Isn't that why you're taking precautions?"

The shoe was on the other foot now, and it fit a little too tight to suit Michele. "How about a truce?" she asked and smiled a beautifully, perfect smile.

"I'd rather have an unconditional surrender."

"A truce is the best I can do."

"Then I'll take it," Andy said. "I don't have room for any prisoners anyway."

48

The sandy soil of the ship channel should have been no harder to bury the body in than the substructure of the condotel. Back in his human form the job should have been a cinch, but the lack of a shovel complicated matters. He had buried and dug up that tool at the condotel for so long that he had taken it for granted. He scrounged around the area near the Sulphur mound and came up with a broken propeller blade and finished the job.

The whole time, both as the beast then as the human, a dark cloud seemed to follow in his path. Even as he threw the last blade of sand on the makeshift grave, he had a feeling of doom. Something was wrong. Something he must have forgotten. He retraced his journey all the way back to the beginning, or at least almost. A large crowd had gathered between the stacks of pallets and the tanker that had brought his victim to the island. He still couldn't understand their language but he could tell by the high pitch tone of their voices that they weren't gathered there for a party.

He listened harder and hoped to hear a little bit of English thrown in somewhere or maybe a familiar voice. Surely with this big of a crowd there had to be someone of authority in the middle of it. But not tonight. Not yet.

He was forced to remain at the outer edge of the pallets. If he ventured in closer he would run the risk of being caught in the middle of something that might prove to be even more dangerous than the beast he had changed from. He carefully climbed to the top of the outermost stack in order to see what he couldn't hear. The crowd seemed to grow by the minute. Men scampered from the tanker like roaches from a rusty drain. He tried to focus on someone who might be doing more talking than the others. Someone who might be in charge. Then he saw him. It wasn't really him he saw but what he was holding. Even in the distance he could see what it was. The cloud of doom that had followed him now brought the rain of realization when he saw the broken camera the man held up by the torn strap for all the crowd to see.

In his haste to move several pallets in order to hide the blood until it had time to dry into an un-recognizable spot, he had forgotten about the camera. His eyes turned a fiery yellow and a growl came out low from the depths of his being, but even the beast, should he change again, could do nothing about it now.

He climbed down from his perch on the pallets and followed the shadows back to his office where he watched from the darkness behind his window until a caravan of flashing red and blue lights turn off Water Street toward the pier.

The long walk carrying the body and the digging without the proper means had left him drained. He laid down on the large couch and fell fast asleep.

49

Andy had already been up long enough to shower and shave when the phone rang. He figured it was probably Michele, who knew his morning routine by heart, calling to tell him good morning as she had begun doing when she had to leave his bed in the wee hours to return to her own. He had felt her soft, goodbye kiss when she had left his condo, but he had pretended not to. When he had heard the front door close he had opened his eyes and looked at the clock. It had been one-thirty.

The new and yet-opened bottle of scotch had still been on the bar when they had arrived which meant Jesse had not taken him seriously. He had made the purchase in case Jesse had decided to make the trip just to spite him. In hindsight he regretted the purchase and even the idea behind it as Jesse didn't have a spiteful bone in his body.

Michele, as a reminder that she was still a little pissed at his delayed question regarding her method of contraception, had taken the birth control pill packet from her purse and laid it on the pillow beside him before they had made love. Afterwards, she was no longer pissed. Not even a little bit.

Just before Andy had dropped off to sleep again, he had thought about Jesse and hoped he hadn't decided to do anything stupid.

Andy thought Michele's early morning wakeup calls were rather juvenile and they did tend to throw his schedule off by a few minutes, but

hearing her voice at that time of the morning
did tend to start his day off on a rather happy
note.

"Good morning," he said with a hint of song
in his voice when he picked up the phone.

"You obviously haven't been listening to the
radio," Jesse said on the other end.

Andy had been prepared for a more sweeter
greeting than he had received, juvenile or not.
"Why? What happened?"

"He's killed again," Jesse said.

"The radio said that?"

"No, of course not."

"Then what?"

"A crewman from an Argentinean tanker has
come up missing," Jesse told him.

"Maybe he just had one too many tequila shots
at Yaga's and is sleeping it off somewhere."

"No, this one didn't even make it off the
pier. They found his busted-up camera about
twenty feet from where he got off the boat."

"Maybe he just got mugged," Andy said. He
wasn't ready to believe the inevitable so early
in the morning.

"For what, a handful of worthless pesos?"
Jesse said. "No, it was him. That's another body
they'll never find."

"Give it a rest, Jesse. Maybe he'll turn up,"
Andy said. "Right now, you're letting your
imagination run away with you. Things like this
have happened before."

"That's just my point, Andrew. Before they were just written off as another crewman jumping ship or drowning or something like that. Who knows how many of those have ended up buried somewhere?"

"The Shadow knows," Andy said in a deep, eerie voice.

"I can't believe you're doing this," Jesse said.

"I'm just trying to keep all this in perspective, Uncle Jesse. So far all I've seen is one dead girl who certainly could have passed as a shark victim and still might. You've shown me some hair but for all I know it could have been from that Chow down the street. The only werewolf I've seen is you and I wouldn't put it passed you to have slipped me some kind of drug to make me hallucinate. After all, you **are** a doctor."

"As far as I know," Jesse said, "they haven't come up with a drug that can make you see a specific thing. You are your own answer, Andrew. You won't let me help you transform. That would give you the answer you are looking for. Tonight is the last night of the cycle. We could do it tonight."

"No, you're gonna have to come up with something else, Jesse. And I don't mind telling you this is all getting a little old."

"What if you see him? Would you believe me then?"

"How are you going to arrange that? I thought that's what your problem was, knowing who and where he was."

"If I could manage it, would you believe me then? Would you transform?"

"Let's take it one step at a time. First I have to see it, and then I have to believe what I see. You're not going to just run some big dog in front of me in the dark and expect me to go running off half-cocked with you trying to catch it. That's what we have the animal control boys for," Andy said.

"If you see it and believe it, will you transform?" Jesse shouted as loud as he could with the phone next to his mouth.

"Yeah, Jesse, I will. But to tell you the truth, I don't think it'll come to that, even **if** I **could** change."

"Fine," Jesse said. "That's all I ask. I'll pick you up at eight tonight." He hung up the phone before Andy had enough time to argue his way out.

"Good move," Andy told himself when the line went dead. "Now what are you going to tell Michele? You can't very well say you can't go out with her tonight because you're going on a werewolf hunt, now can you? You could tell her you have to visit a sick relative, which might not be too far from the truth, but you've beat that dead horse too many times already."

Andy decided to wait until noon. If they found the body by then he would call Jesse and tell him their deal was off. If they didn't, well he would just have to face Michele's music. Either way he had a good five hours before the coin toss.

50

"My don't we look like shit this morning," Amy told Eric when she waltzed into his office with a friendly cup of black coffee.

"Shut up."

"Oh, and chipper too."

"Just put the coffee down and get out," Eric said. "I don't need your crap today."

"What's the matter?" Amy said. "Did you run into someone who wouldn't buy your act?"

"If I ever do," Eric said and paused long enough to take a drink, "you can bet you'll be the last to know."

"Somehow I don't doubt that."

"Is there anything else?" Eric asked.

"Did you run out of pajamas?"

"What does that have to do with anything?"

"Just wondering," Amy said. "You look like you slept in those clothes."

Eric looked down at the clothes had, in fact, slept in. "Let's just say I had a busy night and leave it at that."

"I hear the cops did too," she said.

Eric turned in his chair and looked out the window toward the port. "That's what I understand."

"I hope he ran away or just drowned."

"That sounds somewhat morbid coming from you."

"I didn't mean it like that. It's just that it's too close to home. I don't feel all that safe walking in the parking garage at night as it is now. I'd hate to think we have some sort of maniac lurking in the shadows of our own backyard," she explained.

"I don't think you need to worry about that," Eric said. "The kid's probably halfway to Houston by now. Tomorrow he'll probably be working on some construction site and getting laid after work."

"You think so?"

"I wouldn't lose any sleep over it." Eric took another drink of coffee. "Besides, you can always arm yourself with a bottle of wine."

"I'm serious, Eric."

"So am I. It worked on me."

"But you're different."

"I would hope so."

"No, I mean . . . well, I don't know what I mean," Amy said with a pause.

"That's about par."

"You would understand if you were in my shoes," she said.

"If I were in your shoes, I'd be spending my time trying to latch onto some guy who could take me away from all this, not worrying about whether somebody was going to jump out from behind a car and screw me blind."

"Is that all you ever have on your mind?"

"What?"

"Screwing."

"Only when I'm awake."

"I bet you even dream about it," Amy followed.

"I don't dream," Eric advised her. "It's a waste of time."

"You ought to give it a try."

"Why?"

"It might help you come to work in a better mood."

"Speaking of work," Eric said. "Why don't you try doing some?"

"I think I will. Maybe it'll take my mind off what happened."

"Glad I could be of assistance," Eric said. "And to think you'll get paid at the same time.

With that, Amy left. Eric turned his chair back around to face the port and took another drink of coffee.

51

The morning had passed too quickly to Andy's way of thinking. He was sitting in the Bronco with the radio tuned to the local station for the noon news. When the girl on the radio told him, and anyone else who might be tuned in, that the body of the missing Argentinean still hadn't been found, Andy cringed. He knew it would be easier to tell Jesse no than Michele and with a lot less consequences.

Michele was stationed at Pirate's Beach today and since he still had fifty-five minutes of his lunch left, Andy decided it might go over better if he broke the news to her face to face. He backed around the pavilion and drove out the exit onto Seawall Boulevard and headed west. It was the same route they had taken in the lifeguard parade on the Fourth, only twice as long. Still, it wouldn't take him more than fifteen or twenty minutes to get there even if he caught all the red lights.

As good or bad luck would have it, Michele had decided to lunch on the beach with an apple and a container of flavored yogurt rather than drive back to civilization for a more unhealthier fare. When she saw the Bronco drive up and park she wondered if the visit was going to be a social one. It would have been nice if Andy had gotten out of the truck with a bucket of chicken and a couple of Cokes; even sort of romantic when she thought about it; but when he didn't she got up and walked toward the water. If he couldn't catch up to her, then he couldn't tell her whatever bad news it was that had come along with him for the ride.

"Aw, Michele, come on. I gotta be back in half an hour," Andy whined a decibel or two below a yell.

Michele kept walking as if she hadn't heard him and kicked at the sand with her bare feet.

Andy broke into a run. She saw him out of the corner of her eye and knew she wouldn't be able to outrun him. She could only postpone the bad news if she tried. Instead, she turned to head back and gave him a shocked look of surprise to see him when he trotted up.

"Why, Andy. How nice. What brings you all the way down here?" Her words, like honey, dripped thickly from her mouth.

"Nothing good I'm afraid," he said and tried to catch his breath between words.

"Of course not," Michele informed him. "You wouldn't drive all the way out here just to say hi."

"Look," he said. "Something's come up. I have to see Jesse again tonight."

"Have to or want to? You two got something going?" She knew they didn't but it was the only rude comment she could come up with at the moment.

"I promise this will be the last time." Andy knew he would be able to live up to that promise for at least a month, even if all of Jesse's ramblings turned out to be true.

"How do I know I can believe you?"

"I've never promised before. That's gotta mean something."

"Yeah," Michele said. "It means you're desperate."

"OK, I'm desperate," Andy admitted. "Now am I off the hook?"

"Oh, I see," she said. "Now I've got you on a hook. Are you worried that I'll try to reel you in?" Michele made a fishing movement with her hands.

"That's not what I meant. It was just a figure of speech."

"Then you need to plan your speeches better in the future." She looked at her watch. "And unless you know a short cut, you're going to be late."

"Does that mean I'm forgiven? . . . How's that?"

"Maybe and better," Michele answered, respectively. "I'll have to wait and see if you can keep your promise."

"Thanks," Andy said. He started to lean down and kiss her but he caught sight of one of the other guards looking at them through his binoculars. The guard was too far away for Andy to see who it was and he was in too much of a hurry to ask Michele. He would check the duty roster later if he thought about it, and if he didn't, then it was obviously no big deal.

52

It was almost two o'clock before Eric left the office. The investigation into the missing Argentinean crewman had slowed down the loading process of the tanker; one that held several sugar consignments from his business. It had required him to make several phone calls to make sure the operation would not be halted altogether.

He drove home, changed out of the clothes he had worn for two days and into more comfortable attire in the way of surfer jams. He loaded the Wolfe board on the BMW and ran his hand over the newly painted finish on the car's hood.

Eric was ready for another challenge, especially after having missed a day due to the rain, so he headed to Pirate's Beach. He didn't put much stock in fate but when he parked along the boulevard and caught sight of Michele's familiar figure leaning back against a large rock he decided it might be time to give it some thought.

Michele had been watching two other surfers who had ventured out beyond the limit once before and had been warned, so she hadn't seen Eric walk up behind her.

"Hello, stranger," Eric said and leaned his board against the rock.

Even though Michele didn't recognize the voice her mind did and sent a skin-tingling message to the rest of her body. Se turned quickly out of nothing more than a primal instinct. "What are you doing here?"

Eric looked from Michele to his board and back again. "From appearances, it looks like I might be here to do some surfing."

"Why don't you appear at another beach?" she said. "This one's taken."

"It's a big beach," Eric said.

"Not big enough for both of us."

"Unless my watch is wrong, high noon was a couple of hours ago."

"Listen," Michele said, "I can throw you out of here."

"Not without a good reason you can't," he said. "And that doesn't include a personal one."

"I'll think of one."

"What would happen if I said I was sorry?"

"Nothing."

"How long do you plan on holding this grudge?"

"Until I never see you again."

"You're being sort of petty, don't you think?"

"It really doesn't matter," Michele said. "I'm seeing someone steady now."

"That other lifeguard?"

"Which one?" Michele was stunned by the fact that he knew.

"The one who picked you up that night."

She moved from stunned to frightened but still managed an answer of sorts. "Maybe, but it's none of your business one way or another."

"I could easily make it my business," Eric warned her.

"And you could go to hell!" Michele leaned off the rock and doubled up both fists.

"Hey," he said. "I'm not looking for a fight."

"Just what **are** you looking for?"

"Just a little time on my board. I didn't come here looking for you, if that's what you think."

Michele relaxed her muscles, though not totally. Her hands were still fists but her nails no longer bit into her palms. "Then go ahead."

"Thank you," Eric said and grabbed his board.

Michele took a deep breath and leaned back against the rock to steady herself when he started to walk toward the surf. When he stopped and turned back toward her she stiffened again.

"You **will** try to save me if I look like I might be drowning, won't you?" Eric asked.

"I'll look like I might be trying," she answered.

53

By the time Andy had turned on the TV for the six o'clock news he had made up his mind that if the body had turned up alive or dead, but still in one piece, he was going to phone Jesse and tell him not to bother coming by. He had sat through ten minutes of boring news and two minutes filled with nine commercials before he had gotten what he had been waiting for, only the news had still bn bad. No trace of the missing seaman had been found.

He had jumped into the shower and washed a day's build-up of sand off his deep tan and had then decided on a nap. It hadn't been so much that he had been tired as it was the fact that Jesse might have a longer than usual night in store for him.

His bed had felt lonely but not enough to keep him from dropping off to sleep.

When Jesse arrived just before eight he found Andy still asleep. He looked at the well-proportioned body of his best friend's son as he lay stretched out on top of the made bed and tried to imagine him in another form. He wondered if the form would have the same soft, brown coat as his father or if the bleaching affect the sun had on his hair would transform into the same golden color.

Andy's sub-conscious told him he was no longer alone and he spoke before his eyes were yet half open. "Jesse?" he yawned. "What time is it?"

"Eight o'clock. Time to go." Jesse backed out of the room to allow Andy to dress in private. He went to the bar where the new bottle of scotch still stood guard. He knew he would have to have his wits about him, but decided that one drink surely wouldn't hurt. It might even sharpen his senses. He was pouring a second drink when Andy joined him.

"Where's mine?" Andy asked when he noticed that Jesse had helped himself twenty-four hours later than expected.

"Sorry," Jesse said. "The only thing I know how to mix with booze is ice."

Andy went to the refrigerator and took out a plastic container of orange juice and emptied what little remained into a glass. He went back to the bar and finished filling it up with vodka and stirred it with his index finger. The juice was cold enough to make ice unnecessary.

"What's on the program?" Andy asked as he stood beside Jesse.

"We're going down to the pier and take a look around."

"You think it's safe? I hear the guy's friends are out for blood."

"They've been confined to the ship."

"I see you've been doing your homework," Andy said.

"One of us has to."

"What exactly are we gonna be looking for?"

"I don't know for sure," Jesse told him. "But we'll know if we find it."

"That's reassuring," Andy said. "If there is a werewolf, and that's a mighty big if, you think he'll show up again?"

"Not if he's smart," Jesse answered. "But he screwed up again by leaving the camera which means he might have left something else. He doesn't know we're onto him so he just might make a return trip of his own."

"You don't think there'll be any police hanging around down there? Maybe they're thinking along the same lines as you are. Maybe they think the mugger, or whatever he is, might decide to return to the scene of the crime."

"No, they're already writing it off as another foreigner jumping ship."

"What about the camera?"

"They think he probably hit it against the pallets and dropped it. When he saw it was broken he just left it there."

"Sounds good to me," Andy said.

"I thought it might, but we're going to check it out anyway just the same."

"I can't talk you out of it, huh?"

"Not this time, I'm afraid. You ready?"

Andy downed his drink. "Not really, but I guess I don't have any other choice."

"Not if we're going to catch him," Jesse said. "We have to find a place to start."

"Then let's get the hell out of here and get it over with."

They took Jesse's station wagon in case the police had left someone behind for the reason they had discussed. The coroner's sign painted on the door made it more official looking than Andy's Bronco.

When they got there they found their decision had been unnecessary. Jesse had been right. The pier was almost deserted. There were a few stragglers but none who could be confused with either the law or the crewmen from the ship. The gang plank had also been raised back up to the deck of the ship to make sure none of the missing man's friends could disobey orders and take matters into their own hands.

The full moon already shone low in the summer sky, but its light wasn't yet enough to work by. The wharf light above that section of pier was also of no help to them. It had been broken out by some young, local vandals with nothing better to do but go around chunking rocks at the expensive and somewhat antique equipment. Andy looked down the dock and saw that most of the others suffered from the same fate. It made the area a perfect battleground for muggers. He still told himself that that's all it was, a mugging.

Jesse began to sweep his flashlight over the pier in front of the pallets where the camera had been found. The light went from the dock to the stacks and then back again.

"Found anything yet?" Andy asked.

"Not yet, but give me time," Jesse said as he began his journey through the wooden maze.

"Take all the time you need. I don't have anything better to do," Andy said, sarcastically.

He watched as Jesse disappeared. The light from the flashlight was barely visible through the gaps in the wood.

"Andrew!" Jesse shouted after a little more than five minutes at work. "Come in here!

He had been watching them from his office window across the way. The same window he had watched the police procession through the night before. He had recognized them as soon as they had crossed Water Street and begun their journey across the empty city lot. He yearned for the heart of the younger one but knew they were too smart to just fall into his hands. They were also too many. He had no doubt the beast could kill them both but not with the careful ease it had been used to. Still, it was the third and last night of the cycle. Its last night to taste flesh.

As he left his office he passed the janitor making his usual nightly rounds through the building. He would be an easy prey but it was far too dangerous to transform himself while still in the building, especially if there was a chance some others might be there with overtime on their minds. And with the janitor gone, who would clean up the mess.

The janitor spoke to him as he passed, not realizing how close he had just come to the most horrible of deaths.

On the dock, Andy felt his way through the mountains of pallets to where Jesse was shining the light on the ground. "What is it?"

"Look," Jesse said and moved the beam of light under the bottom of a pallet. "Look there."

Andy bent down and peered at the oblong circle of light. "It might help if you told me what I was supposed to be looking for."

Jesse knelt down beside him and held the flashlight at the edge of the wood. "Blood," he said.

"Give me the flashlight," Andy said. He took it and tried to angle the light through the boards. "I can't tell if that's blood or not. It might be grease or oil or something."

"Touch it," Jesse said.

"You're full of shit! I'm not going to touch it."

"Then I'll do it. Just hold the light steady." Jesse took a handkerchief from his back pocket and reached into the bottom row of boards. The spot was sticky to the touch and held a slight grip on the cloth when he pulled it back out into the beam of light.

"There. What do you call that?"

"Well, it looks like blood," Andy answered. "Maybe something just crawled up under there to die."

"Then check it out."

"I will." Andy got down on all fours and shined the light across the empty floor beneath the pallet.

"Well?" Jesse said.

"Nothing there."

"Of course not. Give me the light and back up."

Andy obliged and was careful to put it in his free hand.

Jesse began to scour the ground with the light. "Look. See the scratches? The pallets have been moved and recently too."

"That's crazy," Andy said. He put his shoulder against the stack and tried to slide it in another direction. "No one could move these things without a forklift."

"**He** could."

The beast had been listening. He had circled the warehouse and come up from the other end where he had stashed his clothes neatly away behind a dumpster. The red hairs on its hump bristled at the sound of their voices. It could take them now. It crouched low and began to nudge its way into the maze. The light from the flashlight served as its beacon, though it wasn't needed. It could smell them. Its nostrils flared from the scent of revenge. When it was no more than two stacks from them the beast froze in its tracks when the dark wooden valleys were suddenly bathed in daylight.

"What the fuck is that?" Andy said as he shielded his eyes from the bright light that shone down on them from the deck of the tanker. There were loud voices coming from the source of the light, but the language was foreign.

"Looks like we've been found out," Jesse said. "Let's get out of here. We got what we came for."

"That suits the shit out of me," Andy agreed.

Jesse folded the handkerchief up and shoved it back into his hip pocket as the blinding light followed them out of the maze and around the corner of the warehouse.

The beast remained perfectly still until the area around it returned to darkness. It pawed at the ground and snarled. It knew its chance was gone, but there would be other chances. It would make sure of it and it would be ready.

"This proves it," Jesse said when they reached his station wagon they had parked on Twenty-fourth Street. He took the handkerchief out of his pocket and showed it to Andy like he was showing it to him for the first time.

"All you've got is some blood," Andy said. "You don't even know if it's human or not."

"Oh, it's human all right. Take my word for it."

"So far, that's all I've been doing; taking your word for things."

"I'll prove it to you. We'll go to my lab right now and put this through the tests."

"If it is human blood, you're gonna have to tell the police," Andy told him.

"No, sir."

"You have to, Uncle Jesse. That could be evidence you're holding."

"Evidence of what? We still don't have a body to put it in."

"No, but they can match the DNA with his personal effects. It'll give them something to work on. At least now they'll start doing some investigating. You can't just hide evidence and pretend it doesn't exist."

"And just what are you going to tell them when they ask why you were down here snooping around?" Jesse said. "This kind of thing is hardly in your line of work."

"I don't care," Andy said. "We have to do something."

"Oh, we will, Andrew, but not just yet."

"Well, you can count me out."

"No, you're in it with me now."

"Unh, uh. That wasn't the deal."

"What deal?"

"You still didn't show me your werewolf," Andy reminded him.

The beast loped along in the shadows of the dock. Every now and then it lifted its snout to smell the air. It was too late to journey to the condotel as it had planned earlier, but not to late to hopefully find a lone stranger sleeping off a drunk in the warehouse district.

It left the docks at Thirty-Third Street and quickly crossed an open stretch of vacant land. It crouched behind a row of bushes and urinated as a car passed in front of it on Water Street. Had the driver seen it he would have thought nothing of a rather large dog pissing on a bush. If he had and stopped he would have died before his foot hit the pavement.

The abandoned warehouses were silent, but the concrete floor of the first one the beast entered was cool beneath its paws. The feeling reminded it of the condotel floors. It was a promising feeling. It loped along with its nose in the air, but the musty smell of rotting gunny sacks was all that filled its nostrils.

The beast was about to venture up the broken stairs when a noise brought its ears to a point high above its head. It waited for the sound again and moved its furry head from side to side. When it came again, the beast recognized it as the tinkling sound made from a glass or bottle when it came in contact with cement. The lack of a scent meant it must have come from the outside. The windows were too high for it to look through, even standing on its hind legs, so it returned to the broken door where it had entered and pranced softly out and to the corner of the building.

The light summer breeze blew in its direction and filled its senses with the odor of human flesh. Its flaming yellow eyes, blue around the center, found the source of the smell. An old, black man was sitting with his back against the warehouse wall. He was looking sadly into an empty wine bottle and mumbling to himself.

The beast, not wanting to be seen, looked up and down both ends of the alley. There were no other signs of life. It could easily take the man without him even knowing how he died, but it wanted revenge. It wanted someone to pay for the two it had let slip away.

The beast crossed the alley and ambled slowly in the shadows of the warehouse until it was directly in front of the man. It stared at the aging wino until he finally looked back. The man's mouth was open and his head was swaying from side to side.

When the beast could control its urge no longer, it padded right up to him until its huge body stood between the man's legs and growled. It looked deep into the man's eyes until it sensed he had finally realized what was about to happen.

And then it did.

Before the shock of realization could stop the man's heart, the beast ripped the flesh and muscles from his neck. The open jugular vein spewed a thick stream of blood against the wall before his chin dropped against his chest and stopped the flow.

Jesse's lab was as cold as Andy remembered it. Too cold to suit him. He preferred open windows and the cool gulf breeze to manufactured air, especially when the room temperature was cold enough to burn his eyes.

"Hurry up, will you, Jesse?" Andy said. "I'm freezing my nuts off in here."

"I've almost got it," Jesse said. "Yeah. Now, come here and take a look at this."

Andy closed one eye and looked into the microscope with the other. He had looked at blood through a similar microscope in high school Biology, but that was too many years ago for him to remember what it was supposed to look like. He lifted his head and shrugged his shoulders. "OK, I'll take your word for it but I still say you should take it to the police to match."

"I am the police," Jesse reminded him. "Sort of anyway, and that's good enough for me."

"That's stretching it a little bit, don't you think?"

"Not when the real police can't do anything."

"What makes you think they can't? You haven't given them the opportunity."

"Fine. You do it then," Jesse said. "Tomorrow you just march yourself into the police station and tell them there's a werewolf running around out there killing people. Hell, I'll even back you up. That way they can laugh us both out of town together."

"I'm talking about giving them the blood to match to the crewman, not divulging your darkest secret."

"We can't just yet."

"Why? I don't understand. We need to do something no matter what the outcome," Andy said.

"We will."

"Well, what?"

"I don't know," Jesse said. "I haven't figured that part out yet, but when I do, you'll be the first to know."

"I don't doubt that for a minute. Now can we please leave?"

His clothes were just as he had left them behind the dumpster. He changed into them quickly. The cycle was now over, but the next one would come as surely as all the others had come; only the next one would be different. The hunt would be different the next time and more challenging.

He already knew his prey.

54

An uneventful week had passed since the last cycle had ended. None of the bodies had turned up and the last one hadn't even been missed. It was as if he had never existed.

The case of the missing Argentinean crewman had been closed for lack of evidence, but Jesse's file on him was still open. It would stay that way until Jesse found the killer.

The authorities had also given up the search for the Covington boy. Their report showed he was assumed drowned. The Methodist minister had said the same thing at his memorial service, so it was now gospel.

Andy was at his usual lunch spot on the pavilion deck deciding whether to have a go at the other half of the cold submarine sandwich or feed it to the trash barrel when Michele walked up behind him. She wasn't alone.

"Hi, boss," she said when she sat down next to him.

"What are you doing here?"

"My day off, remember?"

"My point exactly," Andy said.

"We thought you might enjoy some company."

Andy turned sideways on the bench until his peripheral vision picked up the image of a rather large-chested brunette. His eyes were riveted to the front of her white T-shirt. The words that surrounded the picture of an oyster with a smile on its face said, "Pluck Me, Shuck Me, Eat Me

Raw." Andy had seen the slogan before but the shirt on this girl seemed to give it a 3-D effect.

"Down, boy," Michele said when she noticed she was no longer the center of his attention. "This is Jules."

"Sure is," Andy said back.

Julie walked around the picnic table and sat across from him. His eyes followed her around, much like the eyes in a painting when done correctly.

"Want to go out tonight?" Michele asked.

"I thought we already were."

"I mean out-out. You know, like to a club?"

"Oh," Andy said. "**Out.**"

"Now you've got it," Julie joined in. "We're gonna double."

Andy tried to recall the last time he had gone on a double date, and then gave up trying to remember. "OK by me."

"There's just one catch," Michele said. "Jules here won't tell me who she has a date with."

"It's a surprise," Julie told them both, but directed her answer toward Andy.

"I like surprises," Andy said with a smile and tried to make eye contact with her.

"You never told me that," Michele said.

"You're always a surprise," he said to Michele but kept his eyes glued to the front of Julie's shirt.

"I'm over here, Andrew." Michele waved a hand in front of his face. "I told you not to wear that shirt in public," she said to Julie.

"I guess you're right," Julie said. "I better take it off." She reached for the bottom of the shirt and gave it a tug upward, just high enough to lay her stomach bare. Andy's eyes widened, if that were possible.

"Then I hope you know CPR," Michele said.

"I don't."

"I'll take my chances," Andy said.

"I better not," Julie told him and lowered her shirt. "I don't think Michele could find another date on such short notice."

When the smoke of anticipation cleared from Andy's side of the table he asked the first question that came to his mind. "Who's driving?"

"You are," Michele said. "I doubt Jules' date is old enough to have a license."

Julie stuck her tongue out at Michele and got the same in return.

"You ladies better stick those things back in your mouth unless you're planning on using them," Andy said.

"Oh," Julie said. "Handsome and quick on the draw too. How'd you manage to latch onto him, Mick?"

"He just followed me home one night."

"Speaking of following you home," Andy said. "Does this mean I finally get to pick you up?"

"Not unless you want to spoil everything," she informed him.

"What do you mean?"

"You know what I mean."

"Yeah, but I don't," Julie said.

"You don't need to know," Michele told her.

"You never let me have any fun," Julie said with a pout on her face.

"Don't feel bad," Andy told her. "She doesn't let me either."

"Well, why don't I just let you two go out?" Michele said.

"You mean by ourselves?" Julie said.

"Sure. You two seem to have a lot in common."

"That'd never work," Julie told her.

"Why not?"

"Yeah, why not?" Andy followed.

"I need you there, Mick."

"Why?"

"It's like I've always said. Two's company but three's an audience and you know how I hate to perform to an empty house."

"I think we better leave before Andy gets the wrong idea about you," Michele said.

"Spoil sport," Julie said back.

Andy looked down at his watch. "Oh, shit. I should have been back out there ten minutes ago."

"I'm telling," Michele said.

"Better not," Andy warned her. "They may order me to work overtime to make up for it."

They all three got up in unison. Michele patted Andy on the arm. "I'll be over about seven-thirty."

"You sure I can't pick you up?" Andy asked jestfully.

"You can pick **me** up," Julie told him.

"What about your date?" Michele said.

"What date?" Julie answered then paused. "Oh, him. Well, I'll take a rain check then."

"You better hope it never rains," Michele said.

"I'm just kidding."

"I wasn't referring to you, Jules."

Andy let the two girls walk in front of him as they made their way to the front steps of the pavilion. He couldn't help but notice what the back on Julie's T-shirt said. He laughed at the sight of two oysters in a sixty-nine position above the words, "Oyster eaters make better lovers."

"You gonna wear that shirt tonight?" Andy asked her.

"I will if you want me to."

"You do and you're dead meat," Michele warned.

Julie looked back at Andy and shrugged her shoulders. "Guess I'm not."

55

Michele was right on time. Andy was sitting at the bar and almost fell off his stool when she opened the door. "Where'd you get that outfit?" Andy asked, referring to her brown leather mini-skirt and matching sleeveless, silk blouse.

"You like?" she said and twirled around to give him a look from all angles.

"Let's put it this way, if looks could kill you'd be sitting on death row."

"I'll take that as a yes."

"Good," Andy said, "but you better watch how you sit."

"I got that covered," she said and hiked up the extremely short skirt to reveal a pair of chocolate-colored panties. "See?"

"When are they supposed to get here?"

"Why, you got something in mind?"

"I'd have to be dead if I didn't."

"You like this even better than Julie's shirt?"

"What shirt?"

"That's better," she said. "Now get me a beer. They'll be here in about fifteen minutes."

"That's plenty of time," Andy said, hopefully.

"For you, maybe." Michele walked on by him and into the kitchen. She opened the refrigerator door and got her own beer.

"You still won't let me have any fun," Andy whined.

"Poor baby. You're so mistreated." Michele walked around the bar and sat on the stool next to him.

"You wouldn't happen to have on a brown bra too, would you?"

Michele unbuttoned the top two buttons of the blouse and looked down. "Hunh, uh."

"What color?"

She pulled the blouse apart to reveal her bare breasts and said, "Flesh."

Andy was about to make a sudden, yet expected, move when the door chime spoiled his advance.

"Too bad they're early." Michele made quick work of her blouse and jumped off the stool and ran to the door. She was ready for Julie's surprise to end. When she threw open the door her body turned cold and not from her lack of clothes in the evening air.

"Surprise," Julie said when she took Eric by the hand and led him inside. "I think you two know each other."

Michele stood frozen against the door like an oversized doorstop. Eric winked as he walked past her and into the condo. Andy had come off his stool at a slower pace and stood in front of it.

"Andy," Julie said, "this is Eric."

The two men shook hands. Andy had not yet made the connection. Michele had not yet moved.

Julie turned to Michele and said, "Close the door, Mick. You're letting all the flies out."

"Drink?" Andy asked when Michele finally shut the door.

"Vodka tonic, if you've got it," Eric said.

"I believe that can be arranged," Andy said. "Julie?"

"I'll have whatever Mick's having." It wasn't a chance order as she knew they both shared the same acquired taste in beer.

"Have a seat then," Andy told them. "The bar's open."

While Andy went to the refrigerator Michele walked through the living room and stood behind the bar. She set her eyes on Eric. He looked back and smiled. Andy came back with a beer and a glass of ice. He handed the beer to Julie and reached under the bar for Eric's fixings and mixed his drink. Since no one had said another word Andy decided to take the initiative. "So, Eric, what do you do?"

"He surfs," Michele said for him. She never took her eyes off him. She hoped Andy could count high enough to be able to put two and two together. If he could, he didn't.

"For a living?" Andy followed.

"I'm in the import-export business," Eric said.

"Here in town?"

"Yes. I have an office in the Port Galveston Savings and Loan building."

"Oh, the mayor's building."

"Yes, that's right."

"I guess you get to see him on a daily basis then?"

"Well, not quite," Eric said, "but often enough."

"I'm sorry," Andy said.

"I beg your pardon?"

"Nothing. Just thinking out loud."

Michele's eyes never left Eric during the entire conversation between the two men. Andy hadn't noticed. Julie had.

"What's wrong, Mick?"

Michele moved her stare to the left. "The bedroom," she said to Julie. "Now!"

"It's a little early to get kinky, don't you think?" Julie said. Michele's rabid look told her that her friend was in no mood for her usual antics, but she just couldn't resist the temptation. "Can I take my beer?"

Michele didn't answer. She stormed off for the bedroom instead.

Julie shrugged her shoulders and followed. Michele shut the door behind them.

"Just what the fuck do you think you're doing?" Michele asked in a loud whisper.

"I don't understand."

"You know damn well what I'm talking about," Michele said. "I told you about him."

"So?" Julie said. "I'm going out with him, you aren't."

"Why?"

"Why not?"

"He's an asshole, that's why not."

"That's what you say," Julie told her. "I'd like to find out for myself."

"I thought you had more sense than that."

"Hey, I'm just out for a good time and in case you haven't noticed, I'm not exactly the pick of the litter."

"That's no excuse," Michele said in a much louder voice.

"Don't talk so loud," Julie said. "He might hear you."

"Fuck him!"

"I might if you'll give me the chance."

The room filled with a tense fog of animosity when both girls became uncommonly quiet. Julie remembered her beer and took a drink. Her hand trembled but not from fear.

When Michele finally spoke, her words came out in the form of a warning. "If that's what you want, then you deserve what you'll get and you can bet your sweet ass you'll get it."

"Look," Julie said, "if I'd have known you were going to react like this I never would have brought him here. I just didn't think . . ."

"That's your main problem, Jules, you don't think."

"OK. I'm sorry. I'll go get Eric and we'll just go out by ourselves."

"No, that'll make it worse."

"Then what're you going to do?"

"I'll just have to handle it," Michele said. "That's all."

"Are we still friends?"

"We're going to have to be. You're going to need a friend when he gets through with you."

"Thanks," Julie said. "I knew you wouldn't let me down."

"I feel like I already have," Michele told her, and then opened the door.

Andy and Eric were still at the bar. They acted like nothing had ever happened when the girls rejoined them.

"Let's eat," Julie said.

"Fine by me," Andy said. "Where to?"

"How about The Pelican?" Julie offered.

"No," Michele said. "Gaido's."

"We don't have a reservation," Julie told her.

"We don't need one," Michele said and looked at Julie's date. "We'll let Eric handle it."

"Let's go then," Julie said. She took Eric by the hand again and headed for the door.

Andy took the glasses from the bar to the sink. When he returned Julie and Eric were already out the door. "What was all that about?"

"That's him," she said.

"Him?"

"Eric."

Andy just looked at her with dumb eyes and waited.

"Eric," she said again. "The surfer. The one from the ferry."

"Oh," Andy said.

"Oh? Is that all you can say?"

"You never told me his name," Andy said.

"Oh."

56

Andy knew the front lot of Gaido's would be full but he drove the Bronco through it just the same, and then headed across the side street to their alternate lot. They walked to the restaurant in the same silence they had grown accustomed to on the ride over.

The waiting area was full and there were people standing outside the door.

"Y'all sure you want to eat here?" Andy said.

"Yep," Michele said. "You owe me, remember?" She looked at Eric and said, "It'll take more than a twenty this time."

Eric smiled, told Julie to wait there and walked nonchalantly inside.

"What's he going to do?" Julie asked when the door closed behind him.

"Earn his keep," Michele said.

In two short minutes Eric opened the door and motioned them inside. They followed him in and to one of the hostess' stands just outside the main dining room. From there an elegantly dressed, young woman who could have given Julie a run for her money in the chest department led them to a table in the center of the room.

Once they were seated Michele followed with another shot across Eric's bow. "Didn't have enough for a window table, huh?"

"What makes you think I had to pay for this one?" he asked.

"History has a way of repeating itself," she said.

"Then you flunked the course."

"I don't think so. I've seen you in action."

"Not this time," he said. "A few words in the right ear was all that was necessary."

Michele didn't believe him but she had been on the convincing end of a few of his words before and knew she couldn't totally discount his explanation. "If you say so," she told him and dropped the subject.

When their waiter, a young man of Mexican descent, came to their table they ordered the same drinks they had begun with at Andy's condo. Eric, to Michele's dismay, ordered a dozen raw oysters for himself and the same for Julie.

"Oooo," Julie said to their table. "You know what they say about raw oysters?"

"Yes, Jules, we know," Michele said. "We all read your shirt today."

"Eric didn't," Julie said.

"He didn't have to," Michele told her.

Their drinks arrived followed closely by two plates of shells filled with soft, gray meat. Michele was too far from any window so she struck up a conversation with Andy. "I'm going to have the lobster tail."

Eric saw what she was attempting to do and joined their conversation. He lifted his plate toward Andy, but more in Michele's direction. "Have one."

"He doesn't want one," Michele said.

"How do you know?"

"Because I said he doesn't."

"What if I do?" Andy told her.

"Do you?"

"I might."

"You might like to go home alone too," Michele warned.

"Is that a threat?"

"Did it sound like one?"

"Sort of."

"Then I guess it was," she said. "Sort of."

Andy looked at the plate that Eric still held out toward him. He favored oysters fried or not at all but he also favored making his own decisions. This time he had to choose between something he liked and something he didn't with a little ego mixed in to spice up the flavor. "I guess I'll pass."

Michele took his hand and placed it gently on her bare thigh just below the hemline as a reward for his decision. "Thank you," she said as if her gesture hadn't been enough.

"Suit yourself," Eric said and lowered the plate.

When their waiter returned, Michele and Julie ordered lobster tails and Andy chose the Fisherman's Platter. Michele waited for Eric to order some other oyster delight but he fooled her and told the waiter he'd have the Rock Lobster.

"I guess you expect me to thank you for that?" Michele said.

"Not really, but you can if you'd like."

Their food came slower than a frigid woman. By the time it arrived they had sloshed their way through two more rounds of drinks. Julie was feeling no pain and excused herself for a trip to the ladies room.

"You coming?" she said to Michele.

"Not yet," Michele said. "I'm not even breathing hard."

Julie started laughing then made a mad dash for the facility. Michele followed and found Julie already seated in one of the stalls when she entered.

"You OK?" Michele asked through the stall door.

"No thanks to you," she answered. "You almost made me wet my pants."

"It would serve you right," Michele said when she took the next stall.

"Why?"

"Because you hate oysters and you know I don't even like to look at them."

"I know."

"Then why'd you order them?"

"I didn't. He did," Julie said.

"You could have told him no."

"You know the N-word's not in my vocabulary, Mick."

"You could have made an exception for me."

"I can't do that," Julie said. "If I started now it might become habit-forming."

When they returned to the table their dates stood up.

"Look at this, Mick. Good-looking and gentlemen to boot."

"Not really," Andy said when he didn't sit back down. "Now it's our turn."

"I didn't know men went to the bathroom together," Julie said.

"We do if we need to pee," Andy told her.

The two men made their way through the dining room at a slower pace than their dates had and once inside Andy brought up the subject of Eric and Michele's date.

"I understand you and Michele went out once," he said as they stood side by side at the urinals.

"That what she told you?"

"The whole story."

"I hope this doesn't mean we have to go out in the parking lot later," Eric said with a half-smile.

"Not necessarily."

"Good, because I sort of like you."

"That's a hell of a thing for one man to say to another, considering where we are and all."

"I won't tell if you won't."

"Then, uh, I guess you won't be bothering her anymore?" Andy had tried to choose his words carefully but his choice hadn't come out as well as he would have liked.

"No," Eric said. "I make it a point not to bother, as you put it, another man's property."

Andy didn't consider Michele his property, but he accepted Eric's answer just the same. They both managed to zip up without causing any bodily harm and returned to the table. Andy winked at Michele when he sat down.

"Well, what did you boys find to talk about in there?" Julie asked.

"Nothing of any major importance," Eric said. "We just solved the trouble in the Middle East."

"Oh? Is that anywhere near Tyler?"

Michele choked on a piece of lobster she had been about to swallow and went into a coughing fit. Andy reached over and began to slap her, rather roughly, across the middle of her back.

"You don't have to beat me to death," Michele said when she caught her breath. "I think I'd rather choke."

"Sorry," he said. "Habit."

"Remind me never to drown when you're on duty," Julie said.

When the bill came Andy reached for his wallet.

"No," Eric said. "I started this."

"So," Michele said. "Then you admit you did pay the hostess to seat us?"

"If it'll make you feel better."

"It will."

"Where to now?" Julie chimed in before Eric actually admitted that he had slipped the waitress more than he paid Amy for a day's work.

"How about Kokomo's?" Andy said.

Michele winced and Eric saw her. It wouldn't exactly be like returning to the scene of a crime, but it was the place they had first met. "It'll be crowded by now," she said.

"So?" Andy said. "We'll be dancing most of the time anyway."

Since he **had** let her win the oyster battle she decided to let him have his way. "OK. I need to dance off this dinner anyway."

"Yeah," Andy said. "We don't need any fat lifeguards."

Once outside, Andy slowed his pace until Eric and Julie were out of hearing range. "You don't have to worry about him anymore," he told Michele.

"How do you know?"

"We had us a little talk in the john."

"Are you sure?"

"Uh, huh."

His answer relieved her enough to make light of the situation. "I guess you won't be calling Washington tomorrow then?"

Andy gave her a confused glance.

"The Middle East Crisis?"

"Oh. No, we'll have to save that for another time."

57

Kokomo's was body-to-body bodies and the music was loud enough to wake the dead as far away as Corpus Christi. No IDs in their group were checked. They found a chair-less table near the dance floor and claimed it with the girls' purses and waited until a waitress showed up and ordered their usual round. Eric and Julie hit the dance floor while Andy and Michele stayed at their post until the drinks arrived. When they did, Andy paid for them and Michele moved the purses to the floor under the table before they joined the other half of their double date on the floor.

To Andy's way of thinking, they had timed their arrival just right. The band had just started the first of their two fifties sets with a Buddy Holly tune. He mouthed the words about a girl named Peggy Sue and broke out into an immediate dance sweat.

Michele half-danced and half-looked around in a vain attempt to locate Julie. The dark dance floor offered her no help.

Two songs later the band slowed the pace with the only Procol Harum song people recognize but don't have a clue who sang it. When Andy pulled Michele close she jerked back as if he had suddenly turned to cactus.

"You're sweaty," she said and took a swipe at her arms to brush off the wet.

"Well, what did you expect?"

"Let's just sit this one out. I want to find Julie anyway."

"She's a big girl," Andy said. "She can take care of herself."

"How do you know? You just met her today."

"I'm a good judge of character."

"Not where Julie is concerned," she said. "She doesn't have any. She is one."

They walked back over to the table. The drinks sat untouched in shallow, sweat pools of their own. Andy saved his from a slow and agonizing death by drowning then killed it by a different and more humane method. It was gone in two quick gulps. He looked around for a waitress; found one and pointed at his glass. She nodded and the job was done.

"Let's go out on the deck," Michele told Andy when the slow song ended and Julie and Eric still hadn't shown up.

"I just ordered another drink."

"Then meet me out there." She took her beer bottle off the table and walked around the dance floor to the opening at the back of the room.

The deck was as crowded as the inside had been only with a lot less movement. Michele pressed her way through the bodies until she reached the back railing and looked down into the water as if she half-expected to find Julie floating face-down. When she didn't, she looked down the railing in both directions and caught sight of what she thought could be the back of Julie's dark brown hair at the far end. She squinted her eyes for a clearer look but still couldn't be sure. There were at least a dozen or more people crowded along the rail between them, which made a direct approach impossible. She started back into the crowd when a hand caught her on the shoulder and scared her motionless.

"Find 'em?" Andy said.

"Maybe," she said and breathed out slowly. "Come on."

Michele led interference for Andy until they were two couples from the corner where Julie and Eric were heavily involved in a tongue-wrestling match.

"Damn," Michele whispered.

"Looks like you found 'em," Andy joked.

Michele took another step in their direction only to have Andy stop her in her tracks.

"Where you going?"

"Over there."

"Why?"

"Why do you think?" she told him.

"I don't know," he said. "You tell me."

"Well, look at 'em."

"So?"

"So, he's gone too far," Michele said.

"It doesn't exactly look like she's trying to stop him," Andy said. "So, why should you?"

"She doesn't know him like I do."

"Bullshit! You know what I think? I think you're jealous."

"Get real."

"No, you get real," Andy said. "What if that were you over there, would you want her butting in?"

"You're damn right I would."

"Fine, then," Andy said. "Just go on over there and see what it gets you, but I don't want any part of it."

"I didn't ask for your help," Michele told him.

"Julie didn't ask for yours either." Andy gave her a slight nod. "I'm going back inside and you'd be wise to do the same."

Andy turned and left. He also left Michele to ponder his last warning. She stood and watched until Eric caught her eye and winked.

"Bastard!" she said just over a whisper, then turned and left them. She found Andy at the table. "Come on," she said and grabbed him by the hand. "Let's dance."

"Why the change of heart?"

"Like you said, she's big enough to take care of herself."

Andy and Michele finished the set on the dance floor. She even let him hold her, sweat and all, for a slow song; but only because it was an Elvis cover. She didn't even mind Andy's off-key version in her ear, although she wondered if he was singing it to her or just singing it for his own pleasure. Either way, she held on tight to her fantasy.

Eric and Julie were standing by the table when they walked off the floor for a break.

"Have fun?" Michele said to Julie.

"Yeah," Julie said. "Good band."

"Michele gave her friend a how-the-hell-would-you-know look but it was a wasted effort. She had her arm around Eric like she expected him to break loose and run at any minute.

The waitress came and set four fresh drinks on the table.

"I hope you don't mind," Eric said. "I took the liberty of ordering them."

"I don't mind," Andy said. "But I'm paying. You got dinner."

"Whatever you think is fair," Eric said. It was a good thing since he would have had to break Julie's hold just to be able to reach his wallet.

Michele tried again to catch her friend napping. "Hot out there, huh?"

"Where?"

"The dance floor."

"Oh, yeah," Julie said. "It was. That's why we went outside for a while."

Eric knew what Michele was doing and smiled at Julie's answer.

"Oh," Michele said. "No wonder you look so refreshed."

Andy knew what Michele was doing also, but he had had enough argument for one night. He decided to let her get whatever it was out of her system.

"You should have come," Julie said. "It was crowded, but the fresh air felt good."

"See anybody you know?" Michele asked.

"I did," Eric said and brought an abrupt end to Michele's grilling.

When the band started up their final set, Eric and Julie strolled out onto the floor.

"Happy now?" Andy asked Michele.

"Do I look happy?"

"No, you look like someone just ran over your dog."

"I don't have a dog," she said. "Would a girlfriend do?"

"Come on, let's dance," Andy said when he took her by the arm. "You need to work off some of that hostility."

"If I have to," she said. "But try not to sweat so much this time. You'll have to take a shower when we get home."

"Sounds good to me," Andy said.

"I thought it would."

58

"Y'all want to come in for a final-final?" Andy asked when he parked the Bronco in the carport of his beachfront condo.

"Maybe another time," Julie said. "We need to be going."

Michele wanted to tell her that hell would freeze over first, but didn't. She toned her response down instead and said, "Maybe so, and you're right. I forgot how your father waits up until you get home." The last part had been directed to Eric, but for Julie's benefit, or so she thought.

"He does not," she said. "And besides, Mom and Dad went to Gram's for a couple of days."

It would have been asinine for Michele to have believed that bit of information was meant for her ears only. "Then why don't you just spend the night at my house? The folks haven't seen you in a while."

Andy didn't want to believe what he had just heard any more than he wanted to believe Michele would actually follow through with the invitation, but he did. He waited for Julie's answer.

"That's OK," Julie said. "I've got Eric to protect me from the boogie man."

"That's what I'm afraid of," Michele said into the dark night when she opened the door and got out.

"I'll call you tomorrow," Julie said when Eric opened the door to the BMW.

"You better," Michele said to her. To Andy she said, "I hope she knows what she's doing."

"She's a big girl, remember?"

"Yeah, but even big girls make mistakes."

"That's how they learn to **be** big girls," Andy said and unlocked the door to the condo.

"Some people never learn," Michele answered and walked inside.

"You ready for that shower now?" Andy asked when he flicked on the lights.

"I don't feel much like one right now."

"Feel like a drink?"

"No."

"Feel like sex?"

"No."

"What **do** you feel like?"

"Shit."

"Then you won't mind if I stand upwind," Andy said in an effort to change her mood.

"Can't you just be serious for once in your life?"

"I can't. You've got a monopoly on it."

"I can't help it."

"Hey, at least he's not bothering **you** anymore."

"That's not much of a consolation," Michele said.

"Well, it's all I've got to offer," Andy said.

Michele looked at him and realized she had been taking her anxiety out on the wrong person. "No," she said. "You've got something else to offer."

"I do?"

"Uh, huh," she said and unbuttoned the top of her skirt and let it fall to the floor. She followed with her blouse and stood in front of him with her nipples erect.

"Yeah," Andy said. "I guess I do." He hurried out of his clothes and kicked them into Michele's pile.

"First things first, though," Michele told him when she slipped the chocolate brown panties down across her hips and stepped out of them.

"What's that?"

"You need a shower, remember?" She ran to the bathroom while Andy stumbled out of his underwear.

Michele had the water on cold when he stepped in. "Jeez, Michele, can't we warm this up a bit?"

"No," she said and grabbed his erection. "You're hot enough already."

They made a hurried kind of sex that had nothing to do with love, but had a lot to do with the temperature of the water that rained against Andy's back like thawing icicles in a winter wind.

They fell on the bed cold, wet and out of breath when they were done and laid there a while and listened to their own heartbeats. After a few minutes had passed Michele asked, "Feel better now?"

Michele turned her head toward him for his answer and saw that Andy was fast asleep. "I guess you do," she whispered.

She leaned over and kissed him lightly on the cheek then got up and went into the living room and dressed. She picked up Andy's clothes and took them back into the bedroom and laid them on the rocker. She turned off all the lights and left.

Michele drove to Seawall Boulevard and took a right when a left would have taken her home. She drove by Stewart Beach and on past the burned out condotel until she reached the entrance to Julie's condominium complex. She turned in and drove slowly down the private street until she saw what she hoped she wouldn't. Eric's silver BMW was parked in the drive.

She leaned her head out the window and saw all the lights at Julie's were out. "I hope you know what you're doing, Jules," she said just loud enough for the mosquitoes to hear.

She considered letting the air out of Eric's tires as some sort of weak gesture of retribution, but reconsidered when she realized that would do nothing but prolong the visit. She wished she had been born a male, and then she could walk over and piss on one of his tires. He'd probably never notice but she would know. However, had she been born a male she wouldn't be in the position she found herself.

When Michele finally drove away she couldn't shake the feeling that she had let Julie down.

59

It was an unusually cool, mid-summer day for Galveston Island. It was noon and the temperature was still only hovering around the ninety-degree mark, due mainly to a southerly breeze blowing in off the gulf. Michele leaned against her favorite rock at Pirates Beach. Against her own better judgment, she hadn't called Julie before she came to work at seven. Julie worked at the Beachfront Shirt Shop which didn't open till nine, which meant she didn't roll out of bed until sometime just shy of that.

Michele got on the talkie and told Yann she was breaking for lunch.

"You leaving the beach?" Yann asked.

"Yeah, I need to make a call."

"You gonna be anywhere near the golden arches?"

"I **can** be."

"Bring me back one of them two-story jobs and have 'em run it through the garden, will ya?"

"No problem," Michele told him. "You want some fries or a drink or something?"

"No, ma'am, just the burger."

Michele was about to put the talkie back into the bag when Yann radioed back. "Michele?"

"Change your mind?" she asked.

"No, but have them cut the onions. I got a date later."

"Ten-four," Michele said and grinned to herself as she slipped the talkie into the bag.

The closest McDonald's was at Seawall Boulevard and Sixty-Ninth Street. If they had a pay phone she could wound two birds at once. She threw her bag through the window, climbed into the Malibu and headed east. She pulled into the eatery lot about ten minutes later, no thanks to a stalled car at the One Hundred and Seventh Street intersection.

The lines at the counter were lunch-long so she decided to make her call first. She found a pay phone just inside the door but the metal cord that was usually connected to the phone book was dangling frayed below the phone like the broken fishing line of the big one that got away.

"Shit," she said.

A small boy in the first booth giggled while his mother gave Michele a look that only a mother could give.

"Sorry." Michele opened the snapped pocket of her clutch purse and luckily found two quarters. She put one in the coin slot and dialed the information operator for the number of the Beachfront Shirt Shop. She didn't have a pen in her small purse so she had to remember the number.

"7-4-4-3-6-7-9 . . . 7-4-4-3-6-7-9," she repeated as she put the second quarter into the slot. "7-4-4-3-6-7-9," she said again as she hit the buttons.

"Beachfront Shirt Shop," a girl answered on the fifth ring.

"Julie, please?" Michele said and waited and
assumed the girl was calling Julie to the phone.
Even though the girl had covered the phone with
her hand Michele could still hear her talking in
the background.

"Julie's not here," the girl said when she came
back on the line.

"Did she take an early lunch?" Michele knew
Julie didn't usually go to lunch until one since
she didn't come in until nine.

"No," the girl said. "She called in sick."

Michele's body went cold and numb but she still
managed her next question. "Did she say what was
wrong?"

"I don't know. I didn't talk to her."

"Thank you," Michele said and hung up. She
opened the purse pocket again and fingered through
the change. A dime and three pennies were all she
counted.

"Shit," she said again.

This time the little boy laughed out loud. His
mother wadded up the remains of lunch, took her
son by the arm, lifted him out of the booth and
left. Michele leaned her face against the phone
to hide her embarrassment and could feel the
mother's heated stare as she walked around her and
out the door.

Michele decided against pan-handling for
another quarter. Instead, she took her place in
line in front of one of the three busy registers.
She could have driven to Julie's condo by the time
she finally reached the counter where she ordered
Yann's burger, gave the girl a five and received

her change that included two more quarters. Michele thanked her and went back to the phone. She laid the burger sack on the back of the recently vacated booth, put a quarter in the slot and dialed Julie's number.

After twenty or so rings she hung up and waited for the quarter to drop back down. It didn't. "Shit," she said a third time but the booth was thankfully still empty.

She put the other quarter in the slot and dialed Julie's number again. She let it ring until it echoed out her other ear before she hung up. She got her quarter back this time.

Michele shoved the door open, got in her car and headed back to Pirates Beach. She had less than a half hour left. Not enough time to drive to Julie's. When she got within sight of Pirates Beach she slammed her fist on the steering wheel and her foot on the brake and pulled onto the sandy shoulder. When traffic cleared she made a U-turn and headed back to McDonald's where, with any luck, Yann's burger would still be.

When she pulled into the lot she put the Malibu in park with the motor running and ran in. The sack was gone.

"It just ain't your day," she told herself and took her place in line again. While she waited she noticed two small girls standing at the far end of the counter and looking at a display of toys that would be included in their meals. Next to the display was a sack. She took the chance of losing her place in line and walked over to them.

"Is this yours?" Michele asked and pointed to the sack.

"No, ma'am," one of the girls answered.

Michele was about to open the sack when a girl from behind the counter walked up. "Did you leave that?"

"I hope so," Michele told her.

"We found it over there by the phone," the girl said and pointed in that direction.

"That's me then. Thanks." She took the bag and walked toward the door. She stopped by the phone and looked at her watch. It was one o'clock. Since she was already going to be late she tried Julie's number one last time, only this time she held onto the sack as she dialed. There was still no answer but at least the machine was kind enough to return her quarter a second time.

Yann stood on the sidewalk when Michele drove up. He leaned in the passenger window and said, "Must have been an interesting conversation."

"It wasn't," she said. "Here." She handed him the sack.

"Thanks. How much do I owe you?"

"Nothing. Just don't tell anyone I was late."

"Deal," Yann said.

She drove on down the curb to her end of the beach and parked. She got out quickly and returned to her station by the rock. Before she could open the bag she heard Yann's voice calling to her from inside. She reached in and took out the talkie. "Yes?"

"The deal's off," Yann said.

"Why?"

"There's onions on the burger."

"So, sue me," Michele said and threw the talkie
back into the bag.

60

Sometime between noon and three the breeze played out and the mercury climbed into the second century. Michele had taken her department issue captain's chair with an umbrella attached from the trunk of her car and was in the process of setting it up when a silver BMW with a surfboard on top parked along the boulevard. She recognized it immediately.

Eric got out and unlatched the board. Michele stopped working on the chair and waited. Eric saw her and waved.

"Don't wave at me, you son of a bitch," she whispered and didn't wave back.

Eric hoisted the board over his head and walked down the broken concrete steps toward her. "Have you saved anybody today?" he asked when he stood his board up in the sand.

"What did you do to Julie?" she asked instead of answering.

"What are you talking about?"

"She didn't show up for work and she doesn't answer her phone. That's what I'm talking about."

"Oh," Eric said. "When did you call her?"

"Lunchtime."

"That explains it, then. She wasn't home yet."

"Don't give me that shit. I know she was home."

"Oh, really?"

"Yeah, I . . ." Michele stopped before she gave away the fact that she had driven by Julie's condo after she left Andy's.

Eric waited.

"You . . . you said you were taking her home," Michele stammered.

"And I did," Eric said. "Not that it's any of your business."

"Then why wasn't she there when I called, and why did she call in sick, and why did you say she wasn't home yet?"

"We went out for breakfast," Eric told her. He paused and smiled before he handed her the next line. "Then we went to my place for dessert."

"You bastard," she screamed and took a swing at his face with an open hand. He caught her wrist before it reached its mark.

"Let go of me."

"Not if you're going to try that again."

Michele tried to jerk free, but Eric held on tight. "Let go, damn you!"

Eric loosened his grip and backed away. From over his shoulder, Michele could see Yann running down the beach and regretted her fit of violence.

"You got a problem with this guy, Michele?" Yann asked bravely when he stepped in between them.

"It's OK, Yann. He was just leaving."

"Yann looked at Eric and waited. Eric looked at Michele and said, "You're making a big mistake."

"No, you will be if you don't do as she says,"
Yann told him.

"This isn't any of your concern," Eric told
him.

"Anything that goes on at this beach is my
concern. So, either leave or else."

Eric looked at the muscularly lean and young
lifeguard. "Do you plan on throwing me off?"

"If that's what it takes," Yann said. "But I'd
rather not have to do that."

"Please, Yann. It's OK," Michele said.

"It didn't look OK a minute ago."

"That was my fault," she said.

Her comment wasn't an apology but it opened up
the way for Eric to retreat with dignity. He
walked over and shucked his board from the sand.
"This isn't over yet," he said.

"It is for now, buddy," Yann told him as he
walked away. He noticed Michele was rubbing her
wrist. "You OK?"

"I'll be fine."

"What was all that about?"

"It's personal."

"You mean you know him?" Yann asked.

"Yeah, I'm afraid so."

"That doesn't say much for your choice of
friends.

"I didn't say he was my friend."

"You gonna be OK then?"

"Yeah, but do me a favor, OK?"

"Sure."

"Don't tell Andy about this."

"If you say so."

"Thanks," she said. "I owe you one."

61

When her watch ended, Michele left Pirates Beach and headed straight for Julie's condo. She made a pass through the parking area to make sure there was no silver BMW around before she parked. Julie opened the door before Michele had a chance to ring the bell. It wasn't a good sign. It meant Eric had either been there or had called. She prepared herself for the worst.

"Hi, Mick," Julie said with a spring-like tone in her voice. "You slumming?"

Her attitude caught Michele off guard. She had expected an immediate tongue-lashing at the very least. "How'd you know I was here?"

"I saw you from the window," Julie said. "Come on in."

Her answer gave Michele hope that Eric hadn't been in touch with her. Michele followed Julie into the kitchen.

"Beer?" Julie asked.

"You sure you should be drinking?"

Julie wrinkled her eyebrows. Why would you ask that?"

"Seems your employer thinks you're sick."

"Ah, been checking up on me, huh?"

"You might say that."

"Did you bring me some chicken soup?"

"Not hardly," Michele said.

"Some friend you are. I'll have to settle for a beer then."

"So, you aren't sick?"

"Are you going to leave if I say no?"

"Not without a beer first."

"Now you're talking." Julie took two cans from the refrigerator and handed one to Michele.

"So, how'd it go last night?"

"About a nine on the Richter Scale."

"That bad, huh?" Michele joked.

"Bad, no. A little rough, maybe."

"Rough?"

"Yeah," Julie explained. "He kept changing positions every time I got comfortable. It was hard to stay in rhythm. First I was on my back, then he'd roll me over, then he'd put one leg here and . . ."

"I'd rather you skip the details," Michele said. "I think I get the picture."

"I think I redefined the term multiple orgasms."

"Finally met your match, huh?"

When Julie tilted her head back to take a drink, Michele noticed a red spot on her neck. It was more of a scratch than a spot.

"What's that on your neck?"

"This?" Julie touched the mark with her finger. "You're not going to believe this, Mick, but I think he bit me."

"No," Michele said. "I believe you."

"He actually broke the skin."

"Maybe you should see a doctor."

"Why, it's just a scratch."

"I know, but you may need rabies shots."

"No, but I'll probably need a pound of make-up to cover it up before I go to work tomorrow."

"Is that why you stayed home today?" Michele kept pumping her for information.

"Sort of."

"When did he leave?"

"He didn't," Julie said. "We were doing it until the sun came up. I tell you, Mick, the man's an animal."

"I can see why you stayed home to sleep."

"I didn't really do that either," Julie said. "We went to the Kettle for breakfast and then over to his place for another round. I'm lucky I can walk."

So far, Julie had verified Eric's story, only more so. The fact that she had overreacted at the beach began to devour her conscience like a hungry shark.

"I guess you'll be seeing him again then?"

"Hell, I have to?"

"Why's that?"

"Compared to him," Julie said. "Anyone else would be chopped liver, and you know how I feel about liver."

"I thought I knew how you felt about oysters, too," Michele said. "And look what that got me."

"My you do hold a grudge well," Julie said.

"I know," Michele said with a loud ring of truth. "How well I know."

62

Andy was on the back patio with one eye on the setting sun and the other on two T-bone steaks he had just placed on the grill when Michele walked around the corner of the condo. "Did I leave the door locked?" he asked.

"No, I saw your smoke."

"I never have learned how to operate this thing," he said, referring to the gas grill. "It's not supposed to do that."

"I need to tell you something," she said with a nervous look.

"Well, pull up a chair and take a load off. It'll be a while before these babies are done."

"I think I better remain standing."

"What is it?" Andy asked when he finally noticed the serious look on her face.

"I think I finally let my stupid feelings overload my brain," she said. Michele went on to lay the whole day's events, from Julie's condo to Eric at the beach and back to Julie's condo, out in front of Andy. "So, here I am," she said and finally sat down in the lounge chair that Andy had offered to her before her story began. "And the way I see it, you can do one of two things. You can either say 'I told you so' or you can take that brick over there and knock some sense into me."

Andy got up and picked up one of the bricks left over from when he laid the patio and began to pitch it up in the air in front of her. "I've never been much on I-told-you-so," he said.

"Don't make it quick and painless," she said. "I don't deserve it."

Andy went into his wind-up but let the brick drop behind him before the follow-through. Michele flinched at the invisible pain. He picked the brick up and laid it back in the small stack.

"Did you tell Julie about what happened at the beach?"

"No."

"You should have."

"I know, but I just couldn't bring myself to do it."

"What if Eric tells her?"

"Then I'm dead meat," Michele said.

"You **do** have a phone, you know?"

"It's too late for that," Michele said when she looked at her watch. "He's already picked her up."

"Then I'd suggest you say your lay-le-downs and hope for the best," Andy told her.

"Maybe he won't say anything to her about it," Michele said and looked to Andy for some sign of reassurance. "Maybe he'll be a little sympathetic."

"Yeah," Andy said. "And maybe Hitler was a little anti-Semitic."

63

Michele had kidnapped Julie from a sound sleep when she called her at six forty-five to tell her to meet her at Two Pesos for lunch. When she had been met with no resistance she assumed Eric hadn't told her about their most recent encounter. Now all she had to do was get Yann to agree to swap lunch hours.

"I need another favor," Michele told Yann when she met him at Pirates Beach to begin their watch.

"You keep this up," Yann said, "and you'll end up owing me your firstborn.

"At the rate I'm going you may get to father it."

"Then your wish is my command."

"I need to switch lunches with you."

"Is that all?"

"Yeah. For now, anyway."

"Done."

Two Pesos Mexican Restaurant was on Sixty-First Street about midway between Pirates Beach and the Beachfront Shirt Shop. Michele got there first and took the liberty of ordering two iced teas while she munched on tortilla chips. When the teas, came so did Julie.

"I don't know if I can handle you three days in a row," Julie said when she pulled a chair out and sat down across from Michele.

"I guess you'll just have to suffer," Michele said. "And I'm buying if that'll help ease your pain."

"Can't hurt."

"So, how was your date last night?"

"Ah," Julie said when she dipped a tortilla chip into a small bowl of hot sauce. "The ulterior motive."

"Caught me."

"Well, he seemed a little preoccupied at first, but I got him to come around."

"What was wrong?"

"Hw wouldn't say."

Michele took a deep breath and let it out slowly. It was meant to settle her nerves but it failed miserably. She went ahead anyway. "I think I know."

"Really?"

"I sort of gave him a hard time yesterday," Michele began.

"How's that?"

"I sort of accused him of, I don't know, doing something bad to you, I guess. She stared into the basket of chips as she spoke.

"What do you mean, sort of?" Julie asked.

"Well, you know, he said something I didn't like and . . ."

"And you tried to hit him." Julie finished the sentence for her.

"He told you, didn't he?"

"Yep."

"Why didn't you say something?"

"I could ask you the same question."

"I know," Michele said. "I'm sorry."

"Don't be too sorry, Mick. It made for an interesting conversation. He told me I ought to pick a better class of friends to hang out with, and I told him it wasn't your fault you were born a blonde."

Michele was relieved to see that her friend was taking the situation in her usual give-a-shit manner, so she let her continue.

"He said that was no excuse for your actions and I told him he was lucky you hadn't landed the punch. He said he didn't think that was very funny and I told him I doubted you were laughing when you did it."

"I really shouldn't have done it, though," Michele said.

"That's what he said and I told him you only did it because you were a jealous dyke," Julie said.

"You didn't?"

"No, but I wish I would have thought of it back then. I just told him you were looking out for my best interest, because that's what friends were for."

The waiter showed up and forced a minor detour in their conversation. "You girls ready to order?"

"This girl will have the Super Deluxe Special," Julie said

Michele looked at the menu and cringed at the fourteen-dollar and ninety-five cent price tag that went along with that meal.

Julie caught her looking. "The price of friendship just went up."

64

Almost two weeks had passed since she had spilled her guts to Julie over Mexican food. Michele was due back in Austin in about the same amount of time. Neither she nor Andy had yet dared to bring the subject up. They both knew it; they just didn't want to discuss it. It was like if they didn't talk about it maybe it wouldn't happen.

Andy had checked the roster and found that Michele was scheduled for one of her infrequent days off today, and being the top man on the totem pole he rearranged the roster so that he too was free. They were enjoying their time together fishing off the rocky shore of Sea Wolf Park. Andy was doing most of the fishing while Michele was reading the latest Stephen King novel and trying to build up enough courage to bring up the subject of her returning to school.

The sun was August hot and there was little or no wind blowing in off the channel. Over the last several weeks, Michele had developed a taste for Andy's favorite beverage and between the two of them and the raging sun; they had managed to polish off almost three quarters of the gallon jug by high noon. She was about one vodka and orange juice away from the courage she needed.

"You hungry?" Andy asked as he reeled in an empty line.

"Not really," Michele said. She stuck a chewing gum wrapper between the pages of the book to mark her place and laid the book down. She decided that since Andy had started the conversation, she might as well continue it, although on a different subject, before she lost her nerve completely. "Andy, have you thought much about what's going to happen to us when I have to go back to school?" Her eyes winced behind her sunglasses when she heard her own words hanging out like wet pantyhose in the muggy air.

Andy knew he had, but wasn't sure how to go about answering her question. If he said yes, she would probably question him as to why he hadn't brought the subject up. If his answer was no, she would probably be hurt. He chose a compromise instead. "A little."

"Well, I've been thinking about it a lot lately," Michele said.

Andy chose to remain silent. He could tell by the way her sentence sort of trailed off without really ending that she had something more she wanted to add before it was his turn to talk.

"I'm not really sure I want to go back."

"That's crazy. You can't just turn down a free education, especially when you've already got half of it behind you."

"I know but I'll miss you." Michele was glad she was wearing sunglasses as the tears began to well up in her eyes.

"I'll miss you too but that's not the point."

"Now you sound like my daddy."

"You mean you told him you don't want to go back?"

"No, but you sound just like him if I had."

"He's a smart man, then."

"But what are we going to do?" Michele said.

"Austin's just a couple of hours away," Andy reminded her. "You can always come home on weekends."

"I have to practice on weekends."

"All of them?"

"Most of them," Michele said. "They usually let us off on the Saturdays when the football team plays at home, but then we still have to practice on Sunday."

"Well, I guess I can always come over there," he said.

"What about work? You told me you usually work every weekend when the summer's over."

"I can work that out. You just let me know in enough time when you'll be free and I'll handle it."

"Promise?"

"Yeah, I promise," Andy said. "Now quit crying."

"I'm not crying."

"Then what's that rolling down your cheek?"

Michele brushed the wet trail off with her hand and held it out in front of her as if she were examining it. "That's sweat."

"Oh, excuse me, then."

Andy looked away for a few seconds which was all the time she needed to run her hands up under her shades and wipe away any further evidence.

"What about other girls?" she asked with clearer eyes.

"What about 'em?"

"Are you going to see other girls while I'm gone?"

"I probably will."

She could feel the tears starting to form again. "Why?"

"Hey, I'm a lifeguard," Andy said. "I can't help but see other girls. They'll be running around all over the beach."

"You shithead. You know what I mean." She started to pick up her book and throw it at him but they were too close to the water.

"Yeah, I know, but you just worry about yourself," Andy said.

"What do you mean?"

"You're the one who'll be running around campus with all those young bucks. You'll probably find one or two you'll like better than me. My good looks can only compete so far with age."

"You're not old," she said.

Andy suddenly remembered what Jesse had told him about werewolves and how long they live. "You may be right," he said.

"I know I'm right. Besides, with all the studying and practicing I'll hardly have time to fit any of those young bucks of yours into my busy schedule. I found that out my first two years."

"Is that why you jumped my bones so much this summer? And here I thought it was my good looks and manly charms."

"Oh, just shut up if you can't be serious."

"We've got plenty of time to be serious," Andy told her. "You don't leave for two weeks."

"Ah, ha. So you have been thinking about it."

"I never said I hadn't."

Their conversation was brought to a sudden end when three would-be fishermen set their gear down next to Andy's. "Any luck?" the fatter one of the three asked.

"Depends on what you're after."

The fat man just looked at Andy, then at Michele who shrugged her shoulders and grinned. The fat man began to laugh so hard that he had to put his hands on his over-sized belly to keep it from bouncing off and into the channel.

Andy turned to Michele, but she had already reached down for her book and was flipping through the pages in search of the gum wrapper. She pretended not to notice.

65

Andy was thankful that Michele hadn't been scheduled for Stewart Beach the past week. Very little else had been on his mind since their day off together. It was going to be tough not having her around during the day and even tougher at night. The week without having her share the beach with him had helped prepare him for what was to come. Nothing could help prepare him for the nights without her, though, not even Jesse, who had become somewhat of a nuisance over the past two days.

Tonight marked the first night of the new cycle, and Jesse had done his level best to remind Andy of that fact every chance he got. He had wanted to meet with Andy last night to discuss what he termed as their strategy, but Andy had told him that for the next ten days, he had every intention of spending as much time with Michele as she could handle. Andy had told him that if the werewolf was still around after Michele left, then he might consider joining him in the hunt; that is, if he had nothing better to do with his time than chase shadows.

Andy had finally given in and agreed to meet Jesse at the pavilion during his lunch break. He had told him he could have one hour of his time, but the rest belonged to Michele.

Jesse was waiting for him at the picnic table in the back corner of the second-floor deck. He looked much older than the last time Andy had seen him. Jesse already looked old, but his pale, drawn face gave him the appearance of a man with one foot in the grave and the other about to follow at any given moment.

"No offense, Jesse, but you look like shit," Andy told him when he sat down.

"Nice of you to notice. I was beginning to think you didn't care."

"Get off it, Uncle Jesse. You know my situation."

"And you know mine, Andrew."

"Then there's no sense in us wasting time rehashing it," Andy told him.

"Isn't there anything I can do to make you change your mind?"

"No, sir."

Jesse paused and pondered his next statement. "Then I'll have to do it alone."

"Do what?"

"I thought you weren't interested?" Jesse said.

"I'm interested enough to want to know if you're gonna go and do something stupid."

"I'm only going to do what has to be done," Jesse said. "I'm going after him."

"How? You don't know who or where he is."

"I know where he's been. That's a start at least."

"How are you going to be in two places at once?"

"I can't, but you've left me with no choice."

Jesse's words hit Andy hard, but not with enough force to make him change his mind. "You've got the choice not to do it." He knew his words were falling on deaf ears.

"No, Andrew. What I am gives me no choice. Sooner or later, you're going to have to realize that."

"Or maybe never," Andy said.

"Nevertheless, I'll be on the docks tonight," Jesse said and looked him square in the eyes.

"And what are you going to do if you find him?"

"Fight him."

"Fight him? You said yourself you were too old."

"Maybe, but it's all I can do without your help."

"You're a crazy old man, you know that?" Andy told him. "You'll be lucky if you don't spook yourself at the first thing that moves and fall in the channel and drown."

"Then come with me. That's what they pay you for, isn't it?" Jesse reminded him. "To keep people from drowning?"

"I don't work the docks and neither should you for that matter. If you would have gone to the police like I told you to, at least they might have stationed a few men over there."

"To look for a werewolf?"

"No, to look for a murderer," Andy said. "If there is a werewolf, the sight of a few cops might keep him away from there."

"Then he'd just go to the beach and we wouldn't be any further ahead than we are now."

Andy knew he was again getting nowhere. Jesse had his mind made up, as did he, so he chose his parting remark well.

"You want to be buried next to my dad?"

"**He** will see to my burial, just like the others," Jesse told him.

66

Eric stood in front of his third-floor office window. He had already put in a twelve-hour day. Julie hadn't taken the news too well that he was going to have to put in a little, self-imposed overtime when he had phoned her at work that afternoon. He had told her that between splitting time with her and his surfboard, his business had suffered.

Actually, it had been Amy who had pointed that fact out to him that morning.

"I know you own the company and you can do pretty much what you want to," she had said when she brought him his coffee, "but if you don't start taking care of business, you aren't going to have a business to take care of much longer. It may not matter to you, but I've got rent to pay.

Eric hadn't needed much convincing when it came down to money. From his window, he watched as the Colonel carefully wheeled its way from the dock. In a few minutes, the patrons would be sitting down to a steak and seafood dinner. The thought reminded him that he had skipped lunch, and again, the lights of Fisherman's Wharf beckoned to him from across the way.

He turned and studied his desk. The mountains of paperwork that had greeted him that morning were now no more than shallow dunes. The dunes could wait. It was almost dark, and he was hungry.

Eric closed up shop and headed for the elevator. The lighted circle above the door told him the elevator was stopped at P for penthouse.

He pushed the down button and waited as the light jumped from P to 4 and then to 3, where the door slid open. Mayor Paschall seemed just as surprised to see him as he did the mayor.

"Going jogging?" Eric asked in reference to the mayor's outfit.

"What? Oh, yes. I don't get much exercise sitting behind my desk all day."

"I know what you mean. I prefer surfing, myself."

"I'm afraid I'm a little old for that," the mayor said. "I'll leave that to you younger folks."

When the door opened to the first-floor lobby the two men walked together to the Water Street entrance. Eric opened the door and let the mayor out first. "You be careful," Eric told him. "They still haven't caught that guy yet."

"What guy?"

"The one that got that kid from the tanker last month."

"That kid ran away," the mayor said. "No two ways about it." With that, the mayor began jogging off to the left. Eric crossed Water Street toward Fisherman's Wharf.

The line outside the restaurant was even longer than it had been the last time he was there, so he took his wallet out, retrieved and maneuvered his way inside. "I'd like a table," he told the same hostess who had accepted his bribe before, and showed her the business corner of the bill.

"I'm sorry, sir," she said. "We're full and there's at least a half hour wait.

Just in case she hadn't noticed the incentive, Eric slid the bill further out in his hand for her inspection.

"I'm sorry, sir. I really am," she said and she really was, "but I just don't have any place to seat you."

"Fair enough," Eric told her and reached for his wallet again. He pulled out another five and showed her the pair. "How about twins?"

"I can't, sir," she said. "I can take your name if you want and you can see if you can find a place at the bar."

Eric looked toward the bar. It was already two deep with people just waiting to get a chance to order a drink. He thought about going back to the well for a twenty, but from where he stood, he could tell that the hostess was probably being honest with him. "No, thanks," he said, rather rudely anyway. "It's not worth it."

He pushed his way back out and spilled a woman's drink in the process.

"Hey," the woman's date or possibly her husband said. "Watch out, buddy."

Eric didn't reply, but his eyes fired the man a warning shot before he walked out.

It was now dark. The full moon hung by an invisible thread just above the downtown buildings like a big, yellow yo-yo waiting to be drawn back up. Eric knew there were at least a dozen other hostesses on The Strand who would gladly take his offering and decided to give one of them a chance.

As he walked across the lot he remembered a
phone conversation he had had earlier with the
captain of a Liberian tanker that had been
anchored just outside the mouth of the port for
two days waiting for its turn to load. Another
call to the Port Authority had assured him that
the tanker would be docked late that afternoon and
be loaded tomorrow.

Since he was already down there he decided to
check the docks to make sure.

67

Andy and Michele were just about to leave for dinner at Angelo's when the phone rang.

"I better get that," Andy told her.

"If it's Julie, tell her we're already gone."

"I'm sure she'll believe that." Andy reached for the phone. It wasn't Julie.

"Andrew?" the familiar voice on the other end said.

"What is it now, Jesse?"

"I'm about to leave, so I thought I'd give you one last chance."

"So am I," Andy said.

"You alone?"

"No. Not that it would make any difference."

"Where are you going?"

"Why?"

"I want to know in case I need you."

"You won't need me," Andy said.

"Don't be so sure, Andrew."

"Look, Jesse. We've got reservations and we've been over all this before, so you just go do whatever you think you have to do and you can tell me all about it tomorrow, OK?"

"Is that your final word on it?"

"I don't know how to put it much plainer than that," Andy said.

"Then you go ahead and have a good time and don't bother worrying about me."

"I've given up worrying about you, Uncle Jesse. You're calling your own shots now," Andy said and tried to break off their conversation. "I'll talk to you tomorrow."

"I may not be here tomorrow," Jesse said. "You know that."

"I know that if you don't hang up and let me get out of here, you may wish **I** weren't here tomorrow," Andy warned him.

"Then go. I'll be at the docks when you change your mind."

Andy wanted to tell him not to hold his breath, but the phone went dead.

"What was that all about?" Michele asked. She knew from the middle of the conversation that she had been a party to who it had been.

"Nothing important," Andy said.

"No sick relative this time?"

"No," Andy said. "Not yet anyway, but he's pushing it."

"Did you tell him he could have you all to himself when I'm gone?"

"Yeah, but I guess he just misses my company.

"Not as much as I'm going to."

"I hope you're right."

68

Two tankers were lashed heavily to the dock, end to end. Eric couldn't remember the name of the Liberian tanker, and the nationality of ownership painted on the side made no difference since most freighters were leased. He would have to depend on the flag that usually flew above the control cabin.

The dock was pitch black, but the lights on the deck offered him enough visual support. Eric backed up against the side of the pallets and craned his neck upward. He thought he recognized the flag, but the lack of any wind made it difficult to confirm. He could make out the red and white stripes and part of a blue square in the upper left corner. It was either American or Liberian. The flags were the same, with the exception of the stars. The American had fifty while the Liberian had only one.

He began to walk down the dock toward the stern for a better look when a sudden gust of wind gave him his answer. He began to walk toward the second tanker, but a strange noise made him stop.

The beast crouched low in the shadows of the pallets and breathed heavily. Its heart pounded in its huge chest. A month had passed since it had tasted human flesh and its body ached for the kill and the fresh blood of a human heart. Its front claws scraped nervously across the concrete.

"Who's there?" Eric said. His mind suddenly remembered the warning he had given the mayor. The mayor hadn't heeded it and neither had he.

The beast could feel the fear radiate from the man's body. It brought a rush of fevered anticipation to its own.

Eric thought quickly. "I've got a gun," he said into the shadows.

He didn't, but the beast understood the word and accepted the challenge. More than the kill, it enjoyed the fight. It also pleasured in seeing the eyes of its victims just before they died. From where it crouched, it couldn't see the man's eyes.

"I'm not kidding," Eric said. He stuck a hand in his pants pocket as a weak gesture of deception.

The beast snarled and sprang from the pallets. It could have been over at that moment. It could be tasting the man's blood, but the beast wanted to savor this kill. The others had died too quickly to understand. This one wouldn't.

Eric felt nothing as he stared down at the large animal that resembled a dog, only it wasn't. His body had gone numb. He couldn't feel his legs, much less use them. The only thing that moved was Eric's eyes, and they were filled with fright. A man he could handle, but a dog, possibly a rabid one, was another matter.

The beast growled and wrinkled its snout to reveal its teeth. The hair on its hump bristled. Eric could feel his heart straining against his chest like it wanted to explode. He looked down into the eyes of fire.

With that, the beast lunged into Eric's chest and sent him rolling backward onto the dock. Again, it could have killed him, but it wanted a fight. The sudden impact jarred Eric's brain back from the brink of extinction and sent shock waves of its own to his feet. He kicked wildly at the beast that caught each thrust with its front claws and ripped the material away, taking bits of flesh with it.

"Get away!" Eric screamed and kicked at the air in front of the animal that had reared up onto its back legs.

The beast knew the fight must end when the man screamed. It had toyed with him long enough. The sound would bring others like him. It could also smell the man's blood.

Eric tried to crawl backward, but the sand that lightly blanketed the concrete dock lubricated his movement. The beast pounced on Eric's chest and drove the wind from his lungs. He looked into its eyes as he tried to breathe again. The eyes were replaced by the full moon at the corner of the building when the beast lowered its head.

Eric felt no pain. His mouth opened and closed, but nothing passed through. When the beast raised its head again, he saw why and died knowing.

The beast jerked its head to the left when it heard the noise. It saw a light stretch out against the far end of the dock as if reaching for it. The beast wrapped its powerful jaws around what was left of its victim's neck and drug it into the pallets.

Jesse moved the flashlight's beam from side to side as he walked down the dock. He shined the light into the stacks of pallets, but he dared not go in. If the werewolf was there, he wanted it to come to him.

He took the light from the pallets and moved it to the side of the tanker. It danced against the dull, black metal as he walked. When the light reached the stern, Jesse's feet almost slipped out from under him. He caught his balance and shined the light on the dock until it rested in what looked to be a dark brown pool. Ice filled his bloodstream when the pool turned from brown to crimson in the light.

The beast watched from no less than a hundred feet away. Once in, it had carried the body through the maze of pallets to the far end. It had seen the man almost fall and knew why. It had again been careless. It should have killed the other man when it first had the chance. Now it was too late.

Jesse followed a shallow trail of streaked blood to the edge of the pallets where it seemed to end. He noticed there was a break in the stacks where one building ended on the other side. He took a deep breath and shined the light in. There were no more traces of blood or scrape marks to show a body had been dragged further, nevertheless, he followed the light through the valley and out the other side.

The beast could no longer see the man but it felt a sudden breeze as it blew through the hair on its hump. It lifted its snout and snorted as it caught the intruder's scent. The small was a familiar one. One it wanted. It turned back into the maze toward the scent.

Jesse shined the light across the small alley between the buildings until it came to rest against the bottom of the pallets on the other side, then he brought the light back slowly. There was still no trace of a struggle, nor signs of any more blood. He cursed himself for making the call to Andy. Had he been there sooner, he might have had him. He also might have been able to save whoever's life the werewolf had taken. He walked back through the short row of pallets to where the blood ended and began scraping his feet across the concrete.

The beast watched as the man covered the tracks it had carelessly left behind. Its mind didn't understand. The man's actions made no sense.

Jesse found a discarded paper cup and bent down at the edge of the dock and filled it up. He took it back to the pool of blood and threw the water on it in the direction of the channel. After several trips back and forth he scoured the dock with the light to check out his work. Most all the evidence was gone. By morning it would look like nothing more than a sandy oil stain.

"Sorry, Andrew, but I had to do it."

Jesse started to walk back down the dock to leave, but stopped and turned. "If you're out there," he said, though not loud enough to be heard by anyone who might be standing on the deck of the tanker taking an evening smoke, "I'll be back."

The beast heard and answered with a low growl, then returned for its victim's heart.

A light gray film of mist covered Stewart Beach like a worn sheet from the Galveston County Morgue. Andy was thinking about the morgue's overseer when he drove through the gate. When he rounded the pavilion corner to his usual parking spot, he found it taken. Under other circumstances he would have been pissed but the sight of Jesse's station wagon was more of a relief than an aggravation. Even more relieving was the fact that Jesse was sitting behind the wheel.

Andy parked behind him and got out. He knew Jesse's visit so early in the morning was not a social one, so rather than stand out in the light rain, he opened the passenger door and slid in.

"Well," Andy said when he looked over his shoulder into the back of the vehicle, "I don't see a wolf pelt, so I gather you must have struck out."

"Not entirely," Jesse informed him.

"Oh?"

"He got another one last night."

"You saw him?"

"No."

"Then how do you know?"

"More blood on the docks," Jesse said.

"Behind the pallets?"

"No, out in the open this time."

"Really?" Andy said rather nonchalantly. "That doesn't sound like our boy. You sure you just didn't come across someone's fish cleanings?"

"I really didn't expect you to believe me," Jesse told him.

"I know, so you took a sample and had it tested, right?"

"No, not this time."

"Didn't want to prove yourself wrong, Jesse?"

"I didn't need to. I think I've been around long enough to tell the difference."

"You tested the other one," Andy reminded him.

"The other one wasn't fresh. This one was, and there were signs of the body being dragged away."

"Then I guess the police will finally have something they can sink their teeth into," Andy said. "No pun intended."

"Not anymore."

"Why?" Andy asked. "It hasn't rained hard enough to wash it away yet."

"Doesn't need to. I already took care of that."

"What do you mean?"

"I cleaned up his mess."

"You did what?"

"I cleaned up the blood," Jesse said. "There's nothing left to find.

"So, I could go there right now and I wouldn't be able to find a single clue?"

"That's right."

"Good," Andy said.

Andy's comment sent a clue of its own in Jesse's direction. It meant Andy had accepted the fact he had been denying.

"I'm glad you approve," Jesse said. "I expected you to chastise me for destroying evidence again."

"No," Andy said. "As far as I'm concerned, if nothing's there to see then nothing happened. You just made it all up to hide the fact that you wasted your time last night."

The clue turned into a miscarriage. "I did nothing of the sort."

"Prove it."

"I don't have to prove it."

"Then I don't have to believe it."

"Then you're a fool," Jesse said.

"Maybe so, but I'm not the one who's hanging around the docks at night looking for a werewolf that doesn't exist."

"Oh, he exists all right," Jesse told him. Believe me."

"I think it does, but only in your imagination."

"And what about your imagination, Andrew?"

"What do you mean?"

"Was your imagination running wild the night you saw me change?"

"Could have been, but I still think you probably drugged me."

"You don't believe that for a minute."

"Sure, I do. It makes as much sense as you running around cleaning blood off the docks after dark."

"What was I supposed to do, leave it there for someone else to find?"

"That's the idea, Jesse."

"No," Jesse said. "I want him to come back."

"You're really beginning to worry me now, Uncle Jesse. I think you need to get away from here for a while. When was the last time you took a vacation?"

"I don't need a vacation," Jesse said. "I need your help."

"I'm trying to give it to you but you won't listen to me."

"No, it's you who won't listen."

The sudden appearance of Butch standing by the corner of the pavilion made Andy realize that he had spent more than enough time arguing with Jesse. "I don't have time for any more of this," Andy said and pointed at his watch. "I'm already late."

"Then go with me tonight."

"Not a chance. This is your fantasy, not mine."

"This is hardly a fantasy," Jesse told him.

"What would you call it then?" Andy asked as he leaned out of the half-opened door.

"A nightmare."

"Then wake up, Jesse."

Amy looked at her watch. It was ten-thirty and Eric hadn't come in yet. She knew he had to be somewhere close by since his BMW was in the parking garage. She told herself that he had probably gone down to the docks which he sometimes did for a little hands-on business.

She got up and went into Eric's office and walked over to the window. The rain had ceased and it seemed to be business as usual across the way. The Colonel was already on its morning cruise and tourists milled over the Elissa like ants on a discarded sandwich. She could only make out the front of the tanker at the docks. The rest was hidden behind a row of warehouses. Three men stood near the bow of the tanker, but none of them fit Eric's description.

Amy turned and looked at Eric's desk. He had almost caught up on his work. She hoped the rain would return, assuming he did also. That would keep him in for another afternoon and would be more than enough time to clear away the remaining paperwork that had piled up.

Amy sat down behind the glass desk and went through the small stacks. She separated them into different stacks in order of their importance. When that simple chore was done, she leaned back in his comfortable, leather chair. If Eric came in now and caught her she knew there would be hell to pay, but she liked the way the chair felt. It engulfed her with a feeling of power she knew would never be hers.

The door to Eric's office swung open and Amy gasped when she knew she had been caught.

"It's just me," Ruth said. She looked around the office that she had never before entered. "You've got a call on line one."

"Who is it?"

"Someone from Port Authority. They wanted to speak with Mister Beckett so I thought you might want to take it."

"Thanks," Amy said. Her answer had a meaning other than just for the acknowledgement of the call. Amy was thankful that it had been Ruth at the door instead of Eric. "I'll take it at my desk."

"OK," Ruth said and backed out.

Amy got out of the chair and slid it back under the desk to hide the fact that she had ever been there. She returned to her desk and took the call.

The man from Port Authority told her that the Liberian tanker that was supposed to have been docked last night was next in line and apologized for the delay. Amy thanked him and told him that she would pass that message along to Mr. Beckett.

She wrote the message down, but if Eric was on the docks like she thought, he already knew it.

71

The afternoon had turned an even more dismal gray with low, streaking clouds blocking out any proof that the sun had actually risen. The water, usually a blue-green, was now a murky-brown. Andy wondered if the werewolf couldn't see the moon later then maybe he wouldn't know it was full.

"Come on, Andy, pull yourself together," he told himself as he packed up his gear in preparation to leave his tower.

Butch jogged up to him just as he was about to climb down. "Where you off to?"

"Home," Andy said.

"How about a beer or whatever?"

"Thanks, but I gotta meet someone later."

"Yeah, I know," Butch said. "You and Miss Michele been sorta tight lately."

"You're only young once, son."

"Well, what about later then, or are you two just gonna stay at home?"

"Whatcha got in mind?" Andy asked, more out of courtesy than interest.

"I'm taking Kim to the Reggae show at Yaga's," Butch said. "We'll save y'all a seat if you want. You look kinda like you need to put a buzz on."

The idea didn't sound half-bad to Andy, which meant it wouldn't sound at all bad to Michele. "Why don't you do that? What time?"

"About eight. The show starts at nine but we
need to get there ahead of the tourists." Butch
had hoped he would accept but he hadn't counted
on it.

"OK. We'll see you there." Andy was sure
Michele would welcome the change. Yaga's was
also on The Strand and just a short walk to the
docks in case he felt the urge to check on
Jesse.

He drove straight home and was about to pick
up the phone to call Michele when it rang. He
waited until the fourth ring, thinking it would
probably be Jesse with a last-minute plea for
his assistance. "Hello?" he said without much
life in his voice.

"Well, you don't have to sound so chipper,"
Michele said on the other end.

"Oh, hi. I thought you were gonna be someone
else."

"Oh, really?" she said. "Like who, for
instance?"

"No one, really. Listen, you want to catch
some Reggae music tonight?"

"Funny you should ask," Michele said. "Kim
just called and asked me the same thing."

"Of course she did."

"What?"

"Nothing."

"You sound awfully strange, Andy. Is
something wrong?"

"I've just got a lot on my mind."

"I know. Me, too."

Andy knew she was talking about the fact that she would be leaving for college at the end of next week, and she probably thought that was what was crowding his mind also. He wasn't about to tell her otherwise. "You want me to pick you up?" he asked instead. His question served notice that his mind wasn't exactly tuned into the present conversation.

"Nope," she answered. "Then you'd have an excuse to take me home afterward."

"No chance," he said in an effort to tune himself back in.

"Good. Kim said to be there about eight."

"Of course she did," Andy thought, but didn't say. "Sounds good," he said instead and followed by. "That way we'll beat the tourist crowd."

"How did you know?"

"Lucky guess."

When Andy hung up the phone, he felt a sudden need to call Jesse and tell him he would be close by if he truly needed him, but decided against it almost as quickly. It was bad enough that he knew Jesse was walking the thin line between two worlds. Anyone else might push him in the wrong direction.

72

Somewhere above the charcoal-coated sky, the sun had gone down, and the moon was in full bloom when Jesse parked his station wagon in the lot that was reserved for the patrons of Fisherman's Wharf. It was one of the very few perks of being on the county payroll. He walked past the empty slip where The Colonel was usually docked, but now circled the channel on its dinner cruise. He was about to decide on the best spot to lose himself on the docks when a loud horn blared at him from the city lot. He turned but all he could see were the headlights of a large car flashing on and off in his direction. He looked behind him to see if they might possibly be meant for someone else, but found he was alone.

The car door opened and the driver got out. "Jesse, is that you?"

Jesse recognized the voice of the mayor. "Yeah, it's me."

"Good," Mayor Paschall said. "We've been trying to find you."

When he saw that the mayor wasn't going to come to him, Jesse walked on over to the side of the yellow Cadillac. "Who's been looking for me," he asked politely.

"The sheriff. It seems they've found another body."

Jesse looked in the direction he had been headed for signs of other cars, but a silent darkness was all he saw. "Where?"

"East Beach. Get in. You can go with me."

Jesse cursed himself for picking the incorrect location for his stake-out. He had figured his adversary wrong. It was only he, Jesse, who wanted the confrontation. He should have known. He should have given the werewolf the proper credit. He was obviously of the bloodline and not some rogue who had shown up on the island by chance. "My car's just over there. I'll follow you."

"No, it'll be faster if we go together," Paschall ordered. "Get in." He got back into his car and gave Jesse no alternative but to do the same.

On the drive through the Historical District, Jesse questioned him as to why they hadn't tried to reach him on his car radio.

"We did," the mayor said. "Maybe you have it turned off."

"I don't think so," Jesse said. "I usually leave it on."

"Then maybe it's busted. You better have it checked out in the morning."

Jesse sat back and tried to remember the last time he had used the radio, but couldn't. "Maybe he was right. Maybe it wasn't working," he thought.

Mayor Paschall turned onto Seawall Boulevard and headed east until he got to the road that turned off in the direction of the condotel. Jesse strained his eyes for the usual red and blue flashing lights of one or more of the sheriff department vehicles. As they got closer to the burned-out building Jesse saw that not only were there no lights, there weren't even any vehicles.

"Where are they?" Jesse asked when the car made a quick turn at the side of the building and drove along the packed sand to the back.

"Out there," the mayor said and nodded toward the beach, and cut off the engine. The headlights stayed on.

They both got out together and walked to the front of the car where Jesse got on his tiptoes and tried to look over the sea grape infested dunes.

"What were you doing last night, Jesse?" the mayor asked when the Cadillac's lights turned themselves off automatically.

"When?" Jesse asked back to him. "I think you know when."

Jesse turned to face him. "You mean at the docks?"

"Yes."

"You were there?"

"Yes," the mayor said. "Now answer my question. What were you doing there?"

"I . . . I was looking for evidence," Jesse stammered.

"Evidence of what?"

Jesse had run out of anything that even resembled a believable answer. He hadn't planned on ever having to explain his theory to anyone but Andy. A question of his own struck him. "Where were you?"

"Watching you clean up the blood," Mayor Paschall told him. "Tell me why?"

Jesse could feel the hair on the back of his neck bristle. "So, it's you."

"What's me, Jesse?"

"The werewolf."

The mayor began to unzip his jogging suit. His eyes glowed yellow as the clouds thinned out to reveal the full moon above them. "You know of me?" he said in a low growl as the transformation began. "How?"

"I am one of you," Jesse said and began to tear at his own clothes.

The beast could say no more. The metamorphosis had taken away its human power of speech. It shook its head and snarled, but didn't attack. If what Jesse said was true, it would meet him in their world. It had been at least half a century since it had fought in combat against another of its kind, and it relished the challenge.

Jesse kicked at his remaining clothes as he, too, began to change. He knew the beast would wait. It wanted the battle for blood. When his own transformation was complete the gray beast leaped to the hood of the Cadillac and scratched sharply into the metal and howled into the still night. The full moon showed silver on the gray coat that covered his throat.

The red beast pranced to the front of the car and joined in the ancient ritual to the moon. It was their signal to begin what would spell the end of one of them.

The gray made the first move and leaped fiercely onto the red's back and buried its sharp fangs into the hump. First blood had been drawn but the pain only heightened the red's fury. It threw itself backward and the impact of its strong body, as it forced the gray to the ground, sucked the air from the gray's lungs with a yelp.

The red rolled over and surged into the bare skin of the gray's belly and tore away a section of tight, yet aging flesh. The gray sprang to its feet. Blood trickled freely from the open wound. The red snarled as it chewed at the meat and tasted victory. It was a too-soon taste. The gray sprang at its throat and missed its mark by mere inches. Its teeth ripped into the red's chest, but failed to grip.

The red shook its head and growled at the sight of its own blood, though barely visible on its silky coat. It made another charge at the gray, for the throat this time, but the gray lowered its head and caught the red's muzzle in its own. They tore into each other's flesh with the razor-sharp nails of their front paws as they lifted one another up onto their hind legs. Their teeth scraped against each other's like tiny, but deadly swords as neither one loosened its grip.

The red, being the stronger, drove forward and threw the gray back against the front of the car. It heard the dreadful snap that the other felt. The gray fell to the ground and reached back with its snout like a dog that had just had its back broken under the wheels of a car.

The red backed away for a silent moment and watched the gray's agony. It knew the battle was nearly over. It made a final lunge and tore out the gray's throat, then stood proudly over its victim as the gray's lungs sucked for air through the opening. The red lifted its snout and paid a

final tribute to the full moon, then tore out the
gray's heart.

"You were strong, old one," its mind said. But
not strong enough."

73

Andy had listened and had tried to enjoy the Reggae music through two sets, but his heart just hadn't been in it. During the break before the final set, he told Michele he needed to get some air. "Let's take a walk, you want to?"

"Where?"

"I don't know. I just need to get out of here for a while."

"Where y'all going?" Butch asked when he returned to the table with another round of drinks.

"Andy needs some space," Michele said. "We'll be back before they start up again."

"You better hurry or I'll be forced to drink your drinks."

Once outside, Andy headed them west of The Strand. Michele took his hand in hers.

"Are you sure nothing's wrong?" she asked while they walked.

"Sure. You know how we lifeguards are. We need to smell the sea air every once in a while or we'll suffocate."

They took a right on Twenty-Second Street until they reached Water Street.

"How far are we going?" Michele asked.

"I thought we might walk to the docks and see what The Colonel looks like in the moonlight."

"You're not trying to get romantic on me, are you?"

"Only if you want me to."

When they crossed Water Street, Andy saw what he hoped he wouldn't see. Jesse's station wagon was parked by itself in the late night, empty lot. "Damn you, Jesse," he thought. He gave the car a wide berth and headed in the direction of The Colonel that had long since completed it evening run. He kept his eyes trained on the docks to their left.

"Well, the old boat looks just the same with the lights off," Michele said when they reached the locked gate. "Only darker."

"Huh?"

"That was a joke, Andy," she said. "Now can we go back?"

"Yeah, in a minute." He began to walk to where one of the two tankers was tied to the dock.

Michele let go of his hand and stopped. "I don't want to go over there," she begged.

"Why not?"

"I just don't. It's too dark."

"There nothing there but a big boat."

"I don't care. I'm not going and I don't want you to either."

"OK," Andy said. "But let's just stand here a minute."

"Why, Andy?"

"The breeze will cool us off," he answered.

"I'm not hot," she said. "I want to go back right now."

Andy wanted to call out for Jesse, if nothing else but to see if he would answer, but he didn't. He couldn't. Not without having to explain his stranger than usual behavior to Michele.

"Please, Andy," Michele begged again. "I'm getting scared."

"Oh, OK." As a last resort, Andy picked up a rock and threw it against the side of the nearest tanker and listened as it ricocheted off into the stacks of pallets. He listened for any sign of sudden movement, but the far-off sound of a harbor bell was all he heard. With any luck at all, Jesse would have fallen asleep hours ago and the rock would have woke both he and his senses up while there was still enough time for him to go home where he belonged. "You better be OK, Jesse," he whispered before he turned and took Michele's hand.

"Did you say something?" Michele asked as she gratefully accepted his grip.

"I was just saying we better hurry back before Butch starts in on our drinks."

"Now you're talking," Michele said and squeezed his hand.

Andy took one final look over his shoulder as they walked away, but all he saw was the reflection of the moon in the channel as the clouds parted.

74

Andy watched as the glowing amber lights digits went from 4:59 to 5:00 and wondered just how long he had been staring at the clock as if somewhere in the box there was some magical number that would flash a warning to him that it was high time he did something besides just lay there. Michele had been gone for about three hours, and he couldn't remember falling asleep, just staring. He had to be at the beach in two hours, so if he was going to do something, he had to do it soon.

He got up and walked to the living room in the dark. When he reached the bar, he grabbed the phone off the wall and dialed Jesse's number. He let it ring two dozen times. He knew because he counted each ring, but there was no answer. He tried Jesse's lab but got the same results.

Andy had an uneasy feeling in the pit of his stomach and felt like he was going to throw up. If something had happened to Jesse, it was all his fault. He shouldn't have let him go off alone. It wasn't so much the idea of there actually being a werewolf that tore at his stomach as it was the real possibility that something more human could have been lurking in the shadows of the dock to waylay the old man while he waited.

He went back to his bedroom and dressed quickly in the same clothes he had taken off a few hours before. There was a stale smell of bar cigarette smoke on the shirt but not enough to make him take the time to change.

The low-hanging clouds that had arrived the previous afternoon, only to have parted in the evening, had returned to hide the fading moon. They brought an eerie coolness to the morning, unusual for this time of year. Andy drove to the docks with both windows down and hoped the rush of crisp air would ease the tension in his stomach.

Jesse's station wagon was still parked in the same place. Andy circled it and pulled up next to the driver's door and looked in. He hoped to find Jesse asleep in the front seat. The car was empty and the doors were locked. He whipped the steering wheel to the right and spun the Bronco in the direction of the docks. He brought the truck to a hard stop just past the locked entrance to The Colonel and jumped out.

"Jesse!" he yelled as he ran toward the moored tanker whose crew was obviously still asleep as there were no signs of life on the high deck.

A shrimp boat eased its way down the channel in the direction of Port Bolivar. A flock of hungry gulls circled close behind and seemed to take turns diving in its wake.

Andy stood next to the stacks of pallets, afraid of what he might find if he entered. "Jesse, it's Andy. If you're in there, answer me."

He waited and hoped, but all in vain. He picked up a broken piece of board, no longer than a ruler, and started bravely into the stacks. His sudden burst of courage was fueled only by the fear of what he might find.

The sky below the clouds began to lighten as the sun began to prepare its ascent, but it wasn't enough to penetrate the mountains of wood. Andy reached the spot where he thought they had found the first blood and wished he had thought to bring a flashlight from the truck console. He stood there a moment and listened, but the usual morning sounds of the ship channel were all he heard. He continued on his trek through the maze in no certain order, and as the morning grew brighter, he realized he had gone in a circle of sorts and was back to where he had entered.

Andy heard the creaking sound of a metal door in need of oil and stepped back into the stacks. A lone figure appeared near the ship's railing with a cup of coffee in one hand and a lit cigarette in the other. He moved deeper into the stacks so as not to be seen and waited for the man to leave. Surely the view of the channel from the port side would be better to start the morning off with than having to stare at the side of an old brick warehouse building. The man must have agreed and moved back from the railing.

Andy walked out and down the length of pallets and entered the far end. He made his way through the aisles in a more orderly fashion this time, as one would at a supermarket with a full list of items to purchase. There were no signs of Jesse or that he had ever been there. Rather than go back the way he had come, Andy made his way down a small alley between the buildings and back onto the parking lot. He hurried on past his truck to the pay phone on the wall outside Fisherman's Wharf and made the call he should have made a month ago.

Andy was sitting in the Bronco's driver's seat when a car from both the sheriff's department and the Galveston PD arrived almost simultaneously.

He got out and closed the door when the two cars pulled to a stop next to him.

"Where's Sheriff Danforth?" Andy asked the deputy.

"He's on his way," the deputy said. "He was still asleep."

"Who have we got missing?" the patrolman, who had only been told to investigate the report of a missing person, asked.

"Jesse Spangler," the deputy informed him.

"The coroner?"

"Yep," the deputy said to him. To Andy, he asked, "What's the scoop?"

"If it's all the same to you, Ben, I'd rather wait until the sheriff gets here so I don't have to go over it twice." He also needed more time to make sure he had his story down pat.

"No problem. That looks like him now."

The sheriff's Ford roared across the lot and sprayed a thin wave of loose sand in its wake. The car made a grinding sound when he shoved the gearshift into park before he had come to a complete stop.

"What's going on, Andy? Where's Jesse?" the sheriff asked before he was fully out of his car.

"That's what I'm hoping y'all can find out."

"Well, what the hell was he doing down here at this time of the morning?"

"He came down last night."

"Son, why don't you start from the beginning?" the sheriff told him.

"Yes, sir," Andy said. He went on to tell them of how Jesse hadn't been altogether satisfied that the girl they found in the alley near there had committed suicide, and that when the crewman had come up missing, but his camera had been found broken, Jesse thought the two might be connected in some way. His story wasn't a total fabrication; he just left out the main ingredient. He told them about how he and Jesse had found the blood under the stack of pallets and how Jesse had planned to set a trap last night to catch the killer.

"Why the hell didn't he report any of this to us?" the sheriff demanded. "Or why didn't you?"

"He said he wasn't sure and he didn't want to make a fool of himself if he was wrong."

"Well, now he just might be a dead fool. Come on. You better show me where y'all found the blood. Ben, you call in and get us some more help down here. Officer, you get some of your people and get this area roped off."

Andy led the sheriff to the pallets and through the maze to where the blood had dried to an almost black stain. The sheriff tried to move the stack of pallets but couldn't. "You want to help me with this?"

Andy knew it wouldn't do any good but he followed his boss' order. The stack still didn't budge under their efforts.

"Looks like we may need us a forklift," the sheriff said and rubbed the stiffness out of his arm. "You say you're sure this is human blood?"

"Yes, sir. Jesse took some back to the lab and tested it."

"We may have to fire his ass for this."

"Let's just find him first," Andy said.

They could hear voices on the dock, which meant reinforcements had arrived, so they made their way back out.

"We got us some blood back there all right. Leonard, you round us up a forklift. We gotta get some of this shit moved on outta here," the sheriff ordered.

"Uh, Sheriff?" Andy said. "If it's all the same to you, I'd sorta like to stay and help."

"Like to, hell! You got no choice in the matter. You're in this up to your asshole, son."

"Then someone needs to take my place at Stewart."

"We can handle that."

"I'll call it in," Ben, who had been listening close by, said.

"You do that. Andy, you stay close to me, and you better not be hiding anything else." The sheriff looked at him like he knew he was holding something back and expected him to spill his guts without any further delay.

"Yes, sir."

It wasn't long before it seemed like everyone who owned a uniform was crowded onto the docks, not to mention the crew of the tanker and a horde of on-lookers who had come down to take the morning trip on The Colonel or tour the Elissa. Andy knew it was only a matter of time before the mayor, himself, showed up. He dreaded that moment.

A dozen men from two departments had been assigned to make a thorough sweep of the area, including the abandoned warehouses across Water Street, in search of Jesse. Two motorized rafts that Andy recognized belonging to his department were also brought over and were inching their way along the side of the docks and tankers in search of the body they hoped they wouldn't find.

Andy, doing exactly as ordered, was standing behind the sheriff when the mayor arrived. The wounds from last night's battle were no more than blemishes beneath his business suit.

"Didn't I tell you to talk some sense into Jesse?" the mayor said to Andy, completely disregarding the presence of the sheriff.

Andy jumped at the chance to get even. "I did. That's why he was here."

"What are you two talking about?" the sheriff asked.

"He told me to tell Jesse that the girl might not have committed suicide. That's what gave him the idea to begin with," Andy explained. "So, if something bad has happened to him, you're to blame, Mister Mayor."

Although it was a smoke screen on Andy's part, the mayor knew he was entirely correct.

"Well, Mayor?" the sheriff said.

"I just told him I thought Jesse wasn't performing his duties as he should, that's all."

"Bullshit!" Andy said.

"That's enough, Andy," the sheriff said. "You don't have very much room to talk."

"What does that mean?" the mayor asked.

"I'll explain it all to you later. Right now, we just need to find Jesse."

"Well, this might be a stupid question," the mayor offered in an attempt to seem interested in their futile investigation, "but has anyone bothered to check his lab? Maybe his car wouldn't start and he just walked on over there."

"I called there this morning," Andy said, but realized that had been several hours ago and his call might have caught Jesse on his way, if the mayor was right.

"What time?"

"About five."

"Well, shit," the sheriff said. "Ben, radio the morgue and see if Jesse's there, will you?" He looked at Andy. "Boy, this better not have been a wild goose chase or your goose is cooked."

"If he's there," Andy said. "I'll gladly light the oven myself."

Ben was back before the other three could start another conversation. He shook his head as he walked toward them. "They ain't seen him all morning."

"Well, it was worth a try," the mayor said. He tried not to look pleased at their failure to locate him.

It was noon before the troops were called in. The sheriff left two men in the area just in case Jesse showed up. He told them to keep an eye on his station wagon since that would probably be the first place he'd go if by some slim chance he came after being hit over the head and dumped somewhere further up the way.

As Andy was walking to his Bronco, he noticed a familiar car parked away from the others and a more familiar figure sitting inside. He walked over to where Michele was waiting. "What are you doing here?"

"I heard what happened on the talkie," she said. "Did y'all find him?"

"No, not yet."

"I'm sorry, Andy."

"Yeah, I know."

"Does this have anything to do with why we walked over here last night?"

Andy could see no reason to lie to her now; especially since everything he had told the sheriff was now a matter of public record. "Yeah."

"Why didn't you just tell me?" she said. If you had I . . ."

"I know," Andy said. "I just wasn't thinking."

"Can I do anything to help?"

"No, not right now. Aren't you working?"

"I'm on my lunch break. Have you eaten?"

"No, but I'm not hungry," Andy said. "You go on back to work and I'll see you later."

"Where will you be?"

"I'm not sure," he said. "I'll get hold of you though."

"I've got a better idea," she said. "I'll just go to your place when I get off."

"Why don't you make it a little later?" Andy told her. "I probably won't make it home till after dark."

"OK, but I'll be there when you get home."

"That'll be good." Andy leaned in and gave her a kiss, then stepped back so she could leave.

The mayor had been watching them by the scratched hood of his yellow Cadillac. He had recognized Michele's car from another time and another place.

75

The overcast conditions made dark come sooner than Michele had expected. It also robbed the island of its usual radiant sunset. The driveway of Andy's condo was empty which meant he was still out somewhere in search of Jesse. She pulled the Malibu in under the carport and got out. She knew the spare key, that she had taken to calling her key, would be hiding in its usual place inside the middle of three conch shells in the unkempt garden by the front door.

As she walked around the rear of her car a large arm grabbed her around the waist while a hand covered her nose and mouth with a strange smelling cloth. Then everything went dark.

The mayor lifted her limp body into his arms and carried her to the passenger side of her car and placed her gently on the seat and buckled her in. To the unsuspecting motorist she would just be another tired and happy camper sleeping off a fun day at the beach.

He rifled through her bag and found her keys. It had been a while since he had driven a stick-shift but as soon as his foot hit the clutch it all came back to him like a fond memory. He backed out past the row of oleanders that marked each condo's property line, as well as affording their owners with a bit of privacy, and left without incident.

A half hour passed before the driveway saw any action again. Andy had been ready to apologize for being late, but saw it wasn't going to be necessary. Michele had obviously run into some tome problems herself. He still hadn't eaten and hoped she had decided to stop on the way over for a bucket of chicken. As hungry as he was, he would even look favorably on a cold submarine sandwich from the pavilion.

Andy pulled under the carport and just sat there for a few minutes with the motor running. He was bone tired from a long day of one failure after another. He watched the waves break in the beam of his headlights. When another pair of lights brightened the street behind him he thought it was Michele and turned the motor off and got out. When the lights drove on by his heart sank even lower that it already was.

Next to food, a shower was heavy on his mind when he entered the condo. He had missed his usual morning one, and the clothes he had worn for almost twenty-four hours had grown uncomfortably sticky during the heat of the day. He stripped quickly and was under the water without delay. The noise of the water as it beat against his weary head drowned out the sound of the phone when it began to ring on the wall above the bar.

Andy stayed in the shower longer than usual. He half-expected Michele to join him at any moment. He needed her desperately. When he realized his wish was not going to be fulfilled, he turned the hot water off and let the cold shower shrink his pores for as long as he could take it, then got out.

He had just finished towel-drying his short hair when the phone rang again. It had been so long since that machine had brought him good news, he was almost afraid to answer. When he finally did, the streak continued.

"Hello?"

"I've got something you want," the muffled voice said.

"Who is this?"

"Who I am doesn't matter."

"Jesse? You've got Jesse?" Andy said and threw the towel on the bar.

"No, I've got the girl, and if you don't want her to end up like Jesse, you'll do as I say."

All the voices Andy had ever heard reeled across the recorder in his brain, but none of them matched the one on the phone. "Who are you?" Andy demanded again.

"Be at the condotel on East Beach within the hour and come alone, or you will never see her again. No one will."

"Who are you, damn it? How do I know . . ." The line went dead. Andy yanked the receiver from the wall and threw it across the room. It knocked a chunk of textured sheetrock off the wall by the window.

"Son of a bitch!" he shouted. Even if he wanted to call the police, his sudden burst of temper had destroyed his means of doing so. His head was swimming, near drowning, as the caller's words sank deeper in his mind. Jesse was dead. That he now knew. The fact that Michele, usually overly punctual, had not arrived meant the caller was no doubt telling the truth. He slammed his fists on the bar until the pain informed him that he was accomplishing nothing with his actions. Andy turned toward the clock on the front of the kitchen stove. It was ten to nine and the meter

was running. He knew what he had to do, he had to
do alone, just as Jesse had done and Jesse was
dead.

He dressed hurriedly in jeans and a T-shirt
with no sleeves and was about to leave when he
returned to the closet and took a shoebox from the
top shelf. He opened the box and took out his
father's .45. He had only shot it once on a
deserted part of the beach and then only at cans,
but maybe the sight of it would prove to be enough.
He checked the clip and found it full, then shoved
it into the back of his jeans. The metal felt cold
against his lower back.

The clouds had disappeared, and the full moon
laid a wide swath of yellow ribbon on the waves
that broke behind his condo when Andy gunned the
Bronco's engine and backed out. It was a
frightfully beautiful sight, but Andy never saw
it.

When he reached Seawall Boulevard, Andy
stopped and not necessarily because the red and
white sign told him to. A city police car was
parked in front of the Circle K. The smart thing
for him to do would be to tell the cop about the
call and have them send the SWAT team in. Jesse
wouldn't have agreed with him but Jesse was dead.
Michele would probably be just as dead if such an
outfit showed up in full force. Since Andy didn't
feel very smart and since he wasn't even sure the
Galveston PD had a SWAT team, he stepped hard on
the accelerator and hung a right.

He followed a steady stream of night traffic
down the boulevard and paid close attention to his
speed. He had plenty of time and knew the stretch
of road in the hotel and nightclub area was

heavily patrolled at night. Being stopped for speeding would only delay him. It might also make him change his mind about storming the condotel if he actually came face to face with the law on the way.

He made it through the night spots and then past the amusement park. From there, the road grew dark. When Andy came to the turnoff to the condotel, he pulled onto the drive and stopped. The huge structure was dark and barely visible from the road. He grabbed his bag from the console well and took out the binoculars. He tried to focus them in on the building but all his eyes could see was darkness.

The human figure that stood near a third-floor opening, hidden by the same darkness, had watched as the truck pulled off and stopped. From his vantage point he could also see back up Seawall Boulevard. He was pleased that Andy had come alone. Had he not, the girl who was tied unconscious to a bare, metal stud would have died instantly. It was not the way he would have preferred. It was his wish to have Andy first and the girl for his victory dessert. He wanted to savor her being and possibly toy with her before tasting the young flesh that had escaped his jaws once before. He wanted her to see him as he really was and to know how she was to die.

Andy threw the binoculars back into the well and slammed the lid shut. He didn't need to feel for the gun as he had been reminded of its presence with every bump the rough-riding truck had hit. As he started the truck forward again he could feel his heart pounding in his chest. It told him he had no business being where he was. His brain told him the same thing but he wasn't listening. Jesse hadn't listened either and he was dead for it.

A sudden rush of anger came over him like an unexpected spring shower. Andy put the accelerator to the floor and swerved around the final corner and brought the Bronco to a skidding stop in front of the building. Through the open substructure, his headlights engulfed Michele's car parked in the back. He went to the well again and took out his flashlight and hit the button to make sure it was working before he got out.

He was immediately surrounded by an air force of hungry mosquitoes when he closed the door, but their menacing stings went unnoticed. He was there, just like he had been told to be, but other than Michele's car, there was nothing else to direct him. Andy shined the light into the substructure and followed behind it to the back and then out again to where the Malibu was parked. He aimed the beam inside but it was empty.

The voice directed his next move. "She's up here, Andy."

Andy turned and pointed the light up in the direction of the voice, but no one was there. He moved the beam from side to side, but all he saw were openings where ornate windows would have been had the builder not gone bust.

"The stairs are in the corner," the voice told him from above.

Andy recognized the fact that he knew the un-muffled voice but there were too many other things crowding his mind to allow his memory to identify it. He brought the light back down and found the stairs. He reached back for the gun, but left it there. Whoever it was who had brought him there obviously had something else on his mind. If he was armed at all, the man could easily have killed him where he stood rather than showing him the way up.

Andy kept the light a good distance in front of him as he climbed the stairs. When he stepped out on the first floor landing he pointed the light down the hall. The only sign of life was a skinny rat that scurried off when the beam hit him.

"Keep coming," the voice said, almost as if he could see him through the walls.

"Who the hell are you?" Andy yelled up the stairwell and shined the light in the same direction. When he received no reply he continued his mount. He knew now that the voice was coming from the top floor, but he shined the light down the second-floor hall when he reached the landing just to make sure.

Andy jumped back when his own light flashed back at him from a broken mirror at the end of the hall. "Shit!" he said and caught what was left of his breath.

He leaned back against the wall and shined the light up toward the third floor and kept it there as he made his way cautiously up the side of the wall. The concrete was cold against the back of his bare arms. Just before he reached the top, Andy reached back and wrapped his right hand around the butt of the pistol. He stepped out onto the third floor and flooded the hall with light.

"Where are you?" Andy shouted. "What have you done with Michele?"

"She's in here with me," the voice said.

"Let me see her."

"I'm afraid I can't do that. She's sort of tied up at the moment."

"What do you want?"

"You."

"Well, here I am," Andy said. "Come on out where I can see who you are."

"You mean you don't recognize my voice?"

Andy strained his ears for some sort of recognition as the voice echoed through the vacant rooms. "No, I don't."

"Then I guess you'll have to come in and see for yourself."

"If you've hurt her, I swear I'll kill you," Andy said. He tried to gain courage from the sound of his own voice as he started down the hall. He knew the man was in one of the rooms on the right. He steadied himself then jumped into the first doorway and shined the light inside.

The mayor knew he had done so as the hall became dark again. "One more, Andy," he said. "One more door and you belong to me."

Andy gripped the pistol tighter as he stepped from in front of the first door. He had to do it. He had to go in. He had run out of choices, just like Jesse had; and Jesse was dead. He put his back against the right side of the hall and slid to the next opening, and then just like he had seen the cops on TV do, he drew the pistol and jumped into the doorway. He took dead aim on the bare wall where the light had drawn a circle.

"I'm over here, Andy," the voice said.

Both of Andy's hands moved instantly to the left where the mayor now stood bathed in light. "Paschall? What the hell is this?" Andy asked and lowered the gun out of purely stupid instinct.

"Good move," the mayor said. "The gun won't do you any good anyway."

"What's going on?"

"I was going to ask you the same question."

"I don't understand. "Where's Michele?"

"In there." Mayor Paschall nodded his head toward the opening behind him.

Andy made a move toward the opening.

"Stay where you are!" the mayor said in a low, growling voice.

"I want to see for myself," Andy said.

"Not until I'm ready."

Andy raised the gun in his direction. "I'm going in now."

The mayor's eyes turned into yellow spheres that seemed to glow blue in the centers. "You **don't** understand, do you?"

"I understand you've probably killed Jesse and that's not going to happen to her."

"Jesse's who I'm talking about. He chose to die the way he did, but you don't know why, do you?"

"He was trying to catch you, you fucking murderer! That's why."

"Partly, but that's not all," the mayor said. "Go ahead and shoot me."

"I will if you don't get out of my way."

"Go ahead, please." The mayor unzipped the top of his jogging suit to reveal his bare chest. "Aim right here. Right at the heart."

"You're crazy."

The mayor removed the jacket completely. "No, son, that's not quite true. I am something, but it isn't crazy." He slid down his pants and took his shorts with them. "Here's what I am."

The man began to transform right before Andy's very eyes. "No!" Andy said. "It's not true."

"Then you **do** know," the half man, half beast growled as the hump between his shoulders began to take shape.

"Yes," Andy said and fired the pistol into the form at point blank range. The bullet hit him full in the chest and sent him lumbering back against the wall. Blood began to trickle from the small hole as a coat of red fur began to grow over it.

The beast stuck a claw-like finger into the hole and extracted the bullet and held it out at the light from the flashlight. "Huh. Not even silver."

Andy fired again and this time it hit him in the mouth that had changed into more of a snout. Andy froze when the beast spat the bullet out onto the concrete floor.

"Nooo!" Andy screamed as he raised both arms into the air and squeezed his full hands into fists. The flashlight crushed like an empty beer can in his left hand and the wooden grip of the .45 splintered in his right. He lowered them both and saw what he had done. Andy's body hurt. It was like no pain he had ever felt before, but he felt a power in the pain. He tried to talk but the words sounded too deep to be his. "Nooo!"

The red was now fully transformed and paced back and forth in front of an opening that should have been a picture window. It saw what was happening and was glad.

Andy tore at his clothes with hands that were changing into claw-like paws covered in a light brown, almost blonde, fur. He could feel his shoulders folding together and his back becoming heavy. Again, he tried to speak, but the snarl that came from the mouth he could actually see below his eyes told him it was useless.

Andy's body finally doubled over and he found himself standing on all fours, but his mind was still his. He could still think, just not speak. He was still Andy, but Andy was now a werewolf.

The red howled from the opening then pranced to the side and waited. The brown waited too. It remembered Jesse telling him how he needed to learn how to be a werewolf; how to act and how to control the power. It needed Jesse, but Jesse was dead. The brown felt a primeval urge growing inside it. Its lungs ached. It fought back what it though was a cough, but when it emerged the sound of its own howl filled the room and overflowed into the night.

The red charged to begin the battle for blood. The impact sent the brown back against the wall and sheared the rivets from a metal stud. The red had only been testing him and backed away as the brown shook off the pain. It wished he had believed Jesse. It could feel the power of the beast but had no control over it.

The red attacked again, this time with its jaws open. The brown moved to the side at the last minute and the red buried its teeth in the brown's hip. The brown shook the red loose and limped to the opposite wall. It turned and looked at the blood that ran down the hair on its back leg. The brown knew it should be hurting worse than it did, but the pain was no more than he had experienced many times when he had hit his leg against a chair or a door. It had hurt for a few seconds, then the pain was gone. This pain was no different.

"So, this is the power," the brown thought.

When the red charged again, the brown crouched low and sprang at it with all its might. The red, not being prepared for such a return, was caught in the air and flipped. It landed with all its weight on the back of its neck.

The brown suddenly became the hunter. It was learning to control the power, much like he had learned to block a charging linebacker in football. Still, it wished he had listened to his coach when the offer of assistance had been given. The coach was dead, but the killer wasn't.

The red got to its feet and began to circle the room. The brown turned with its every move. The red charged again but this time the open doorway to the adjoining room was its target, not the brown.

The brown stood in the center of the room, unsure of what was to come until it realized the meaning behind the red's exit. It wasn't trying to escape. The brown ran through the opening with no fear for its own safety and saw the red standing over Michele's tied and limp body. Its drooling mouth was poised at her throat.

The brown lunged for the red as the red's jaws moved in for the kill. The brown's legs became tangled in Michele's but the movement caused the red to miss its mark. Its teeth closed on nothing but stale air.

Before the brown could get it feet back under it the red attacked again and buried its fangs into the brown's shoulder. It missed the heavy vein in the brown's neck by scarce inches. This time the brown felt a burning pain as the red ripped out the hairy flesh and backed away for another charge.

Through weary and unsure eyes, the brown thought the red's contemptuous snarl looked like a grin as it came at him again. The brown ducked when the red lunged and bit into its head. The brown could feel the warm blood as it ran down the snout in front of its eyes. The brown's front legs buckled and it went down. It was dizzy from the pain in its head.

The red again backed off and sized up its victim for the final strike. The brown could feel the soft flesh of Michele's thighs under its neck and its nostrils filled with her sweet scent. Then came the surge; not of the red but of the power. The power overtook the brown's entire body. It lifted its head and looked into Michele's calm,

yet unknowing, face. It was the same peaceful face
he had watched as she slept beside him in his bed.

The brown turned and growled at the red and
waited for the charge. It wanted the charge. It
was now ready for whatever was to follow.

The red saw it was time and dived under the
brown. It tried to reach the soft under-skin of
its belly, but the brown leaped upward, turned in
mid-air, and came down on the red's back. It dug
its claws into the red's side, unsure if it could
hang on. It bit into the back of the red's neck
and for the first time tasted blood. It was a
sweet taste. Almost enjoyable. Almost.

The red tried to shake the brown loose, but
with every move the brown's teeth sank deeper into
the muscles of its neck. The red ran to the far
wall and slammed them both against it, but the
brown's grip only tightened with the blow.

The red realized it had finally met a
formidable foe. One that could kill it if the
battle continued. The red could feel itself
wearing down under the weight and strength of the
brown. It was then that the red saw the opening;
its one and only chance to break free of the
brown's hold. The red ran to the front of the room
and sprang out the window and into the moonlit
night, three floors above the ground.

The brown let loose its death-grip in mid-
flight and pushed itself off the red's back. It
balled itself up, much like doing a cannonball
from the high dive, and prepared for impact. Its
move propelled the brown across the drive and into
the soft sand on the other side. It hit and rolled
and bounded up on all fours.

The red had not fared so well. With the weight of the brown suddenly lifted off, it had lost its sense of balance and had fallen headlong onto the asphalt where it lay with the broken bones of its shoulders sliced up through its hump.

The brown walked cautiously toward the broken body and sniffed at the wound. The red rolled over on its side and lifted its legs in the air and bared the underside of its body in defeat and waited.

The brown could hear Jesse's voice. "The heart. You've got to take the heart."

When the red whined its final plea the brown tore into the flesh under its ribcage and tore out its heart.

76

Andy sat in the rocker by his bed where Michele lay in an unconscious state. He had found the handkerchief soaked with chloroform in the pocket of the mayor's jogging suit when he had put it on. His own clothes had been pretty much torn to shreds and he had been left with no other alternative but to borrow the outfit. The mayor wouldn't need it any longer since he, too, would be found on East Beach in the morning; another apparent shark victim.

Jesse wouldn't be there to discount the story or offer any opinions to the contrary. He knew they might never find Jesse's body, but wherever he was, he hoped he was proud.

The mayor's jogging suit, handkerchief and Andy's own torn clothes were now a soft mound of smoldering ashes in the barbeque pit on Andy's back patio.

Getting both the Bronco and the Malibu back to his condo hadn't posed much of a problem once Andy remembered the Bronco was equipped with a tow-bar that had been used, though rarely, to free vehicles that had been driven too far back off the beach and had become buried up to their axles in the soft sand.

The problem had come when Andy realized he didn't know where the mayor had abducted Michele. He had only presumed it was from his condo, but if so, where had she parked? If it had been in the carport, then he needed to pull her car in first. If it had been in the street, then he needed to leave it there. He had taken the easy way out, flipped a coin, and drove the Malibu under the carport.

As Andy rocked slowly in the rocker, a screwdriver held comfortably in one hand, he thought back over the story he would feed Michele when she came to. If she didn't buy his tale about her almost being kidnapped and him driving up just as she was about to be thrown into a car, and fighting them off but letting them get away rather than leave her lying in the street . . . well, he could always tell her the truth.

THE END